POISON

Also by Molly Cochran

Legacy

POISON

MOLLY COCHRAN

A PAULA WISEMAN BOOK

SIMON & SCHUSTER BFYR

NEW YORK   LONDON   TORONTO   SYDNEY   NEW DELHI

SIMON & SCHUSTER BFYR

An imprint of Simon & Schuster Children's Publishing Division
1230 Avenue of the Americas, New York, New York 10020

This book is a work of fiction. Any references to historical events, real people,
or real places are used fictitiously. Other names, characters, places, and events are products
of the author's imagination, and any resemblance to
actual events or places or persons, living or dead, is entirely coincidental.

SIMON & SCHUSTER BFYR is a trademark of Simon & Schuster, Inc.
For information about special discounts for bulk purchases, please contact Simon &
Schuster Special Sales at 1-866-506-1949 or business@simonandschuster.com.
The Simon & Schuster Speakers Bureau can bring authors to your live event.
For more information or to book an event, contact the Simon & Schuster Speakers Bureau at
1-866-248-3049 or visit our website at www.simonspeakers.com.
Book design by Krista Vossen
The text for this book is set in Bodoni.
Manufactured in the United States of America
2 4 6 8 10 9 7 5 3 1
Library of Congress Cataloging-in-Publication Data
Cochran, Molly.
Poison / Molly Cochran.—1st ed.
p. cm.
"A Paula Wiseman Book."
Summary: Katy receives a "gift" of poison that turns her into a killer,
while powerful witches stir up trouble, not only at Ainsworth School, but in
a world known as Avalon, as well.
ISBN 978-1-4424-5050-9
ISBN 978-1-4424-5052-3 (eBook)
[1. Good and evil—Fiction. 2. Supernatural—Fiction. 3. Witches—Fiction. 4. Poisons—
Fiction. 5. Morgan le Fay (Legendary character)—Fiction. 6. Boarding schools—Fiction.
7. Schools—Fiction. 8. Massachusetts—Fiction.] I. Title.
PZ7.C6394Poi 2012
[Fic]—dc23
2012006736

FIRST
EDITION

For Warren Murphy, who taught me everything
I know about anything

Acknowledgments

Many thanks to my talented and hardworking editor, Alexandra Penfold; my brilliant and amazingly organized agent, Lucienne Diver; to my initial readers, Pam Williamson and Lynne Carrera, who make sure my course steers true; to BFF Michele Horon, without whom I could plot nothing; to all the bloggers who took the time to read and review my first YA novel, *Legacy*; and finally, to my new readers whose support has given me a new future.

PART ONE
THE EMPORIUM OF
REMARKABLE GOODS

CHAPTER

·

ONE

I probably went to the only school in the country with a rule against practicing witchcraft.

That wasn't really as crazy as it sounded. The Massachusetts town where I lived was sort of known for its rumored history of magical residents. Some said it was even more haunted by witches than Salem, our famous neighbor. The story went that while the Pilgrims in Salem were burning innocent women at the stake, the real witches went to Whitfield and vanished into a fog.

Of course, that wasn't entirely true. Nobody had actually been burned at the stake in Salem. Oh, there had been plenty of murders, jailings, and torture of women who hadn't done much more than piss off their neighbors. Lots of widows had their property stolen, and one guy got crushed to death. But the burnings were pretty much left to the Europeans. The part of the story that *was* true was the part about the real witches going to Whitfield.

I knew because I was the descendant of one of those witches. A lot of us were, although we kept quiet about it. That was because even there, in the town where at least half the population were witches, we had to live among *cowen*, aka non-magical people. Actually, we thought of ourselves as *talented*—we could all do different things—rather than *magical*. But that wouldn't have mattered to cowen. They had a nice tradition of destroying anything they couldn't understand. Look at Salem.

At school there were two kinds of students, the Muffies and the witches. Muffies were the kinds of girls you'd find at every boarding school in the Northeast: fashionable, promiscuous, and clueless. Okay, that wasn't fair. There were plenty of cowen kids at Ainsworth School who weren't Muffies. Half of them weren't even girls. But those non-Muffies generally left us alone. It was the Muffies who were always making life difficult.

They sneered at us. They called us names. (Yeah, these were the same people who were legally named Bitsy, Binky, and Buffy.) "Geek" was probably the most popular name for us, since it was pretty much true, at least from their point of view. We generally didn't have problems with drugs, alcoholism, reckless driving, kleptomania, credit card debt, or STDs. To be fair, we did sometimes have issues with ghosts, apparitions, disappearing, transmogrification, rainmaking, telepathy, demon rampages, telekinesis, and raising the dead. And maybe a few other things.

Hence the injunction against performing witchcraft at Ainsworth. This rule had been in place ever since my ancestor Serenity Ainsworth had founded the school. (I liked to think that one of her pupils had given some Puritan Muffy a pig nose in a catfight.)

The Muffies didn't know about this rule. They didn't know that Whitfield was the biggest and oldest community of witches in the United States, or that the geeks at Ainsworth School could summon enough power to make a hydrogen bomb seem like a fart in a bathtub if we wanted to. They thought that Whitfield was an ordinary place and that Ainsworth was an ordinary school.

Or did they?

I'd often wondered if they knew. . . . I mean, how could they *not* know? On every major witch holiday the Meadow—that was a big field in the middle of Old Town—filled up with fog so dense that you couldn't see through it. It was the same fog that saved the witches from being grabbed by the Puritans back in the day. When the fog appeared, the witches all tumbled into it like lemmings, but cowen couldn't—physically *couldn't*—enter. And that was only one of the weird shenanigans that went on there. Even the dumbest Muffies must have had an inkling once in a while that Whitfield, Massachusetts, was a little different from wherever they called home.

At least that was my theory about how the whole mess started. With a jealous Muffy.

And an idiot who should have known better than to forget the no-witchcraft rule, since it was her relative who'd made it in the first place.

Right. It was me. But in all fairness I had a good reason. I was
protecting my friend Verity from Summer Hayworth, the most
evil of the evil Muffies at Ainsworth. More accurately, I was
protecting her boyfriend, Cheswick, from expulsion, and possibly arrest, for what he was about to do to Summer in Verity's
defense.

I could still see it—Summer, who had the taste level of
a dung beetle, laughing when Verity opened her locker and
found a stuffed witch doll hanging by its neck. The doll had
been made to look like Verity, with striped stockings and red
hair. Its eyes had been removed and replaced by *X*s, and someone had sewn a red tongue hanging out the side of its mouth.

There was no doubt about who'd done it. Even though none
of them had classes near Verity's locker, Summer and her three
main cohorts—A. J. Nakamura, Tiffany Rothstein, and Suzy
Dusset—just *happened* to be hanging around the area. Aside
from Verity, me, and our boyfriends, Cheswick and Peter, the

evil Muffies were the only people within a hundred feet of the locker in question. As for the witch doll itself, well, it had "evil Muffy" stamped all over it. A.J. was an artist, and the tongue definitely looked like her work, but the idea had to have been Summer's because nobody else in the school could possibly have been so crass.

If it had been my locker, I wouldn't have thought much about it. The witch doll was actually kind of cute, X-ed out eyes and all. But Verity was, well, sensitive. More to the point, she was a QMS—a quivering mass of sensitivity—of the highest order. She got emotional if someone swatted a fly or squashed a mosquito. She went into coughing fits if anyone in the room was wearing perfume. She was a vegan, of course, and only wore plastic shoes. Frankly, she wasn't the most fun person to party with, but that wasn't the point.

The point was, she was from a very old witch family, and being outed by Muffies in high school was, for Verity, pretty much on a par with being ravaged by wild dogs. She went all pale and started shaking so hard that Cheswick had to hold her up. Her eyes filled with tears. Her nose ran. Her fingertips turned blue.

"She needs something to drink," Cheswick said. He was looking at me, but Summer answered:

"What would she like? Bat's blood?"

"Shut up, Summer," I said.

"You going to make me, or are you just going to turn me into a frog?"

"I'd turn you into a jerk, except someone must have beat me to it," I said. Peter poked me in the arm. He thought I asked for trouble. Not true. I never had confrontations with horrible people if I could help it. Peter was just more of a "go with the flow" kind of person than I was.

Tiffany almost laughed at my little comeback, but she checked herself. Summer had no sense of humor, especially about herself. A.J. and Suzy just stared, as bored and clueless as ever.

"Let's get out of here," Peter said.

"Yeah," Cheswick agreed, slamming Verity's locker with a little more force than necessary.

"Oh, yeah. Go with your cool boyfriend," Summer said. A.J. and Suzy smiled. Cheswick, who looked like a dandelion puff and was the all-school champion in *Lord of the Rings* trivia, was not considered cool, even by the geeks.

I think this, more than Summer's offending Verity, was what set him off. Before any of us knew what was happening, Cheswick hurled Verity at Peter like he was passing a football, and threw five fingers at Summer.

The Muffies laughed at that, which showed how dumb they really were. When witches did that—flicked their fingers at someone—it was like aiming a wand at them. And when the witch was as pissed off as Cheswick was, the result usually wasn't good.

"Cheswick!" I whispered, but it was too late to stop him. All I could do at that point was try to weaken his spell by throwing out one of my own to cross his.

"Stink!" I shouted. Don't ask me why I chose that one. It was probably at the core of what I felt about Summer and the skank girls. Anyway, at that moment A. J. Nakamura, Japanese-American princess that she was, let loose with this tremendous salami-scented belch. Tiffany sniffed at her armpits, and then gagged. Suzy Dusset grabbed her belly and headed for the bathroom, sounding like a Formula One race car the whole way.

"What the hell do you think—" Summer began, then stopped to sniff the air she had just fouled with her breath. The rest of us shrank backward. Verity started to retch. Summer narrowed her eyes at me. "You'll be sorry," she said. Then she smiled at Peter and made the *Call me* gesture with her fingers. That was how crusty she was.

"Er . . . you wouldn't happen to have some air freshener in your locker, would you?" I asked Verity.

Cheswick led her away. Figuring that Verity didn't need a repeat of what had just gone on, I opened the locker and took out the doll.

"I don't think you should be touching that," Peter said.

"Hey, somebody has to get rid of it."

He sighed. "Okay, but why does that person always have to be you?"

"It's just better if we avoid complications," I said. "Look, I'm not doing anything wrong, okay?"

"Exactly what *are* you doing, Katy?" a pleasant voice behind me asked. It was Miss P, the assistant principal.

"Oh, no," Peter muttered.

"Move along, Peter," Miss P said, her eyes never leaving mine. "Is that your locker?"

Quickly I stashed the doll behind my back. "Miss P, I can explain."

"I don't think so," she said in a tone she might have used to discuss the weather. "I saw you using special ability on those girls." "Special ability" was code for "witchcraft."

"Then you know I didn't—" I thrust out my arms, having forgotten about the doll, whose head bobbed in mute accusation.

"I'll take that, please."

Abashed, I handed it to her as I watched Peter recede into the distance, shaking his head.

"Do you have a minute?" Miss P said cheerfully. That was code for "Bend over and kiss your butt good-bye."

CHAPTER
·
THREE

Actually, it wasn't so bad. Miss P was pretty decent most of the time. She rounded up everyone who had been near the locker and heard us all out. Of course, no one said anything. Peter said he hadn't seen anything, Cheswick wouldn't admit to throwing out five fingers, Summer didn't confess to putting the doll in Verity's locker, and naturally, the Muffy posse would die before they'd say they smelled bad.

In the end everyone was dismissed except for me.

"I needn't remind you about your responsibilities as a member of this community," Miss P said. That was all code. Translation: "Do that again, and you'll not only get kicked out of school, but you won't be welcome in Whitfield anymore either."

Witches were strict. If you didn't fit in—that is, if you weren't magical enough, or if you broke one of the million unwritten rules that had been passed down through the centuries, most of which had to do with not drawing attention to yourself—then the whole town stopped talking to you, and you had to go live among cowen if you wanted any kind of life at all.

Fortunately, that didn't happen often. Peter had been afraid it might happen to him last year because he wasn't very proficient in witchcraft (sorry, guys, but it was one area in which females seemed to have a slight edge), but his friends helped him through that. Besides, it was better to have too little magic than too much. No one was kinder, smarter, or more loyal than Peter Shaw. Or better-looking, if truth be told. To be honest, if he got kicked out of Whitfield, I wouldn't want to stay there either.

But Peter wasn't the problem this time. I was.

"I understand," I said. I tried to sound reasonably contrite, but I knew that causing four nasty girls to have BO wasn't going to put me on the FBI's Most Wanted list, especially since the Muffies hadn't even complained about it.

"I'm aware that the infraction wasn't severe," Miss P said. "It's that it happened at all. This is an open school."

I nodded. Ainsworth needed the Muffies, because most of them came from rich families. Without them (and their sizable tuition checks) a lot of us would have to go to Liberty High, the area's twelve-hundred-student public school, where we'd stick out like sore thumbs and probably end up being beaten into jelly.

"You really should try not to involve your friends in your misadventures," she said crisply.

That hurt. "Involve . . . They involved *me!*" I protested.

Miss P sat back in her chair. "Really?" she asked quietly. "How did Peter Shaw involve you in this?"

I swallowed. "Well, not him, maybe," I said, reddening. I

didn't want to drag Peter into anything. He had enough problems of his own.

"I understand you're considering applying for early admission to Harvard next year."

"Uh, yeah," I answered warily.

"So is your friend Peter," she said. "However, despite his excellent academic record, he lacks some of your advantages."

Meaning, I suppose, my father, who had been lobbying to get me into Harvard since the day I was born. An academic himself, he planned to pull every string he could get his hands on to guarantee my early acceptance and a hefty scholarship.

Peter wasn't so lucky. The poorest relation of the richest family in town, he'd been disowned by his relatives and regarded as an outcast by the Shaws after his parents had died.

Miss P leaned forward and looked earnestly into my eyes. "I want to help Peter get the education he deserves," she said. "I'm sure you do too."

"Of course," I said. She knew that Peter Shaw meant more to me than anything else in the world.

"So you must know how important it is that Peter's record not be marred by disciplinary issues." Her eyes bored into mine.

"Oh." She'd struck a nerve. If my stupidity caused anything bad to rebound onto Peter, I'd never forgive myself. "I get it," I said quietly. "There won't be any more . . . issues."

"Good." She smiled at me as she got up and held open her office door for me.

Peter was waiting by my locker when the final bell rang. "Hey," he said softly, touching my hair.

"Hey," I answered. I wrapped my arms around his waist and leaned my head against his chest. Just hearing his heart beat, as deep and steady as Peter himself, made me feel as if I'd gone into a safe place.

"Are you okay?"

I nodded silently, afraid that my voice would betray me.

"No, you're not," he said, and lifted my chin. He was smiling, his gray eyes twinkling beneath his thick honey-colored hair. "Listen, if you're going to break all the rules, you'd better get used to being yelled at."

"Thank you, Judge Shaw."

"So what'd you get, detention?"

"Not even." I got out my coat. "Miss P gave me a pass this time."

"Well done," Peter said with mock admiration. "Now if you can just avoid flying through the halls on your broom . . ."

"Ha-ha," I said humorlessly. I closed my locker and turned to leave—Peter and I were both due at work in half an hour—but I couldn't get out of my mind what Miss P had said. "Peter, I'm so sorry," I said, throwing my arms around his neck. "You know I'd do anything for you."

"Oh?" He grinned, wiggling his eyebrows suggestively. "Want to prove it?"

I pulled away and thumped him on the arm.

"It was worth a try," he said with a shrug.

"I was hoping you'd take me seriously," I said hotly, heading for the exit.

"Come on, Katy." He loped after me. "You know I was kidding."

We walked through the doors into the crisp late-autumn air.

"I guess," I said. There was a cold drizzle falling, which felt good after the superheated classrooms of the school's ancient building.

"So tell me what's up." Casually Peter took my books and tucked them under his arm with his own.

I shook my head. "It's just that Miss P said I was involving you in my . . . infractions or whatever, and that you were going to suffer for it."

"Me? Suffer how?"

"By not getting into Harvard."

He burst out laughing. "Because you gave Summer Hayworth BO?"

"Or something. Miss P was serious, though."

"I doubt that. Besides, we're not even allowed to apply to colleges until next year."

I stopped in my tracks and turned toward him. "She *wants* you to go to Harvard, Peter. She's going to help you. But everything we do from here on in is going to count. Don't think it won't."

"Okay, I get it. No fraternizing with criminals. But I hardly think you fit into that category." He put his arm around me as we walked into the Meadow.

Hattie's Kitchen, where Peter and I worked after school, was on the far side of the grassy expanse that had stood in the middle of Whitfield since the town's founding three hundred and fifty years ago. For cowen it was just a nice little park with a quaint old cemetery that had headstones dating from the sixteen hundreds, and a lot of twisting, narrow pathways leading into the woods that protected the town from the Atlantic winds blowing off Whitfield Bay. But to the witches whose families had settled the area, the Meadow was the wellspring of their magic.

I've mentioned that on Wiccan holidays the Meadow filled with a supernatural fog so thick that only the descendants of those original settlers could enter it. But even on ordinary days the place exuded a sense of peace that always made me feel better.

I put my arm around Peter, matching his arm around me, and we walked together through the wet fallen leaves. "I love you," I whispered.

"I love you, too." He pressed me close to him and kissed the top of my head. "Even if you are a bad influence."

"I'm really sorry about what happened today," I said. "The next time you see me doing something stupid, don't bother trying to talk me out of it. Just run the other way."

"I promise," he said, crossing his heart. "Although I really had hoped to see you beyond next week."

I scowled.

"Oh, come on." He ruffled my hair. "You're the smartest person in school. You can't even *do* anything stupid."

Right. Which is why I had been almost burned at the stake last year. If it hadn't been for Peter—and a few helpful ghosts—I'd have finished out the summer as an ember, thanks to one of my bright ideas.

"So I'm officially asking the smartest person in school to Winter Frolic."

I looked up at him. "The dance? Really?" I tried to look enthusiastic, but actually I hated events like Winter Frolic. People looked forward to it so much, and then when it finally came around, everyone was too nervous to have a good time.

So they would just hang out pretending that they were having fun. Plus there was always somebody who cried in the bathroom all evening, somebody who acted like a jerk, somebody whose dress ripped, and somebody who got reamed out by a teacher in front of everyone. *Please.*

"You don't want to go?" Peter asked, knowing full well how I felt about Winter Fwow-up. "Zounds."

"I get it," I said. "You don't want to go either. You only asked me so I'd feel good about being invited."

He smiled. "I'd do anything for you." He kissed me on the lips. Our books fell to the ground in a *whoosh* of slick leaves. Some boys who were passing by whistled and whooped at us, but we ignored them. All I could think about was the touch of his soft lips on mine and the feel of his body pressing so closely against me. "How about ten minutes?" he asked.

"Huh?" I just wanted to keep kissing him.

"We can go to the dance for ten minutes," he said. "That way you can at least put on a pretty dress. Unless you don't want to do that."

I licked my lips. They felt chilled in the cold air now. "I guess I could handle ten minutes," I said, loving him more than ever. "Then can we go for pizza?" I leaned against him.

"Sounds like a plan," he said. "An excellent plan."

CHAPTER

•

FOUR

Hattie's Kitchen was warm and dry and brightly lit. "We're here!" Peter yelled as we hung up our coats and put on our aprons.

"Good," Hattie answered, brushing flour off her ebony-colored arms as she bustled into the room.

Peter gave her a kiss on the cheek.

"You have a good day at school?" she asked, straightening his collar. Hattie had raised Peter since he was six years old. She still kept his room in the cottage attached to the restaurant, even though, like most other witches, he had a room in the school dorms.

"I did," Peter answered. "How's Eric?"

"Sleeping."

Eric was Peter's eleven-year-old brother. He was a witch too, and about a thousand times more powerful than Peter. He was more powerful than just about anyone in Whitfield, really, even though he couldn't speak or walk or feed himself.

Nature is weird in the distribution of genius, but there it was. The greatest magician in a town filled with magicians was a brain-damaged eleven-year-old kid.

Hattie consulted the menu she'd been writing. "Katy, start on pies," she ordered. "Six pumpkin, six Dutch apple. And a cheesecake. Peter, you go call Jeremiah Shaw."

Peter and I looked at each other. "What?" we asked in unison.

Hattie raised her hands in submission. "Don't ask me. His secretary called to command you into the old coot's presence. You have to negotiate when that's going to happen."

"I don't think I want it to happen at all," Peter said. "He stood me up the last time."

I remembered vaguely that Jeremiah Shaw had invited Peter to meet him at Shaw Enterprises last summer, but that hadn't amounted to anything. When Peter had shown up, he'd been told that his great-uncle was out of the country.

"Well, that's up to you," Hattie said. "But if you ask me, enough bridges have been burned. Maybe you ought to hear old Jeremiah out."

Peter puffed out his cheeks. "All right," he muttered. He shot me a look as he left the kitchen. His expression looked like that of a drowning man going under.

I felt for him. Peter had been dealt a bad hand from the beginning, with both parents dead and a brain-damaged brother who would never be able to take care of himself. Their father, the lowest-ranking member of the patrician Shaw family, had left both children in the care of Hattie Scott, who was not only poor and cooked food for a living, but was also known even to tourists, although half jokingly, as the village witch woman. It wasn't a set of characteristics that appealed to the upper-crust Shaw family, who all seemed to have been born with long sticks up their butts.

When he couldn't reverse his nephew's will, Jeremiah, as head of the family, had disinherited Peter and had seen to it that none of their relatives would have anything to do with either of Hattie's wards again.

"So why would Jeremiah Shaw want to contact Peter, after all these years of ignoring him?" I asked out loud.

"Just tend to your pies," Hattie snapped. "Lord, but that girl is nosy," I heard her grumble.

It seemed like forever until Peter came back. He looked dazed.

"Well?" I demanded. Hattie was looking at him expectantly.

"He—he apologized," Peter stammered. "For everything. Just . . . everything. He wants me to go see him."

"Again?" I asked skeptically.

"You hush," Hattie said.

"I think he wants to train me to work for his company." Peter's hands were shaking. "He says he'll put me through college."

"Oh, my stars," Hattie whispered, looking heavenward.

"Harvard?" I asked breathlessly.

He nodded. "If I can get in." He bit his lip. "And if I work out with Shaw Enterprises."

"Meaning what?" I wanted to know. Hattie waved me away.

"He says I've been gone from the family for too long," Peter said. "Maybe he wants to adopt me. Or *re*-dopt me. Whatever."

The phone rang. Hattie held up her index finger, then went to answer it.

"You've already been adopted," I spat, casting my eyes toward Hattie. Peter looked pained. "But I guess it wouldn't hurt to see what's what," I relented.

Peter nodded mutely.

Then Hattie got off the phone and came over. "Don't you worry about a thing, Peter Shaw," she said gently, hugging him. "Everything's going to work out just fine."

So things were more or less okay until the next day, when my hamburger turned into slugs.

Let me stress that I am *not* kidding. I was eating lunch with Peter and noticing how his calm gray eyes had flecks of gold in them, when Becca Fowler, who'd been sitting across from us, suddenly stood up shrieking like a prom queen in a horror movie.

My first thought was that maybe Verity had puked in the food line—it wouldn't have been the first time—but Becca was pointing at *me*. That's when I noticed that my bun had sprouted antennae and was traveling. My fries, too, had taken on a new appearance. They had become a pile of severed fingers.

I jumped up so fast that my chair fell over behind me. Everyone at my table—all witches—was either staring and speechless or scrambling toward the exits, because there was no question at all about this being an unnatural occurrence, and a fairly advanced one. What I mean is, most of the witches at Ainsworth School, even seniors, wouldn't have had the skills to pull this off. Whoever made fingers out of potatoes knew something about the Craft.

I looked around. By this time the place was in a state of utter confusion, with a lot of shouting and laughter and gross sounds of all descriptions and people getting up to check out the spectacle for themselves. The only ones who didn't seem to be at all perturbed were Summer and the Muffies, sitting on the other side of the cafeteria. All of them were facing me. A.J., Suzy Dusset, and Tiffany were giggling behind their napkins, but Summer was just watching me with this little half smile on her face.

"Summer?" I was basically talking to myself, but the thought was so surprising to me that I guess I spoke out loud.

"What?" Peter asked. Apparently he hadn't made that connection at all.

Becca did. "Don't be ridiculous," she said. "Summer may be heinous, but she's still cowen. Besides—"

At that moment a huge black dog leaped through the open cafeteria doors and bounded down the aisle, stopping momentarily near my table to shake mud on everyone and help himself to a half dozen hamburgers.

"Ewww," someone said as the dog belched dramatically.

"Hey, he left yours alone," Peter said with a grin.

"Very funny."

"Everyone calm down," Miss P commanded, the heels of her shoes clicking across the floor. Actually, she didn't exactly *say* anything. She only *thought* those words, but that was enough. Even though the room was practically vibrating with noise, all we heard was her voice in our heads and the sound of her walking through the silence.

"What is going on here?" she demanded in her real speaking voice, moving unerringly toward my table.

"N-nothing," I stammered.

"I do not wish to warn you again, Katy."

"But I didn't . . . " I gave up. I couldn't explain anything anyway. "Sorry. I guess I knocked my chair over by accident."

Miss P studied me for a moment, trying to figure out what I'd done to cause so much commotion. *Well, sorry, kemo sabe,* I thought. *Can't help you there.* My eyes drifted toward Summer.

Miss P caught my look. "Do you have a problem with someone here?"

No issues, I thought. "No."

She clacked away. "You." She pointed to the dog that had been sitting obediently, licking his chops. "Out!" The dog barreled through the caf doors like he was on fire. "Carry on," she said aloud.

Right. Business as usual. Welcome to my world.

"I don't suppose you feel like dessert," Peter said finally.

I shook my head. Most of my hamburger had fallen—or crawled—onto the table. "Go ahead," I said miserably. "I think I'll go to the library."

Summer!

How could that be? She was not only cowen, she was über-cowen. *Math* was magical to Summer Hayworth. If her parents hadn't donated the school's auditorium, she'd have been in someplace like Las Palmas High in south Florida, where I used to go to school. There were no witches at Las Palmas, only surfer dudes with six-pack abs and brains the consistency of warm oatmeal. Summer would have fit right in there.

She couldn't have slugified my burger. I don't know if *I* could have done that, and I was supposed to be pretty proficient for my age.

But her face . . . She'd known what was happening. Even from that distance, I'd been able to see the look of triumph in her eyes. Not to mention the giggling Skankettes having a hearty laugh at the miracle their leader had wrought.

It had to have been Summer. But how had she done it? I had to find out.

That night, I lurked.

I often wished I had the gift of invisibility. I guessed almost every witch wishes that. It's a rare talent, and I'd never met anyone who could do it. So in lieu of vanishing I had to make do with skulking around the corridor of dorm C, pretending to be visiting Muffies whose names I didn't even know. Whenever someone came out of one of the rooms, I'd face a random doorway, smiling and waving, as if I were just saying good-bye to whoever was inside. Fortunately, that happened only twice—it was after midnight—before I reached Summer's room.

I could smell incense. That was a cowen thing, thinking that the trappings of magic—incense, candlelight, incantations, talismans—were what made the magic work. In truth, you could do magic in a supermarket, with fluorescent lights and announcements about red dot specials.

That is, if you were a witch. These girls weren't. They were incanting like crazy, and burning enough incense to choke a horse.

"Spirits, grant us power!" That was A.J.'s reedy little voice, presently shouted down by Summer.

"*Me,*" Summer corrected as I heard a loud thump. "Give *me* power!" Then she added, less stridently, "We don't want to dilute it."

"Jeez, Summer, it's only a stupid Ouija board," Suzy Dusset countered. "I don't even think you're doing it right."

"How would you know?"

"A Ouija board's for contacting the dead, doofus. It doesn't give you power."

"Well, it worked before, didn't it?"

"Then let me do it."

"No way. You'd only use it to get boys."

"Yeah," Tiffany agreed. "That's why they call you Sleazy Does It."

I almost choked over that. As it was, it pretty much signaled the end of their session. Suzy started cursing like a sailor at about the same time the room resounded with the crashing of various items against the walls.

One of them screamed in the high-pitched tone only girls who weigh less than ninety pounds could achieve. A.J., I figured.

"Shut up!" Summer stage-whispered.

"But there's something on me!"

"It's only a stupid bug."

More squeals and thumping. "So get it *off* me!" Slaps and snuffles. "Get it—"

"Okay, okay. Just hold still while I open the—"

At that moment, the door swung open and a large moth—undoubtedly the creature that had unhinged A.J.—flew past me as I knelt awkwardly with my ear to what had been the keyhole.

Clearing my throat, I stood up slowly, trying desperately to think of something cool to say.

The four of them stared at me. Beside an abandoned circle of flickering candles stood a jar half-filled with what looked like oregano. A broken Ouija board lay in pieces on the floor.

"Can we help you?" Summer asked, as if I'd just walked into a White House state dinner wearing spandex and big hair.

"Er . . ." It took me a moment to gather my thoughts.

"Maybe you're lost," A.J. offered.

"The kitchen's that way," Tiffany added.

This was a reference to my job cooking in a restaurant after school. I actually liked it, but to Muffies all work was demeaning and to be avoided at all costs.

"I want to know how you did what you did in the cafeteria," I said as evenly as I could.

"Why?" Summer asked innocently. "Do you want the recipe for tomorrow's blue plate special?"

"Look, I'm only—"

Then it began, the nightmare that I thought would never end. A.J. was the first to drop. I mean *drop*, out cold, onto the floor in a heap.

"Hey, what are you doing?" Tiffany snarled at me a second before she also collapsed.

I heard sounds behind me. When I turned around, I saw that half the dorm had gathered around the doorway, probably drawn by A.J.'s scream, but now focused entirely on me.

I ran inside. "Summer?" Suzy croaked. Then she hit the floor.

Summer was the only one left. "Summer, are you all right?" I squeaked, putting my arms around her.

Her eyes rolled back in her head. "Oh, snap," she said. Those were her last words.

CHAPTER

•

SIX

Miss P wasn't nearly so lenient this time. "Those girls are in comas," she said in hushed tones. Her face was drawn with worry. "Summer's parents took her home today."

"Miss P, I swear—"

"Don't speak," she snapped irritably. "I've explained to everyone concerned that we must not jump to conclusions. Any number of things might have caused this. We are beginning with medical inquiries, and all the girls are receiving excellent care. The cafeteria food is being analyzed, as well as anything the girls might have . . . consumed in Summer's room."

My thoughts went to the herbs in the jar Summer was keeping in her room. Suddenly I doubted very much that she was storing oregano for a rainy day. I was pretty sure Miss P and whoever else had searched the room might be thinking along the same lines.

"However, if nothing is found to account for this phenomenon—

and I reiterate that every effort is being taken—then we will have to consider a supernatural cause."

My great-grandmother fanned herself with her handkerchief. "Goodness gracious," she said.

"I'm terribly sorry to burden you with this, Mrs. Ainsworth."

"I'm afraid it's you who has the burden, Penelope," Gram said. "And Katy, of course." She patted my hand.

Gram never considered for a moment that what everyone was saying—that I'd bombed into Summer's room and put a killing hex on all of them—was true. I loved her for that.

"I'm sure there's a reasonable explanation, and that we'll find it," Miss P said, smiling tightly.

"I hope so, dear. Otherwise the effect on the school will be calamitous, I'm afraid."

Miss P cast a glance in my direction. "I'm aware of that, Mrs. Ainsworth," she said.

"Can you imagine what would happen if four wealthy cowen families believed that their daughters were killed by *witchcraft*?"

I could. I would go to prison. The school would close. The laws would change. And eventually the persecution against our kind would begin again, just as it had more than three centuries before.

"I'm trying not to think about those possibilities," Miss P said.

"Well, I suppose it might have been the food," Gram said halfheartedly, although she knew as well as I did that it couldn't have been that, because all of the students had eaten the food.

Almost all of us. Everyone except me. I'd been working

at Hattie's Kitchen during the dinner hour. That was another reason why so many of the students were accusing me.

"They were using a Ouija board," I whispered.

Both Miss P and Gram gave me bored looks.

"They were talking about how it gave them power."

"I told you not to speak, Katy."

"I'm sure she's just trying to be helpful," Gram said.

"The Ouija board in question has been examined. It has no intrinsic magic whatsoever."

Gram looked up at Miss P. "You're quite sure these girls were cowen?"

"Quite," Miss P said.

"Still, somebody turned my hamburger into slugs," I insisted.

"I beg your pardon?" Gram's handkerchief halted midwave.

Miss P gave me a cold stare.

"Well, it's true."

"But not those . . . same individuals, surely," Gram said.

"It had to have been them," I said. "I saw it on their faces."

"Oh, for pity's sake!" Miss P picked up her paperweight and dropped it with a thud. "Listen to yourself, Katy!"

"I'm telling you, they used magic!"

"And you didn't?"

"I just made them stink!"

My great-grandmother blinked several times. "Excuse me?"

"There was an incident at the lockers, in which Katy played a prank on . . . some girls," Miss P admitted.

My great-grandmother was not stupid. *Those* girls?"

Miss P nodded. "In addition a number of residents in Dorm

C saw her behaving suspiciously prior to her encounter with Summer and the others."

"I see," Gram said.

"I'm not accusing you, Katy. In fact, I'm fairly certain that you haven't the ability to cause the kind of damage we're talking about. But you have drawn attention to yourself."

"Oh, dear," Gram said. She patted her face with her handkerchief.

That was it, of course. The first, last, and most important rule of witchcraft: Don't get noticed. There was even a motto about that:

KNOW, PLAN, ACT, KEEP SILENT.

Most witch households had those words on display somewhere in their homes as a reminder that their way of life, and sometimes their lives themselves, depended on secrecy.

I hadn't held strictly enough to that motto, and now there were going to be consequences. I just hoped they wouldn't involve Peter.

Also, although it probably shouldn't have bothered me so much, practically no one in the school was talking to me anymore. I began to hear people yelling "Stink!" behind my back in the halls. I heard a rumor that I had changed my lunch into slugs and fingers myself because that's what I secretly liked to eat. I guessed even witches weren't immune to the myth of the evil hag who raises toads and roasts children.

But the worst thing was that even my best friends didn't believe me.

"You used *magic*," Verity said breathlessly at the door to

my room. Becca Fowler was with her. I guessed the two of them had come to tell me why they'd decided to stand against me.

"The only magic I used was to keep Cheswick out of trouble that day at the lockers," I said.

"That's still against the rules," Verity said. Verity always followed the rules. Every rule, including not talking in the library and not using more than five sheets of toilet paper.

"Maybe you ought to be lecturing your boyfriend, then," I said icily.

"Oh, I have," Verity said. "Count on it."

"Cut it out, both of you," Becca said. "You know it wasn't about the locker thing."

"That's right." Verity looked pained. "Those girls are *cowen*, Katy. They couldn't defend themselves." Injustice affected her like indigestion. Any hint of unfairness brought out Verity's inner protester.

"I'm telling you, I didn't use any magic."

"Maybe you did and you didn't even know it," Becca offered.

"Huh?"

"It could happen," she said. "I mean, you can do a lot of things no one else can." She gave a little shiver. "It's scary."

I rolled my eyes.

"Well, it's true, isn't it? What about last summer, when you called up all those dead people?"

"They were spirits," I corrected.

"Spirits of dead people," Verity said, as if there were any other kind of spirits.

"Whatever," I said. I could feel the tension practically

crackling in the air between us, so I ignored them and leafed through a magazine until they left.

And then I burst into tears. I felt just the way I had before I'd moved to Whitfield. For most of my life I'd been an outcast, a motherless freak who'd had to hide my "gift"—though at the time I'd thought it was a curse—from everyone. And then, even though I'd come to Whitfield and Ainsworth School kicking and screaming, I'd discovered that this place was where I really belonged. This was where I found my great-grandmother and my aunt, two people who had loved me since I was born. This was where I'd met Peter, and where I'd learned that there were other people like me in the world. This was where I'd found magic.

But now it was as if none of that had ever happened. The people here didn't want me any more than the jocks at Las Palmas High had. Even Peter was supposed to keep his distance from me, if he knew what was good for him.

Know, plan, act, keep silent.

As if outcasts like me had any other choice.

Then there was the matter of dog poop. I think every Muffy in dorm C made me a gift, presented in one way or another, of dog poop. There was so much poop in front of my door that I had to move out of the dorm and in with my aunt and great-grandmother until I could clear my name.

"Try not to be persuaded emotionally," my aunt Agnes said as I sat with my head in my hands, recalling the bags of dog poop with which my fellow students had conveyed their feelings about me. "Feelings aren't facts."

"It's a fact that everyone hates me."

"Now, now, dear," Gram said sweetly. "We don't hate you."

That's when you know you've hit rock bottom, when your relatives are the only people who can stand to be around you.

"Oh, stop sniveling," Aunt Agnes said irritably. "Your universal unpopularity, whether true or not, is of no importance. What *is* a fact, however, is that actions leave traces. Even magical actions."

I looked up. "Do you think it was magic?"

"Of course it was magic. Four healthy sixteen-year-old girls don't suddenly keel over within ten seconds of one another from food poisoning."

"I thought that was rather far-fetched myself," Gram interjected. "Even if the food was dreadful."

"They'd been *dabbling*," Aunt Agnes pronounced, as if she were accusing Summer and her friends of injecting heroin. "There are ways magic can be worked through cowen. They're perfect dupes, after all. Since they have no knowledge of magic, they have no fear. The question is, who worked it?"

That was the question, all right. "Well . . . the Ouija board may have had something to do with it," I repeated stolidly.

"Please, Katy," Gram said. "Even in the hands of real witches, Ouija boards have all the power of a camera battery."

"Not necessarily," Agnes said with a reflective tilt of her head. "Spirits have been known to manifest through a Ouija."

"Yes, *spirits*," Gram said. "Insubstantial thought forms. Spirits can hardly knock one unconscious."

Agnes tapped on the dining room table with her long no-nonsense index finger. "That room must be explored, because there are almost certainly traces to be found."

"Traces of what?" I wondered.

She raised an expressive hand. "Dust, often. An odor, perhaps, or a stain."

I blinked. Dust, odors, and stains? Had she ever seen a high school dorm room?

"But surely Penelope—Miss P," Gram said, nodding at me, "would know to hire a scenter."

"I'm sure she has already," Agnes agreed. "Or at least is looking for one."

"A center?" I asked. "Like the tall guy on a basketball team?"

Gram burst out laughing. "I keep forgetting you haven't been here long," she said.

"A lot of young people don't know about them, Grandmother," Agnes said. "After all, there isn't much use for them these days." She turned toward me. "We're talking about *scenters,* as in 'scent.'" She wrinkled her nose. "Although a scenter employs much more than a sense of smell."

"A scenter is a sort of detective," Gram added excitedly. "Someone skilled in the use of many senses."

"Many?" I asked. "Like five?"

Agnes *tsk*ed. "There are more than five senses, Katy. You should know that."

"Of course she does!" Gram leaned forward. "How does it feel when you push, dear?"

"Pushing" was a slang term for telekinesis, or moving objects with your mind. It was not that big a deal as far as special abilities go, but it was something I could do. "Er . . . I don't know," I said. Actually, it felt sort of like sending a whip out from my brain and feeling it wrap like a tentacle around things, but I didn't want to gross out my great-grandmother. "Weird, I guess."

"Well, a scenter would know that feeling, and a number of others as well. She—or he, since many of them are male—would be able to perceive traces left in that poor girl's dorm room from whatever magic occurred there."

"By sensing dirt and things." I was still trying to get my head around that concept.

"By focusing," Aunt Agnes said. "Focusing is the core of all magic. The scenter concentrates on whatever has been deposited in the room—hair, skin, breath—and then sorts out what is relevant from what isn't."

"Breath?"

"Nothing is lost, Katy. The breath from your body will remain, in one form or another, until the end of time."

"Gracious, I hope Penelope doesn't have too much difficulty finding one," Gram interrupted. "There hasn't been a scenter in Whitfield for years."

"Let's hope we find one in a hurry," Agnes said. "It's been nearly two days. Traces are evanescent, you know. They remain, but they fade quickly, and soon become impossible to perceive, even for a scenter."

As it turned out, the lone scenter in the tristate area was on vacation at Club Med in Aruba, so Summer's room would be yielding no new information. Everyone was disappointed, especially me. The scenter might have exonerated me. Better yet, he might have figured out what had really happened to the Muffies, so that they could wake up. I hadn't liked Summer, but I wouldn't have wished what had happened to her on anyone. If there were just something I could do!

I began to think about scenters, and how they were the detectives of the spiritual plane. Actually, I could see myself doing that, solving crimes by using my highly honed sensitivities—being in demand wherever people were in need of psychic help, a Sherlock Holmes of the magical realm. I'd be welcomed into the highest circles of society because of my extraordinary skill. I'd even make inroads among enlightened cowen, bringing our disparate worlds closer together. Yes, I could see myself answering that call.

Katy Ainsworth, finder of lost souls.

"There are traces of everything everywhere, of everything that's ever happened," I explained to Peter while we were shucking oysters. Fall was the big season for oysters at Hattie's. "Like Napoleon's breath," I said, elaborating on Agnes's information with something I'd thought of on my own. "It's still here, somewhere."

"His farts, too?" Peter inquired.

"I'm serious!" I shouted, banging my knife on the bucket.

"Okay, I was listening. Traces. They're everywhere."

"But they're evanescent."

He looked over at me. "Like those baking soda volcanoes?"

I gave him a hard look. "No, not *effervescent*," I said, as if I didn't know he was pulling my chain. "Evanescent. The traces fade. They're made of things like dust and odor, so they fade."

He shrugged. "I don't think they fade very fast," he said. "Not in my room, anyway."

"Believe me, I know. I've been there." I put down my knife, thinking. "Still, it's worth a shot."

He sighed. "What sort of shot, exactly, are you thinking about, Katy?" he asked.

"I have to get back into Summer's room," I whispered. "To pick up the traces."

"I thought you said it took an expert to spot that stuff. To smell it or whatever."

"Well, an expert isn't available. The room's scheduled to be cleaned tomorrow."

"So? What would you be able to do?"

"I don't know. Check it out. Maybe I'd be able to pick up a vibe."

"What kind of vibe?"

"A *supernatural* vibe, Peter. If we knew that magic was involved, Hattie and Gram and Miss P might be able to help Summer and her friends. Besides, we might find something else. A clue."

"I doubt that," Peter said. "The police have already . . . Did you say 'we'?"

"No. My mistake. Me. Just me. I wouldn't want you to be involved."

"Frankly, I'd feel better if I *were* involved," he said.

I stopped what I was doing. "Why?"

He rubbed his chin. "Um, don't take this the wrong way, but . . . well, I'd feel safer if you weren't going to . . . whatever . . . all by yourself."

"Thanks," I said. "But I'm not about to be accused of being a bad influence on you."

"Just what are you planning, anyway?"

I bent close to him. "I'm going to break into Summer's room before the janitor gets there," I whispered. "That'll be a piece of cake. Moving locks is really elementary magic."

Peter nodded. "Fine," he said. "Only, nobody in dorm C is going to let you past the front door after what you . . . what you allegedly did."

I swallowed. "Maybe no one'll be around."

"Katy." He gave me one of his *Be reasonable* looks.

"Anything can happen."

"That's what I'm afraid of." He took a deep breath. "Look, if you're going to do something so crazy, I can't let you go alone."

"But what can you do that I can't?" I nearly shouted.

He looked right, then left, then crossed his arms over his chest. "I can get you past the girls who live there."

He explained how we were going to pull this off. In my mind's eye I could see Miss P shaking her head, blaming me once again if Peter and I got caught.

"But we won't get caught," I said aloud.

"I sure hope not."

"No way. Won't happen. It's a great plan."

It was a stupid plan. I realized that while I sat crouched inside the garbage bin that had contained, among other revolting things, the remains of the three hundred oysters Peter and I had just shucked.

"Can't you go any faster?" I hissed, peering out from under the stinking lid.

Peter was steering the bin on a dolly toward dorm C. "I don't want to draw attention to myself," he said, pulling a baseball cap over his eyes. That, plus the zip-up coverall that he wore when he worked on Hattie's truck, was the closest we could come to a janitorial disguise.

"I'm gagging in here."

"Sorry. I washed it the best I could. Get down." He pushed the lid down on my head.

"Howdy," he said in an unnaturally low voice. After a while he lifted the lid.

"Howdy?" I repeated.

"It was the school electrician. I didn't want him to recognize me."

"So you *talked* to him?" I sank back down. Maybe this wasn't going to be as easy as I'd thought.

"Okay, we're in the building, in front of Summer's room," Peter whispered finally. "Open the door."

I peered out of the bin and looked around. If anyone saw me, I'd be dead meat, and I'd be dragging Peter to the butcher with me. But the coast was clear. This was as good as it was going to get.

I threw five fingers at the lock. It clicked open. "Okay, go in," I said.

It was sad-looking inside. Summer's bed was folded up so that the metal frame showed above the wheels. It could have been anyone's bed, bare and ready for storage. You'd hardly know Summer had ever existed, except for the posters that had been left on the wall, one of Taylor Lautner with no shirt on, and one of Lady Gaga wearing black boots and a mask made of mirrors.

I wondered where Summer was now. A hospital room, probably, surrounded by monitors and poles with bags of hanging liquids, and maybe a vase of flowers that she wouldn't be able to see.

Who had done this?

My heart shivered. I knew I was innocent, but right then, that didn't make any difference to Summer or the others. They were living only in the strictest sense of the word, and no one knew how long they would go on that way. I'd read that people in prolonged comas rarely woke up.

I had to find out why this had happened. Not just for me but for them.

"Should I clean up here?" Peter asked. "To give us a reason for coming in."

"No!" Sometimes Peter could be so *dense*. "We don't want to disturb anything. Besides, I have to scent the place."

He sniffed. "Sorry, but the only scent in here is you." He made a face. "Oysters."

I waved him into silence, but he was right. Once I stepped out of the jumbo plastic garbage bin, the possibility of detecting subtle mystical fragrances was pretty well obliterated.

I decided to concentrate on the dust. There was a lot of it. My guess was that the jar of herbs I'd seen, which had no doubt been confiscated, may have been smoked in that room.

It didn't work, though. As hard as I tried to focus, I didn't really know what I was looking for. A pattern? If I looked hard enough, would I see a picture, the way gypsies read tea leaves at the bottom of a cup?

"Maybe we should move the bed," I said.

"I thought you didn't want to disturb anything."

"We'll put it back."

The bed rolled away easily, revealing a debris-filled corner. "The mother lode," I said, sifting through it.

Disappointingly, there didn't seem to be very much of value there—an expired coupon for T.G.I. Friday's, a Victoria's Secret ad cut out of a magazine with a circle drawn around a purple racer-back bra, a receipt for $15.80 from Fred's Bargain Mart, a sewing needle (probably the one A.J. had used to sew the tongue and stockings onto the witch doll), and a crumpled wad of paper that had once covered a drinking straw. I picked it up and smoothed it out. Written across it was a phone number.

"Found it," I said, dropping it along with the other items into a box I'd brought along for the purpose of collecting evidence.

"I've got something too," Peter said, showing me two broken pieces of brown plastic. "They were lodged behind the radiator. I think they're from a hair thing. A barrette."

"Looks like it. Toss them in." I held out the box.

"I think that's everything," he said.

"Then let's get out of here."

I knew that most of what we'd found was junk, but there was one object that had made this whole smelly excursion worthwhile. Magical scenter or not, the phone number would probably yield more information than all the dust patterns in the room put together.

The number turned out to belong to some guy at Yale whom Summer had met at a bar in Boston. He acted sad when I told him about Summer's medical condition, but I could tell by his answers to my questions that he didn't even remember her. It was only after I'd divulged her approximate bra size—he'd asked me—that he seemed to get a picture of who I was talking about. When he asked for my name, I hung up. I figured it'd be a lost cause anyway, unless I also e-mailed him a picture of my chest.

So that was a dead end. I went through the other things I'd found. The Victoria's Secret ad wasn't worth much. I figured that maybe Summer had been planning to impress the boob-crazed Yalie with a purple push-up. There was nothing strange about the needle, either. I even jabbed it into my own thumb to see if it was tipped with poison or something, but it wasn't.

Then I checked out all the T.G.I. Fridays within a ten-mile radius of Whitfield, but no one I spoke with knew Summer or the others. I considered passing on all my finds to the police, but then I'd have to admit that I'd gone into Summer's room.

That left the broken barrette and the receipt from Fred's Bargain Mart.

CHAPTER

•

NINE

Saturday morning I walked into town. Now, Whitfield is a hot spot on the Haunted New England trail, although the tourists we get are generally wackier than the ones who go to Disney World. They like witches, or think they do. Some of them want to *be* witches. And some of them really *are* witches and don't even know it, but there's nothing we townies can do about that. Anyway, because of the tourists, most of the stores along Main Street have silly names like Haircraft (beauty shop); the Cauldron (diner); the Green Man (florist); Bell, Book, & Candle (New Age literature and assorted woo-woo gift items); Sybil (women's clothes, mostly garments of the one-size-fits-all variety, and long velvet robes with big hoods); and Fred's Bargain Mart.

It was pretty easy to figure out the one thing that didn't belong. Fred's, with its torn awning and window crammed with out-of-print books and dingy knit pot holders and dusty statues of elves and bluebirds, was one of the most unattractive

storefronts imaginable. But the place had been around forever—so had the inventory, I think—so no one even noticed
it anymore.

That's why I was so surprised when I stood across the street
and saw . . . not Fred's but a charming little boutique with gera-
niums flanking the shiny red and brass doorway. Its sparkling
window was divided into sections like an advent calendar,
so that every individual mini-doorway displayed something
different—a pair of earrings made of seed pearls in the shape
of stars, a pink retro princess phone, a silver snake brace-
let with eyes the same shade of green as my own, a filigree
box containing painted clay figurines of animals. I can't really
explain why, but everything was so *inviting*. I didn't even like
to shop, but I couldn't wait to go inside.

I looked up. Past the new awning—black with red trim—
was its new sign:

The Emporium of Remarkable Goods

And beneath it, a banner reading:

Grand Opening
Free Gift with Purchase!

As I reached for the doorknob, I remembered—vaguely—
that I was really coming to find out what connection Fred's
Bargain Mart had with Summer Hayworth and her friends, but
somehow that part of it just didn't seem so important anymore.

Just then a high wind gusted up, smelling like spring and
the sea and green places far away. I closed my eyes and shiv-

ered. Music danced somewhere in the back of my mind, just out of reach—songs of yearning and loss and the slow passage of time.

I shook my head. For a moment I'd forgotten where I was. I'd forgotten everything.

A hat blew toward me, and I grabbed it. It was more like one of those old-timey helmets worn by biplane pilots or football players from a hundred years ago than a real hat. Made of coarse cloth, it looked like it was designed to fit closely over the head and then hang loosely on the sides like dog ears, sort of Elmer Fudd meets Birkenstock.

"Oh, thank you," huffed a red-haired kid about my age as he jogged up to me. "I was afraid I'd lose it for certain." At least I think that's what he said. His English was so strange that I could barely understand him.

I took a step backward. His clothes were even weirder than his hat. He was wearing a sort of monk's habit, a shapeless burlap robe that came down to his ankles. On his feet were what looked like leather bags.

His face cracked into a nervous smile. "Would you tell me where the high priestess of the village is, then?"

"The high priestess?" I repeated archly as I realized what was going on. Screw-loose tourist. Roswell, New Mexico, must be overrun by people claiming to have been abducted by aliens. Graceland had to be a mecca for Elvis impersonators. And Whitfield, Massachusetts, drew visitors like this. "The chamber of commerce is that way," I said, pointing down the street.

"But you . . ." Looking puzzled, he raised his head and sniffed the air. "You're one of us, aren't you?"

I resisted the urge to open my coat and check my arm-pits. "I don't know what you're talking ab— Oh." He took my hands in his, and even through my mittens I could feel a warmth and power and a strong sense of kinship with this person. I was also getting a picture of a strange and beautiful place with starry skies and clear water. When he withdrew his hands, I felt a sense of loss.

"Please," he whispered, his face as angelic and innocent as a child's. "The high priestess. I must see her. My mission is urgent."

Actually, Whitfield did have a high priestess: Hattie Scott, my employer at the restaurant and Peter's guardian. I normally wouldn't have thought of giving her name or revealing her status to a stranger, but I knew from his touch that whoever he was, he was of my kind and could be trusted. I gave him directions to Hattie's Kitchen.

"My thanks," he said, bowing formally. "Fare thee well, mistress."

I watched as he walked down the street, his curly red hair shining in the winter sunlight. *What have I done?* I thought, instantly sorry about blabbing so much. But he had been so warm, so . . . *trustworthy*. It occurred to me to maybe follow him to Hattie's to make sure he wasn't an ax murderer or something, but then a bell jangled behind me and the door to Fred's—that is, the Emporium of Remarkable Goods—opened.

In the doorway stood a girl with long black hair and the reddest lipstick I'd ever seen. She was tall and slender and wore black four-inch-high spike-heeled boots, black leather pants, and the kind of nubbly, slouchy sweater that would have looked like a sweatshirt on me but seemed ridiculously glamorous on her.

Total intimidation. I couldn't get away fast enough.

"Hold on," she said, gesturing with her head toward the interior of the store. "You know you want to come in."

"No, really. I thought this was . . . someplace else." She stared at me, looking amused. "The library," I finished, fully aware of how lame I sounded.

"You thought this was the library?"

I tried a laugh. It sounded so phony, I wanted to gag myself. "I guess I wasn't paying attention," I babbled, backing away. "All righty, then—"

"Oh, come on," she said. "Nobody's been in all day. I'm bored stiff. How about a soda?"

"Root beer okay?" the girl called over her shoulder. "There's Mountain Dew, too."

"Root beer's fine," I shouted. While she was gone somewhere in the back of the store, I took a look around. I wasn't really much of a shopper, but the array of gorgeous things in the store was . . . well, breathtaking. I turned in a slow circle, unable even to walk as I took in the one-of-a-kind objects that surrounded me. There were fancy soaps, exotic-looking clothes, pocketbooks and shoes, lace collars and fishnet stockings. Cute jewelry that I longed to wear, even though I never wore jewelry. Unusual perfumes with names like Baby, New-Mown Hay, Snow, and Gold.

My overwhelming desire to buy something was quelled as soon as I saw the prices. Everything was expensive. It was about as far removed from Fred's Bargain Mart as you could get.

"Hey! Catch!" she bellowed as she threw a can at me overhand. To my amazement I caught it before it crashed into one of the pricey display cases.

"Good save." She plopped down on a suede sofa and patted the seat cushion beside her. "How's about taking a load off?" she asked, propping her booted feet on a coffee table.

Obediently I came around and sat down. "You've got some beautiful things here," I said.

She shrugged. "It's my aunt's store," she said. "She's in Beirut or someplace, fighting over a shipment of silver."

"And she left you in charge?"

"Why not? It's not as if people are beating down the doors to get in."

I took a drink of my root beer. "My name's Katy," I said.

She extended a perfectly manicured hand to me. "Morgan." I'd never known anyone my age to shake hands before, at least not girls.

"I guess you're not from here," I said.

"You got that right. Hey, what's with this place, anyway? Is everybody crazy for witches here or what?"

"Oh, you noticed?" Through the front window I could see the bar called Magick Brewski. "It's even worse than this during the summer," I said. "And at Halloween . . ." I rolled my eyes.

"I get it," Morgan said, nodding. "So, are you a witch?"

I choked on my drink. Fizz poured out my nose. Very cool.

"Okay, take it easy. It was just a question. You don't have to answer."

So I didn't. I mean, if I'd been a little more prepared, I might have come up with a believable lie, but since I was pretty sure she was only trying to make conversation, silence seemed to be the best course of action, especially since I was already in trouble for magical showboating.

"Actually, I came to ask about something," I said finally. "I don't suppose you worked here while the place was still Fred's Bargain Mart."

"No, I just got here." She shrugged. I nodded. "But my aunt took over the inventory, and I've cataloged it all, if that helps."

Well, that was something, anyway. "Did you—er, Fred— sell Ouija boards?"

She raised her eyebrows. "Sure did. Still have three of them in the back." She got up and gestured for me to follow her. "They're not in the best condition, but my aunt thought someone might want them for their retro value." After a walk through more enticing merchandise, she handed one of the boxes to me. "Do you want to examine it first?"

I didn't know what I'd be examining it for, since I'd never actually seen a Ouija board. "No, that's all right," I said. I took out the receipt from Fred's Bargain Mart that I'd found in Summer's dorm room. "I just need to know if this was for a Ouija board. It would have been last week. On the twenty-third. Whatever she bought cost fifteen dollars and eighty cents. She used a credit card."

"No problem," Morgan said. She compared a number on the box with one on the receipt. "That was it."

So Summer had bought the board here. But I already knew that.

"Mystery solved?"

I took a deep breath. "Well, it explains what the receipt was for," I said. I'd been hoping that Summer had acquired the Ouija in some weird way. That it had been a magic board.

But it looked like it was exactly what Miss P had said it was, a perfectly ordinary toy. "I guess it helps. Thanks."

She cocked her head. "So what are you checking out? Or are you on some secret quest?"

"Nothing like that. It's just . . . Well, these girls at school . . . " I didn't know how much to tell her. Or how. Or if. *Probably not,* I thought, rubbing a dark spot on the rug with my toe. "They sort of . . . *Aak!*"

Beside me, in Morgan's place, sat a spotted jaguar.

I leaped down the length of the store like a demented sprinter and took refuge behind the sofa.

"Jeez. Relax, will you?" she said as she turned back into a girl again. "You were just kind of losing me there, you know? Got to work on the social skills, Katy."

"You turned into a jungle cat because you were bored with my conversation?" I asked huffily.

"Nah. Just trying to spice things up a little, that's all."

I shook my head to clear it. "So you're a witch too," I said finally.

"Shape-shifter. What's your thing?"

"Er . . . "

"Come on, out with it."

"I don't know," I said, waffling. You didn't just go around telling people you were a witch, even if you knew they were.

"For crying out loud, Katy, I smelled you coming down the street."

"Smelled?" I thought of the oddly dressed red-haired guy who'd sniffed around me. "Do I smell like—"

"You smell like a witch," Morgan said.

This was the weirdest thing I'd ever heard. I'd never noticed that witches smelled any different from anyone else. I doubted that even the major league witches of Whitfield—people like Miss P or Hattie Scott or my great-grandmother, Elizabeth Ainsworth—could *smell* the difference between witches and cowen.

"How about closing your mouth?" Morgan teased. "You're drawing bats."

I guessed I'd been gawking. "Just how do we smell?" I asked quietly.

She laughed, a big, raucous guffaw that was so at odds with her sophisticated appearance. That laugh dared me to stay mad at her. In another second I found myself laughing along with her.

"We smell *fabulous,*" she said, throwing her leg over the top of the sofa. "As cool and clean as running water, with a touch of mystery. Deep and earthy. Passionate. Wise. Exciting."

"All that? Hmm, maybe I'll quit showering." She'd said "we," I'd noticed. "Seriously, though, how did you know?"

"Hmm?"

"You know, that I might have, er, special ability."

"Special ability?" She laughed. "Is that what they call witchcraft here at Massachusetts Witch-a-Rama?"

I shook my head. "Just at my school."

"Are you kidding? You go to witch school? Is it like Hogwarts?"

"No. Ainsworth is a regular school. Well, it's private, and a lot of us board, but the classes are all the standard academic stuff. Where do you go? Liberty?"

She stuck her finger into her mouth. "Please. The rah-rah isn't for me."

"Are you homeschooled, then?"

She tossed her long hair. "Yeah, you could say that."

I thought there might be more behind that answer, but I didn't want to pry.

"What's your last name?" she asked suddenly.

"Er . . . Ainsworth," I said uncertainly. The issue of my name was always difficult to explain. "I grew up with a different name—my father's—but after moving here, I found out that the women in my family always keep the Ainsworth name."

"Like the school you go to."

"Right. It was founded by a distant ancestor of mine, Serenity Ainsworth."

She made a face. "Imagine being stuck with a name like Serenity," she said.

"Well, actually, that's my name too," I admitted. "Legally, anyway."

Morgan shrieked. "Your name is *Serenity*?"

I nodded glumly. "That's why I go by Katy."

"I can see why," she said, and laughed. "Hey, don't worry. Your secret is safe with me. So, what's your talent?"

I supposed it wouldn't be any big deal to tell her. "Telekinesis," I said with a shrug. Admittedly it wasn't a very big talent. "And psychometry."

"Psy what tree?"

"I can read objects. Like their history, or the people who owned them. No big deal," I added. "Not like shape-shifting."

"Are you kidding? Your magic is with *objects*. You're the Mistress of Real Things!"

I laughed, although what she'd said made me feel a lot

better about my gift. The Mistress of Real Things. Yes, I liked that.

"But you can't practice psycho-whatsis at school, right?"

"God, no. We can't even talk about witchcraft there. It's not allowed. Of course, the witches all know who the Muffies are—"

"Muffies?"

"Cowen." I explained about Muffies, which led to my telling her about what had happened in Summer's dorm room and why I was looking into Ouija boards. "All four of them just sort of keeled over," I said. "And the only thing even a little bit strange about the room was that they were playing with a Ouija board. Plus they might have been stoned."

She gave a dismissive wave.

"So what do you think?" I asked.

Morgan gave me a thoughtful look. "Did you really make them *stink*?" she asked.

I blushed. "Come on, Morgan."

She lay down on the couch, holding her sides. "And they turned your fries into fingers?"

"That's the point. They were Muffies. They shouldn't have been able to do anything like that. That's why I think the Ouija board had something to do with it."

She was still laughing as she got up and retrieved one of the boards we'd been looking at in the back of the store. "Well, okay. If you think it'll help, take one." She tossed it at me.

"No, that's okay," I said. "I really just wanted to know if Summer had—"

"Go ahead."

"No, I couldn't accept it. Really."

"So buy it," Morgan said.

"Huh?" Of all the wonderful things in the store, a Ouija board was about the last thing I would choose to spend money on.

"Let's see it, Katy. Cash on the barrelhead." She crashed her fist onto the coffee table.

"Okay, okay," I said, counting out fifteen dollars and eighty cents, which left me with four dollars. Fool, thy name is Katy.

"Huh! I knew I'd get your money sooner or later." Morgan gloated, pretending that my bills were some kind of vast fortune. "There's a sucker born every minute, I say."

"Yeah. Great," I said.

"Oh, now you're mad." She handed my money back. "I was just kidding."

"No, it's okay," I said, trying to be polite. "I'll take the board."

"Don't be dumb. I can palm it off onto someone else. Take the money." She waved the bills at me. "I'll give you the free gift anyway." She reached behind the cash register. "Grand opening special."

I almost gasped. It was gorgeous, a ring with a blue oval stone the size of a dime that seemed to glow from within. And it wasn't just about how it *looked*. It may have been my imagination, but as soon as the ring was on my finger, I felt suffused with a feeling of well-being, as if all my jangled nerves had been instantly coated with honey. "Are you kidding?" I asked. "This is a free gift?"

"Cool, huh?" She laughed. "It almost looks real, doesn't it?"

"It's not real?"

"Five bucks retail."

"Wow." I tried to take it off to look inside. "It's so . . . Ow." I felt a jolt like an electrical spark when it left my finger. "It almost hurts to take it off," I said, laughing.

"So don't. It suits you, anyway."

The stone had changed. When it was off my finger, it didn't glow at all. I put it back on. The stone came to life again. "Amazing," I said.

"It's some new resin or something. The band's a metal alloy, but it has real weight."

"It looks like gold."

"No lie. My aunt gets them from this company in California. Isn't it fabulous?"

I nodded, feeling that same sense of contentment coursing through me again. "Fabulous," I whispered.

Then I saw a clock in the display case, and gasped out loud. "Is that the time?" I threw on my coat. "I've got to get to work."

"Oh, you have a job?"

"In a restaurant called Hattie's Kitchen. I'm a cook."

Morgan put her hands on her hips. "Well, aren't you enterprising," she said.

"What I am is late." I raced for the door.

"Will you come back?" she asked.

"Sure," I said. "When are you here?"

"I'm always here." She cut her eyes toward the ceiling. "I live upstairs."

"Don't you get . . ."

She shook her head. Her eyes didn't meet mine. She knew I was going to say "lonely," and she didn't want to go there.

I don't know how I knew that; I just did. Maybe it was from being lonely myself. Anyway, nobody who's lonely wants other people to know it, so I let it drop. Besides, I was in a hurry. "Maybe we can hang out together sometime," I said, stepping outside.

"Sounds good."

The door jingled behind me. I jogged to Hattie's feeling— for a while anyway—as if all were right with the world.

CHAPTER

•

ELEVEN

I just had time to get to work in time for the dinner shift. I didn't like to make it just under the wire like that, because there was always a lot of prep work to get out of the way before the place got crowded, especially on a Saturday. I was hoping to have at least a few minutes alone in the kitchen, but when I arrived, the place was already humming, humid and redolent with the aroma of something that reminded me a little of beef stew, only better.

"That smells great," I said to the room in general.

"Thank you," answered a voice that sounded sort of like a cross between Justin Bieber's and Dracula's. I blinked as he stepped out from behind the pantry door. It was the same guy I'd met in front of Morgan's store. "Oh, hello again," he said with a smile. He wiped his hands on his snow-white apron and walked over to me, as graceful as a cat.

His strange outfit had been replaced by a pair of jeans and Peter's Foo Fighters T-shirt, so I guessed that Hattie had hired him. "So, are you a work-study student too?" I asked, taking a clean apron off a peg on the wall.

"A what?"

"Katy!" Hattie bounded into the kitchen with Peter's little brother, Eric, in her arms. "Have you met Bryce?"

"Biii," Eric cooed.

"Bryce de Crewe," the red-haired boy elaborated.

"I'm Katy," I said. "Whatever you're cooking smells good."

Bryce de Crewe grinned proudly. "'Tis an easy task with instant fire," he said.

"Huh?"

"Never mind," Hattie said. "What we're making's almost finished, so we won't need you."

"Are you kidding?" Saturday night was our busiest service.

"No. Take the night off. Bryce and I will manage."

"What about Peter?" I asked, wondering if I still had a job.

"He's off too," Hattie said. "Bryce and I can handle the dinner service."

"But it's Saturday," I said. I didn't see how two people could prepare all the food, especially since nothing seemed to have been started except for a pot of broth.

"It's a limited menu," Hattie said.

"Limited to soup?"

"That's right," Hattie said, sounding dangerously annoyed. "Have you got a problem with that?"

"No . . . Just asking," I said.

"It's a special project that the two of us have to attend to." That was, I knew, the closest thing to an explanation that I was going to get.

"Uh, sure," I said. "No problem. I'll just . . . go." Hattie was already bustling, putting Eric in his extra large high chair and taking down some infrequently used ingredients from a special pantry at the far end of the kitchen.

Then it occurred to me. "You're making a potion," I said.

"Get!" Hattie shouted, waving a wooden spoon at me. "Go on, get!" she shouted. I skittered backward as Eric burst into peals of laughter.

Bryce looked alarmed, as if he believed Hattie was going to beat me with her spoon. I knew that wouldn't happen, but something was bothering her. Something she wasn't about to tell me.

"You're working brunch tomorrow," she called as I headed out the double doors.

No one was home at my great-grandmother's house. Gram and Aunt Agnes were consulting with florists or bakers or something, getting ready for my aunt Agnes's wedding. She was thirty-eight years old and "not the marrying kind," so getting married was a pretty big deal. Actually, it was more like the biggest deal in the history of the world as far as those two were concerned.

Normally Agnes was a very sensible person. She was the chair of the Ethnobotany Department at Stanford University, to which she commuted via astral projection, although I doubted the chancellor knew that. Gram was a Therapeutic Touch practitioner in the Alternative Healing section of Whitfield Hospital. Neither of them was what you'd ever think of as flaky. But this wedding thing had turned them both into lunatics. They'd spent so much time on preparations that Jonathan—Agnes's fiancé, who was a carpenter—had taken on extra work just to fill up all his free time, since Agnes was hardly ever available.

It was the same with me. Coming to Gram's house used to mean baking cookies together and tending the garden and watching movies at night. Now it meant heating up a frozen dinner by myself and pondering how many bags of dog poop had accumulated outside my dorm room that day.

With a sigh I opened my laptop and clicked on e-mail. There was something from my father. For a moment—a very brief moment—I entertained the idea that it might be a personal note. *Hi, Katy. Hope you're enjoying your new term at school. Can't wait to see you during break!*

But no. It was a lengthy article about the monodic madrigals of Carlo Gesualdo (1566–1613). I guessed he thought that was something I needed to know. *Thanks, Dad. Try not to be so sentimental next time.*

Well, at least there was Peter. Whatever awful thing might happen, Peter could always make it better.

I called him on his cell. He'd spent the afternoon with his great-uncle, and he'd been nervous about that. Most people don't have to prepare to visit their relatives, but this was a special case. Aside from all the complicated family issues that had come up in the years since Peter's parents had died, there were other problems. For one thing, Peter's great-uncle Jeremiah was the richest man in Whitfield, and maybe all of Massachusetts. It couldn't have been that easy for a guy who'd never shopped anywhere besides Wal-Mart to hang out with an old man who owned a Learjet and lived in a mansion that was bigger than most hotels.

But that meeting had been hours ago. I should have heard

from Peter before now. "Are you okay?" I asked when he answered the phone.

"Uh, yeah," he said. He sounded weird, so I asked him if he could talk. "Sure," he said. "It's just that I'm in a . . . a car."

"Whose car?"

"Jeremiah's, I guess." He whispered, "Katy, it's a limo."

"Where are you going?"

"To New York."

"What?"

"He said I needed clothes. So I'm going for a fitting. At Armani."

I choked. "Are you kidding me?"

"No. Not unless he was kidding *me*."

"Maybe you can get a tux for Winter Frolic," I said, reminding him about the big midyear school dance.

"I do have to get a tux. It's on the list."

"He gave you a list of clothes to order?"

"Right. Then he gave me fifty dollars for coffee and told me to go with the driver. Oh, God. I think we're here."

"Peter—"

"I'll call you later, okay?" He broke the connection.

For a long time I just sat with the phone in my hand, trying to wrap my head around things. I mean, it was great that Peter's coldhearted but rich relative was finally paying attention to him, but it was a lot to take in. The day before, my boyfriend had been an orphan who'd lived above a restaurant. Today he was being chauffeured to Armani for a fitting.

The two of us had enjoyed our mutually low status as kitchen workers because we'd had each other and Hattie, who had taken me under her wing after I'd been dumped into a boarding school because my father had been too busy with his love life to put up with me. But now that Peter's Uncle Moneybags had surfaced, all that might have been changing.

Don't get me wrong. I was glad that something might finally be going Peter's way. It was just that, as selfish as it was, I missed him then, that night, when I had no friends and no work and nobody in the house except the ten thousandth generation of Whitfield mice to keep me company.

My life was going through a black hole or something, what with my soiled reputation at school. I didn't feel welcome there. My family was doing wedding things. My dad—well, that was the same as ever, his idea of a warm relationship being an e-mail forward. My job at Hattie's Kitchen had always allowed me to take my mind off my problems, but it looked as if I might have been replaced there, too.

And now Peter, who would be wearing an Armani tux to Winter Frolic while I graced his arm in a gown from the consignment store, was too busy to talk to me.

Did that suck or what?

CHAPTER

•

TWELVE

I made a sandwich and took it to my room upstairs. My French textbook was open to a review of irregular verbs, in preparation for a test on Monday.

Great. I'd be spending Saturday night studying for a verb test two full days in the future. Just call me Miss Party. In a dramatic (and, okay, childish) gesture, I threw the French book against the wall. On its way it knocked over the box where I'd stashed the debris from Summer's room.

With a sigh I crawled under my desk, where the various "clues"—all having proven to be worthless—were strewn, and tossed them one by one into the wastebasket—the bra ad, the sewing needle, the T.G.I. Friday's coupon, the sex-crazed Yalie's phone number. From my jeans pocket I took the receipt for the Ouija board and tossed that in too. While I was retrieving my French book, I spotted the two broken pieces of plastic that Peter had found. They had fallen behind the desk, and I had to reach for them with a back scratcher. When I finally got hold of them, I hit my head while extricating myself, and cursed through clenched teeth while the jagged pieces of plastic dug into my palm.

"Calm down," I said out loud, forcing myself to lean against the bed. I knew that I was having a klutzdown—a meltdown of klutziness, not unfamiliar to me—and that if I stood up at that moment, I was sure to stub my toe, spill coffee on my books, and probably poke myself in the eye. "Breathe," I commanded myself, closing my eyes. "In, out, in, out . . ."

In my mind's eye I saw a beautiful meadow filled with wild-flowers. The sky was a soft, cloudless blue, and the air was suffused with the scent of violets. "Yes, yes," I whispered. "Good thoughts . . ."

Into the picture I'd created walked a man of late middle age.

Huh?

A dark-haired young girl, eight or nine years old, held his hand and skipped alongside him. At a spot in the meadow where a profusion of daisies grew, the girl stopped, picked an armful of flowers, and offered them to . . . her father. Yes, of course he was her father, despite his advancing years.

The longer I held on to the image, the more certain I became, although I still had no idea why I was having this vision in the first place.

The little girl loved him more than life itself. His visits, though infrequent, were filled with surprises and affection. And magic. Oh, the magic! The girl tossed the daisies over her head and—whoosh!—they changed in midair into butterflies. Shrieks of laughter. The man applauded appreciatively.

What was this? I wondered. A dream? Had I fallen asleep? Or was my subconscious telling me something about my relationship with my psychologically distant father? If so, why was this man so much older than my dad, who was thirty-eight, looked like Hugh Jackman, and was cowen to the core? Why was the little girl doing magic? Before I'd come to Whitfield, I'd never mentioned a word about my abilities to anyone.

Still, only a small part of my mind asked those questions. The rest of me just wanted to watch.

The girl held up her arms, and the man picked her up and whirled her around in a cloud of butterflies. Then he set her down, admonishing her with an upheld index finger to stay.

The girl's face fell. She ran toward him, her arms outstretched once again. But this time he did not pick her up but pushed her away gently, shaking his head. She cried as he moved farther and farther away, growing dimmer with each step as if he were being enveloped in mist.

"Da," she called, but she knew she could not bring him back. He would return when he wished, when he could spare the time from his other life, his other child, whom he loved more than he loved her.

"Please don't go," she whispered, sinking to her knees. No one heard her. Strands of her long hair fell across her eyes and stuck to her teary face. "Don't leave me—"

And then she heard them. Looking skyward, she saw vultures flying toward her, their huge wings making shadows on the earth beneath them, surely coming for her.

"No. No," the little girl rasped, staggering to her feet and stumbling forward, her head craned to see the creatures behind her. "No!"

She ran as fast as she could, but she could not outrun the gigantic birds. They swooped down on her, their ragged wings enveloping her as they grasped her thin bones with their claws and screeched into her ears.

"Da!" she called helplessly as she tried to cover her head. "Come back for me, please, Da."

I jumped up so fast that for a moment I didn't remember where I was. My hands were trembling. I opened them slowly. In my right palm, which was marked by their sharp edges, were the two pieces of plastic I'd found under my desk.

It had been a long time since I'd "read" objects without thinking about them. I guessed it was because I'd forgotten that I was holding those plastic bits. But what exactly *had* I been reading? Almost reluctantly I let the pieces fall back into the box where they had been since Peter had found them. Even in the box they seemed to be vibrating with energy. And my ring . . .

The ring from Morgan's store was glowing again, a bright opalescent blue.

Still breathing hard, I put the lid on the box and placed it on top of my dresser. Psychometry was strange that way. Usually the vibes I got from objects were pretty drab, but occasionally, if the thing I touched had a lot of emotion attached to it, it could be a pretty intense experience.

One thing I knew, though, was that the emotions I'd gotten through those bits of plastic hadn't belonged to Summer Hayworth. Those thoughts had come from a witch, one who could turn flowers into butterflies at an age when most children were learning to roller skate.

So how had they gotten into Summer's room?

• • •

After finishing my sandwich, I tried to call Peter again, but this time he didn't answer at all. He was probably getting his pants fitted, I thought.

Or else he just didn't want to talk to me.

Suddenly all thought of my psychometric experience vanished, replaced by paranoid thoughts about Peter Shaw. Did he even love me anymore? My "Insecure Katy" voice kept piping up. *Well, why should he?* it said. I was okay for Tuesday evening, maybe, but why should Peter stay with me now that he was a part of the great Shaw family again? He wasn't the poor little orphan boy anymore. The richest man in town was re-inheriting him.

I wondered how long it would be before the Muffies at school started to treat him like one of their own. They'd always liked Peter—you couldn't look like he did without having girls fall all over you—but now he was in their league. Becca Fowler had told me that she'd overheard a group of Muffies comparing notes about Peter. Two of them had asked him to Winter Frolic, but he'd turned them both down because, as one of them had said, he was stuck with "the kitchen girl."

That was me, I guess. There was no way they could understand that cooking was something I liked to do. Not to mention how the extra money I was making would come in handy when I went to Harvard after I graduated the following year. Me. With Peter. Alone, since there was no chance that any of those Barbie doll cretins at Ainsworth School would be going there.

Still, it was a long time between high school and college, and with his recent ascent in social status, my guess was that Peter was going to start looking more like Muffy candy and less like someone who'd want to spend his life with the kitchen girl.

Insecure Katy wasn't someone I liked to listen to.

To get rid of her I called my great-grandmother's cell. "Where *are* you, Gram?" I demanded. "It's almost seven o'clock."

"Oh, dear," she said, sounding dismayed. "Are you at home? We thought you'd be working tonight."

"I was supposed to, but—"

"Agnes and Jonathan and I are on our way to Heath's for dinner, and then afterward we'll be stopping at the hospital. Jonathan's agreed to put up some bookshelves in the children's play area. Do join us, Katy."

"Er . . . thanks, but I've already eaten," I said. It was a pretty safe bet that Heath's had been Gram's idea, since it specialized in soft white food for old ladies. Jonathan must have been loving that. Not to mention working at night for free. But hey, maybe that was what happened when you got married. You ended up living a life you didn't even want. Maybe that was what Peter was afraid of. Maybe the prospect of throwing his future away on the kitchen girl—

"Oh, stop it!" I said out loud.

"What was that, dear?" Gram asked.

"Oh, nothing. A bug. Er, crawling up my leg."

"Good grief."

I figured I'd better get off the phone before I lied myself into the emergency room. I made my apologies to Gram and Agnes—not that any were necessary, since they hadn't planned on inviting me in the first place—and left the house. I just couldn't stand my own company any longer.

CHAPTER

•

THIRTEEN

All of downtown Whitfield looked like a scene cut out of paper and set against a star-filled sky. Cars were starting to fill up the parking lot in front of Hattie's Kitchen, their owners no doubt expecting real food. Whatever she and Bryce de Crewe were concocting, it was probably going to come as an unwelcome surprise to the diners.

That was a bad move, in my opinion. Hattie's Kitchen had a reputation, deserved or not, for giving everyone what they needed. That meant a lot of different meals and custom everything. How could you run a restaurant where you served everybody the same thing? And soup, at that?

The thing that bothered me most, though, was that she hadn't trusted me enough to let me help her. She preferred relying on a total stranger.

Who was this Bryce guy, anyway? Some dude who blew in from nowhere, and clearly didn't have all his marbles, either, I thought irritably as I passed the last of the restaurant's twinkling lights. Against the dark sky my ring glowed fairy blue on my finger.

I moved on purposefully toward the lineup of Main Street stores, where the Emporium of Remarkable Goods stood out like a beacon. Even from across the street I could see the CLOSED sign on the door. Well, duh. It was nearly eight o'clock at night, and the summer tourists were long gone. What had I expected?

I was about to turn around and go back home when I saw some movement in the store. Maybe she was still there. As I crossed the street, a thought floated into my mind: *What am I doing here?* When Morgan had told me to come back, I doubted that she'd meant come back *that night*. I mean, girls who looked like her always found something to do on Saturday night, even if they were new in town.

What had I been thinking? *Oh, God,* I thought, *I've got to go home before I start bibbling my lips or walking down the street doing the chicken dance.*

"Katy?"

Morgan was at the door, smiling. "Couldn't stay away, huh?"

"Oh, no," I said airily. "I was just . . ." I made a vague gesture meant to indicate that I hadn't intended to be there at all but was only strolling past the closed storefronts on a whim.

"Looking for the library again?"

I felt myself blushing so hard, I thought I would combust.

"Come in," she said, laughing.

"No, really—"

She grabbed my sleeve and dragged me inside.

On the coffee table was a tray of fantastic-looking frosted cookies. "Did you make these?" I asked.

"No big deal," she said.

Unfortunately, she was right. I took one bite, and it was all I could do to choke it down. It tasted like a year-old gingersnap.

"Yuck?" Morgan asked.

I had to help my peristalsis by massaging my neck. "No, they're great," I lied.

She laughed that wild, hearty laugh that made me want to laugh with her again. "Actually, they're year-old gingersnaps," she said. "I put a glamour on them."

"Man, I got it right on the nose," I whispered as the platter took on its original appearance. Mold was even growing on some of them.

"I was hoping I'd be able to fool you."

I finished choking. "Did I tell you I'm a cook?" I asked.

"Wonderful. Cook for me."

"And deprive you of creating these?" I pushed the cookie tray her way. We both laughed.

"Seriously, I'm glad you're here," Morgan said. "I've been thinking about you."

"Thinking what?"

"About you being the Mistress of Real Things. How about showing me what you can do?"

I felt myself blushing again. "You're kidding," I said.

"No, I mean it."

"It's not very interesting. Mostly the history of tables and chairs."

She shrugged. "How about this?" she asked, handing me a pewter and ceramic tankard. The pewter was pitted and thin, and the ceramic was so ancient, it looked like smooth stone.

"It's really old," I said.

"You think?" she said sarcastically.

"How old is it?"

She shrugged. "Fourth or fifth century. British, but of Roman design. Probably from the occupation of Britannia under one of the later emperors. Valentinian the Third, maybe."

I set it down gingerly. "Wow," I said. "You really know your history."

She waved the compliment away. "So, what do you see? Or do you want me to go first?"

"Huh?"

"I'll show you what I've got, and then you show me."

That took off a lot of the pressure. "Okay," I said. "Just don't turn into a gargoyle or anything this time."

"Okay. Sit over there." She pointed to a chair with carved wooden arms and a seat upholstered in mauve velvet. Next to it was a small marble-topped table on which rested a cage containing a delicately worked bird made of silver filigree.

I almost reached over to touch it, but I stopped myself. *What's with me?* I wondered. Why the sudden fascination with *stuff?* I'd never cared at all about things like jewelry and decorative objects. I didn't even use bubble bath. Peter was always complaining that it was hard to buy presents for me because I'd rather have a bottle of saffron than a bottle of perfume. He gave me a pen for my birthday, and even that was too frilly for my taste.

But here everything was different. Celtic harp music quietly filled the room as Morgan took the bird out of the cage. "It's Bengali, about a century old," she said, gently stroking the fine metal filigree of its wings.

Just then I saw what looked like a movement of the bird's head. I blinked, and it happened again. "What—"

"Shh."

The bird looked at me. *Saw* me. I could see into its eyes. It flapped its silver wings and flew around the store, fully alive now, its metallic color replaced by the gray feathers of a living sparrow.

"Omigod," I said. "You can bring inanimate objects to life."

She laughed. "No. Hell, no. That would be like raising the dead. No one can do that."

Well, there was one person. Peter's little brother, Eric, could do exactly that. Which was why no one who knew about it ever, *ever* talked about his talent, even to other witches. Eric was only eleven years old, and had enough problems without having the whole world beating down his door. So I didn't see any reason to tell Morgan—or anyone else who didn't already know—about him.

"All I can do is change something's appearance," she said, standing up and holding out her hand. The bird flew by. Then, with a movement too swift for me to follow, she snatched it out of the air. When she opened her hand, the bird had become a metal sculpture again. "It's all about appearance anyway, isn't it?"

This time I did reach out to touch it. As I did, I caught a fleeting glimpse of the bird's eyes. They were panic-stricken.

"The bird—"

Morgan pulled it gently out of my grasp. "Convincing illusion, huh?"

"But it *looked* at me. It was alive."

"Was it?" She handed the bird back to me. I looked into its eyes. There was nothing. No sign of life at all.

Everything felt very still for a moment. Finally I said, "I guess you're right," and gave it back to her. "I didn't mean to . . . *accuse* you or anything," I said, waffling. "It was just—"

"God, girl. Lighten up."

"So . . ." I swallowed. The whole episode had left a strange feeling in my belly. "You can make things look any way you want?" I asked.

She made a small gesture. "Like what?"

"Could you make the bird look like a bear?"

"Why would I do that?"

"Because you could," I answered without thinking.

"My, you're ambitious," she said.

"What do you mean?"

"It's your turn," she said.

"I can't do anything like . . ." I looked at the bird. It still gave me a queasy feeling. "Like you did."

"Too bad," she said. "A deal's a deal. Get cracking."

"Okay," I conceded, picking up the tankard and focusing on it. I used to not have to focus. At one time everything about the object, including everyone who'd ever touched it, would come rushing at me as soon as I picked it up, so I'd learned to control that. Now I didn't get anything unless I was trying. It was a lot better that way, believe me.

"I meant it when I said it was old. Its vibes are dim, as if it hasn't been touched in a very long time. *Your* imprint isn't even on here."

"I cleaned it," Morgan said.

I pushed a little harder. "I can hear music," I said. "Someone's singing. Someone who's blind drunk, from the sound of him. He's got brown hair and a beard, and . . . and he smells really bad." Seriously, this dude's body odor was nearly overpowering in the humid mist of the lake.

"The lake?" I said aloud.

"Go there," Morgan said.

"What?"

"You can see it, right? The lake, the tankard, B. O. Plenty?"

"Uh-huh." I was trying to keep the image in my mind while talking to her. It wasn't easy.

"So take it one step farther. Go into it."

"Go into what? The tankard?"

"Yes."

"But how would I get back?"

"Don't be stupid. You're not really *going* anywhere in the first place. You'll be here."

"Oh."

"So go ahead."

"You mean now?"

"No. Next week."

"Okay, okay."

"On the count of three."

"No. That's too—"

"One."

"Morgan, I told you—"

"Two."

"I can't. I need more—"

"Three. Go."

OMG. OMG. OMG.

I was there.

Chapter

·

FOURTEEN

At first I felt really constricted, as if I were squeezing through a vacuum cleaner hose. For a second it seemed as if I would be crushed like a nut, but then . . . *foop*. Suddenly I was standing in a boat, which was not my favorite place to be, since I couldn't swim very well. The last time I'd gotten into a boat, it had crashed, and the only reason I'd made it home alive was because Peter had carried me through a mile of mud.

So there I was, trying to figure out how large I should be. Since I had no body in this place, it was hard to tell what size I was. I swung from being tiny, crawling around the wet boards, to being gigantic and hovering over the craft like a cloud.

Finally I was able to get a vague fix on things and take in the scene. It was night, a dead, starless, moonless night. I wondered what this fool was doing in a rowboat at night, but since he was so drunk, I figured he probably didn't know himself.

He took a swig and belched loudly. *God, men can be so*

gross, I thought. Then he laughed and started rocking the boat from side to side.

"Like that, do you?" he slurred.

"Hold still, you moron!" I yelled, but of course he couldn't hear me. He just kept rocking until water started sloshing over the side. This really wasn't a fantasy I wanted to live out. "I can't swim!" I shrieked.

He responded by spitting.

Okay, I can handle this, I told myself. I was perfectly aware that this was magic I was doing, that some part of my mind had gone through the tankard to the time and place where the tankard had come from. I knew that my body was really perfectly safe inside the Emporium of Remarkable Goods, and that Morgan was . . .

"Morgan?"

She was *there*, in the boat with him. With me. At least it looked like Morgan, except that her clothes were completely different. She was wearing a long gown with a sash. I think it was green, but the night was so dark that it was really hard to see anything clearly. There was just something about her eyes, gleaming as if she were enjoying this macabre midnight boat ride, that made me think . . .

But no, it couldn't be. It was all too weird.

"Give us a kiss, love," the drunk man said, sloshing beer or whatever it was all over himself as he stood up and squat-walked through me to where the girl (was it Morgan?) was sitting.

"Go back to your end of the boat, you lout," she shrilled, laughing. "You'll tip us over."

It couldn't be her, I decided. My mind was doing that, making it seem to be Morgan because of some psychological connection. The question was why.

Her head swiveled to face Mr. Charm. Unfortunately, I was wobbling directly in front of the man, so it looked for all the world like she was staring straight into my eyes. Then, with a big grin that sent shivers running though me, she said, "It would not do for you to drown, my dear."

I knew in that instant exactly what she was going to do, but it was too late to stop her, even if I'd had a real body to stop her with.

She stood up suddenly and straight-armed her date right in the neck. He had just taken a drink from the tankard, and that mouthful spewed all over the place while his eyes bulged out and his arms began to windmill.

"No!" I shouted as he lost his balance. "No!" the woman shouted at the same time, scrambling toward him on all fours while the boat swung crazily around in the water. I guessed that she'd changed her mind about throwing the drunken fool into the lake, but she didn't reach for him. Instead she grabbed for the tankard. I felt a brief moment of relief. If the tankard didn't fall into the water, there was much less chance that I'd drown. But then the man grabbed it right out of her hands before lurching toward the side of the boat.

I needed time to go back into the tankard. Without it I'd be lost. But there was nothing I could do. I was tethered on a psychic level to the tankard. Wherever it went, I had to follow. If I didn't, I knew, I would die. The guy bellowed like a crazed bull as he fell into the water, still clutching his drink, and I felt myself being pulled behind him, through the dank air toward the algae-covered water. The last thing I saw was the girl, who looked so much like my new friend Morgan, standing in the boat with her hands on her hips, shaking her head in anger.

"Morgan!" I called. I couldn't even reach the tankard now.

I was in the middle of a lake in an unknown place and an unknown time. Even if I lived through this, I'd never be found. "Help!" I screamed. "Get me out of here!"

Her eyes met mine, and I saw her mouth move. "Goodbye," she said.

Well, maybe her eyes didn't meet mine. Maybe she was looking at her date. Her date, whom she might have just murdered.

Water shot inside every opening in my body—up my nose, filling my mouth, blinding my eyes. I came up sputtering, flapping my arms uselessly as I tried to teach myself to swim then and there.

It wasn't working. For a moment the moon came out, and I saw the girl's face again, bathed in cold light. "Morgan!" I called. I was hoping, praying that she could see me, but she gave no sign of it. She just kept standing on the boat as it drifted away.

"Please help me," I squeaked.

The man, finding his way to the bank, climbed up and shook himself like a dog. "I'll see that you pay for this, you harpy!" he shouted.

The woman responded with a rude gesture. "Idiot!" she shouted. "'Tis *you* ought to have drowned!"

Even though I was panicking, a part of my mind registered the way she had emphasized the word "you," and it struck me as odd. It was as if she knew that someone besides the man had been in the boat with her.

But none of that mattered now. All I knew was that the water was invading every part of me. In the last glimpse I had of her, she was standing like a statue in the boat, a shawl wrapped around her shoulders. As I sank beneath the water, I watched her pull the shawl more closely around her arms.

I don't know how long I stayed there, but when I came up, I couldn't breathe. The boat was gone. Crickets chirped along the distant shore. A mosquito droned near my face. I was so tired, too tired to do much besides allow the water to drag me down again.

Chapter

·

Fifteen

"Katy."

Someone was hugging me. Or punching me. I couldn't tell which. Water poured out of my mouth. But it was still all around me. I would have screamed if I'd had the strength, but all I could do was stiffen my limbs.

"Stop it. Relax. Listen to me. Relax."

"Who . . ." I managed to turn my head. "Peter!"

The sight of him did a lot to bring me around. "How . . . How did . . ."

"Shh. Just listen," he said. "It's the ring. You've got to concentrate on the ring, okay?"

"What?"

"The ring will take you back. To the store, remember?"

"The . . . store . . ." I shook my head and coughed. "Okay. The ring." I looked at my finger. The ring Morgan had given me was glowing a bright opalescent blue.

"But . . . I don't know how . . ." Suddenly I was coughing

again, but not from the water in my lungs. The place had a horrible smell. "Are we in a swamp or something?"

"Never mind," Peter said. "Just concentrate on the ring."

"Okay," I breathed.

"The ring will take you home."

Like Dorothy's ruby slippers, I thought, focusing on the ring. *Take me home. Take me home.*

Peter was still holding me, but his grip was loosening. Somewhere in the corner of my consciousness, I could hear him coughing. Then he let go of me, and I slid out of his arms and into the deep water.

Take me home. I touched the slimy bottom of the lake, and the tankard was there, calling to me like sonar. *Yes, yes. Home.*

I felt myself constricting again, being sucked into the molecules of the tankard. With a huge sigh of relief, I just allowed myself to go.

And then I felt as if someone had just smacked me across the face with a plank. *Peter!*

Where was he? Hadn't he come with me? *Couldn't* he?

"Peter!" I screamed. "Peter!"

"Calm down," someone was saying.

I opened my eyes. I was on the couch in the store.

"Sheesh, what a drama queen."

I propped myself up on one elbow and tried to swallow the furriness in my mouth. "I'm back," I whispered.

"Keenly observed," Morgan said. "Who's Peter?"

I cleared my throat. I could still taste the lake water. "My . . . my boyfriend," I said, looking around. "I was drowning. In a lake that smelled like a toxic dump. And Peter came. He rescued me."

Morgan laughed out loud. "And they lived happily ever after," she said. "Is that how it ends?"

"What?"

"Your fairy tale. The handsome prince has to make the scene, is that right? I mean, you couldn't possibly have made it back by yourself, on your own two feet."

"I wasn't on my feet. It was a psychic journey."

"Whatever. Barbie goes metaphysical."

"Who are you calling Barbie?" I demanded, sitting up.

"You," she said, looking at me levelly. "Because nobody rescued you. You went into the tankard, and you came out, all on your own power. You didn't need a *guy* to make it okay."

"I needed *someone* to tell me how to get back," I said angrily. "It sure wasn't you."

"Oh?"

"Peter told me to use the ring. Otherwise I'd never have known how to leave that place."

"What ring?"

"The ring you gave me. It's a magic ring, isn't it?" I sounded like an interrogator.

"Of course it isn't. Going into that tankard must have burned up some of your brain cells."

"How else was I supposed to get out?" I shouted.

"How would I know?" she shouted back at me. "You're the one with the gift."

I was so frustrated, I crammed another cookie into my mouth. "These suck," I mumbled, spitting into a napkin.

"Okay," she said. "Let's be reasonable. Call Peter. He'll tell you if he was there or not." She handed me a phone.

"Good idea." I dialed his number. If he didn't answer, I'd

take that as a sign that he was still at the lake. *Or in it*, I thought with a frisson of horror.

"Hello?" Peter mumbled on the other end.

"Where are you?"

Smacking of lips. "I'm back in the limo," he said with a yawn. "What's the matter?"

"Nothing. What are you doing?"

Silence. Finally a sigh. "I'm sitting here," he said. "I'm going home. To bed. Because it's late, Katy. Any other questions?"

"Oh," I said. "Then you weren't . . . somewhere else?"

"I might have been," he said patiently. "Can you give me a clue as to where?"

"Like in a lake? Rescuing me from drowning?"

"Is this some kind of prank?" he asked crankily. "I think you pretty much know everywhere I've been, since you've called me just about every hour on the hour since I left."

That hurt. I'd called only three times. "Okay," I said contritely. "I'm sorry I bothered you. I really am."

"Hey, sorry. It's just been a long and boring day," he said, his voice softening. "You never bother me." I could hear the sleepy smile in his voice. "How about breakfast tomorrow?"

I laughed. We were both scheduled to work the six a.m. shift at Hattie's. "Sure," I said, and hung up.

"I owe you an apology," I said to Morgan.

She arched an eyebrow. "So Peter wasn't your knight in shining armor, huh?"

I shook my head. "He was in New York. Actually, I knew that, but everything just seemed so . . ." I caught myself. "I was going to say 'real,' but . . ."

She laughed. "I know. Who's to say what's real and what's not?"

"Especially here."

"Especially," she agreed.

"I guess I *wanted* Peter to rescue me," I admitted. "I wanted him to . . ."

"To care?"

"Yeah," I said hoarsely. I was ready for her to make fun of me, call me a Barbie again or worse, but she didn't. Instead she took a scarf off one of the display tables and wrapped it around my neck. "We all want that," she said. "Sometimes it happens, and someone does care. But when it doesn't, we have to be enough for ourselves. Do you get it?"

I nodded. "Be my own hero," I whispered.

"Yeah, baby. Shoot, you're the Mistress of Real Things, aren't you?"

"Damn right," I said, although I didn't feel as cocky as I tried to sound. I looked over at the tankard and shuddered. I could still feel that brackish water flooding into my lungs.

"You okay?"

I took the scarf off and gave it back to her. "I'm fine," I said.

She wrapped the scarf around her own shoulders. The moon shone through the skylight above and lit her face. I thought of the little filigree bird with the living eyes.

PART TWO
THE MISTRESS OF
REAL THINGS

I moved back to my dorm room after the first snow, even though nothing had changed. Summer and the other three Muffies were still in vegetative states, and I was still being blamed for what had happened to them. The witches at Ainsworth believed I'd used magic against Summer, and the Muffies just thought I was generally weird and evil. Since there was no real evidence against me, I hadn't been kicked out or anything, but my popularity rating had dipped from maybe a two on a scale of one hundred to absolute zero.

Nevertheless, Aunt Agnes convinced me that running away wasn't going to help anything and that the best way to prove my innocence was to act as if I weren't guilty. The school tried to help. Mr. Midgen, the custodian, had complained about the bags of dog droppings in front of my door, so the halls were now monitored regularly and I could at least walk down the hall for a shower without stumbling through an obstacle course of smelly paper bags with my name on them.

I tried to concentrate on my schoolwork and convince myself that being friendless had an upside, but I still felt rotten. I thought I'd found a friend in Morgan, but every time I went to the store to see her after that first day, the place was closed. I guessed that maybe her aunt had gotten held up longer than she'd thought, and that Morgan had gone home.

I didn't even know where that was. It would have been nice if she'd told me she was leaving, but to tell the truth, I was getting used to being ignored.

Speaking of being ignored, my relationship with Peter had become, to say the least, uneventful. Half of his free time was now spent sucking up to his uncle Jeremiah, who showered Peter with expensive gifts—a laptop, a Wii, a smartphone, an iPad, plus a new wardrobe, haircuts at the best salon in Boston, and a couple of sessions with a cosmetic dentist, who managed to make Peter even better-looking than he'd already been, if such a thing were possible.

The other half of the time that Peter had once spent with me was now devoted to hanging out with Bryce de Crewe.

It was Hattie's idea to enroll Bryce at Ainsworth, even though he didn't have any records or ID of any kind. Not only was he accepted and all fees waived, but to my amazement, Miss P herself volunteered to tutor him privately to bring him up to grade level.

"But who *is* he?" I asked Hattie one day before work. "Why does he sound weird and dress like a monk?"

"He doesn't dress any differently from anybody else," Hattie answered, skirting my questions.

"That's because he's wearing Peter's clothes." His *gorgeous, expensive* clothes, I might have added, since Peter dressed in only designer labels these days. "When I first saw Bryce, he looked like Friar Tuck. And he acted like a gas stove was a miracle of modern science."

Hattie sniffed. "You sound pretty snooty for someone who's known as the dog poop queen."

My eyes narrowed. "Not fair."

Hattie smiled in spite of herself. "You're right," she said. "But you're nosy." I was about to object, but she stuck a finger in my face. "Don't try to deny it."

She had a point. "Okay. I guess you're right. But I won't say a word. I swear."

"Oh, really?" Hattie mused. "The way you didn't say a word about Peter's brother, and almost caused him to get killed?"

She was referring to something that had happened the previous year, before we had known what the little kid could do. "I paid for that. Big-time," I said. "And I haven't said anything since. You know that."

She sighed. "Lord knows I'd be crazy to tell you anything," she said, "but since you'll be working with him, maybe you ought to know."

"Yes?" I asked eagerly.

"But you'll have to keep this to yourself."

I crossed my heart. Hattie gave me a skeptical look but told me anyway. "Bryce de Crewe is from a different plane of existence," she said quietly. "At one time all of our ancestors lived in his world, so there will always be a connection between our two planes."

"The land where witches originated?" I asked, spellbound.

"Something like that, yes. So as high priestess of Whitfield, it's my responsibility to help Bryce with his mission."

"Which is . . ."

"Which is something he'll tell you himself when he's good and ready," Hattie said. "Now, I don't want you to go blabbing about that, because the poor boy's going through enough of a culture shock without being treated like some kind of freak. Especially at school. Whatever he's been sent here to do, I want him to feel like a normal teenager. For once."

"For once?"

"Now, that's all I'm going to say about it."

"Okay," I said. "Er . . . thanks." I had to be—or at least pretend to be—content with that.

Bryce moved into Hattie's living quarters at the restaurant. At Hattie's request Peter moved back in too, even though he had a room at school. In fact, he moved out of the dorms at just about the same time I moved back in.

Great. Just great.

In a strange turn of events, Bryce—far from being considered an outcast, as Hattie had feared—quickly became one of the most popular guys at school. Girls were crazy about him, especially Becca, who thought he looked like Prince Harry. Peter liked him too. In fact, for two guys with a lot of extra-curricular work to do, Peter and Bryce managed to spend a lot of time together. Time Peter could have spent with me.

There, I'd said it. Sometimes I just got tired of being understanding and non-clingy and self-sufficient. I missed the old, poor, awkward Peter. Old Peter once carried me down the ivy-covered wall of a burning building on his back. New Peter couldn't eat lunch with me because he was either taking etiquette lessons from his great-uncle Jeremiah's butler or else hanging with Bryce and fighting off the girls who were all over the two of them like a coat of paint.

That was my state of mind—insecure, dejected, and melodramatically depressed—when my two so-called best friends, Becca and Verity, plopped down next to me in the cafeteria. It was the first I'd seen of them since I'd fled the dorms.

Since then I'd been alone so much that I'd stopped thinking about having friends, but here they were, uninvited and . . . Well, I was going to say "unwelcome," but that wasn't true. I'd missed them. Even Verity, who was usually a pain.

"Is this seat taken?" Becca asked, smiling. She always looked like she was in a shampoo commercial. Her curly blond hair literally bounced. With her dark eyes and pouty lips, she was as close to movie-star gorgeous as anyone at Ainsworth could get.

"What do you think," I answered dryly. Since it was common knowledge that I was the school leper, I figured she'd get my drift.

Verity blushed as she placed her napkin on her lap in preparation for chowing down on the radishes and cucumber slices on her plate. "We need to talk," she said in her usual breathy whisper.

"So talk," I said, taking a bite of my cheeseburger.

"Are you really going to eat that?" Verity asked, looking queasy.

"No, I'm going to smear it all over my body, and then I plan to swim the English Channel."

"All right, all right," Becca said, leveling her soulful brown eyes at me. "Katy, are you okay?" She took my hand. I started to pull away, but I decided not to because I knew it wasn't just a gesture. "We came to your room earlier, and you were out cold on your bed."

"Maybe I was asleep," I suggested. "It's been known to happen."

"But we couldn't wake you up," Verity said.

"So?"

This, I admit, was bravado. Actually, I'd spent the previous couple of hours walking through a Moroccan pillow into a street bazaar in Fez. Ever since Morgan had shown me how to walk through objects, I'd been practicing. So far I'd gone to a Native American powwow through a feathered dream catcher, to a hippie commune through a beaded lamp, and, most surprisingly, to a nineteenth-century English drawing room, where some awful woman kept screaming at her daughter to sit up straight.

I wanted to see how far I could go with this new skill. Of course, my body wouldn't be very active while I was visiting these places with my mind. I guessed I'd look pretty inert to the casual observer, but there usually weren't any observers, so what did it matter? Also, it was a lot more fun than studying all the time.

"We thought maybe you were drunk."

"Right. Thanks, Verity," I said. "As supportive as ever."

Becca looked down, blushing, but Verity got all steely, which was funny, considering how timid she was. It was like one of those cartoons where the mouse squared her shoulders and marched off to face the cat.

"I really thought you did it," she said. "Zapped Summer, I mean."

"So did everyone else," I said. "With no proof at all."

"That's just it. I thought I had proof."

I put down my burger. "What are you talking about?"

"I went into Summer's room a couple of days after it happened," Verity said.

That would have been after I'd been there with Peter. "Why?"

"I thought maybe I could help you. With a defense or something." Now she blushed. "You see, sometimes I can . . . I can sense things."

Right, I thought. Verity claimed to have sensed plants screaming as they were being harvested. "Like what?" I asked, in what I admit may not have been a very respectful tone of voice.

"Like . . ." Verity took a deep breath. "Like the fact that those girls lost their souls."

"Lost their whats?" Sometimes Verity was so vague and inarticulate that you couldn't tell what she was talking about.

"Well, maybe not *lost*, exactly. It's more like their souls were pulled out of them."

"Pulled . . ." I couldn't get my mouth to close long enough to form more words.

"Out of them," Becca finished for me.

"I could see their traces," Verity said. "Well, not *see*, exactly . . ."

"Omigod," I said, finally understanding. "You're a scenter."

"Not yet," Verity protested. "That's why I didn't say anything. My parents don't want me to tell people about this talent until it's more developed."

"But you . . . you saw Summer's soul?"

"Not *saw*, exactly—"

"Okay, okay," I interrupted. "Whatever. Where did they go?"

"That way, I think." She pointed vaguely out the cafeteria's north-facing windows. "I couldn't follow the traces for long."

"So you don't know what happened to them?" I asked.

She shook her head.

"There was nothing else? No other traces?"

"Just fish," she said. "It's like someone had brought a lot of dead fish into the room."

That had been me, of course, in the garbage can where I'd hidden after dumping out the oyster shells that had filled it.

"And one other thing," Verity said after a long pause. "Although I don't know if it means anything."

"What was it?"

Verity looked embarrassed. "It was an image I got. A picture."

"A picture?"

"Or maybe it was a dream. Or something I saw in a book. See, that's why my parents don't allow me to—"

"For God's sake, what was it?" I demanded. Sometimes Verity's dithering could drive you crazy.

Her head swiveled, panic-stricken, between me and Becca. "It was . . ." She lowered her eyes. "It was *toys*," she said at last.

"Toys?" Becca looked at me. "Summer's soul went to Toyland?"

"I knew I shouldn't have said anything," Verity said bitterly.

"What kind of toys?" I prompted.

"I don't know. All kinds. Old toys. A jack-in-the-box. A doll with a lace collar. I don't know."

"Think."

"I *can't*, okay? That's all I can do. These . . . things I get, the pictures, whatever . . . they're like ribbons or something, floating through my mind. I can see them for a second, and then they float away again. And then I don't know if I ever really saw them at all. And it wasn't really *seeing* in the first place."

"Okay," I said. I'd never met a scenter before, but it seemed to be a really amorphous talent. Perfect for Verity. "So you don't know if you really experienced it or not."

"That's it," Verity said, seeming to have grown a little calmer. "Maybe when I get older, I'll understand it better." She smiled hopefully.

"But why didn't you tell Miss P?" I wanted to know. "Even that much might have helped."

Verity made a face. "I told you," she said. "I thought you'd done it!"

"What? Taken their souls?"

"Yes. I thought that by keeping quiet I *was* helping you."

There was a long silence. "Wow," Becca said finally. She turned to me. "And I thought *you* were scary."

"Anyway," Verity went on after chewing her cucumber slice exactly fifty times and then dabbing her lips with her napkin, "that's why I didn't come around while you were having that trouble. I'm sorry."

"Me too," Becca said. "Not that I thought you'd done it or anything. But my mother . . ."

"I get it," I said. Most parents weren't perfect, but Becca's mom was something else. Wherever there was blame, Livia Fowler could be counted on to stick it on someone. After growing up with her, Becca was lucky not to have been a raving lunatic. As it was, Becca had been pulling out her hair since she was twelve. Until last year she wore a red wig—because her mother liked red hair. We'd finally burned the thing one night after Becca had decided to face the world as she was, blond and semi-bald. And with me as her friend.

Her hair started to grow back after that. In fact, Becca was so beautiful that her short hair became her trademark and something other girls copied. But I think what really saved her was that, after the wig-burning incident, Becca was allowed to board at school. The farther away from Livia Fowler you got, the healthier you became.

"Yeah. It's really hard to go up against Clytemnestra," she said. I could tell that it really troubled Becca to admit her fear of her mother. "But when I heard that you'd moved back into the dorms, I had to see you."

"And I don't think you did it anymore either," Verity chimed in.

"Oh?" I asked. "What changed your mind?"

"Miss P. I finally did go to see her. With my parents, of course."

The light dawned. "To turn me in," I guessed.

Verity turned bright red. "It was a matter of justice," she said. "I wrestled with my conscience."

"Good for you," I said, wondering why I bothered with her.

"My dad says that the truth is always the best way to see that justice is done."

Verity's father was the attorney for Ainsworth School. "Good for him," I said acidly.

"So what did Miss P say?" Becca asked, trying to diffuse the situation. "About the losing of the souls or whatever?"

"Nothing. But she said that magic of that magnitude couldn't have been performed by a student, no matter how gifted," Verity parroted.

"I got that too," I said.

"Besides, the school board has decided to drop the investigation."

"What?" I coughed. "You've waited till now to tell me this?"

"I really shouldn't be telling you at all," Verity said. "Miss P will probably—"

"Tell me!" I demanded.

"Well, they've decided to go with the findings of the non-adepts."

This was news. "Non-adepts" was the traditional term for cowen, or normal people. In this case, they were the families, doctors, and lawyers of the coma girls.

"Why?" I asked. "They wouldn't know anything about the magic that knocked them all out. *We* don't even know."

"That's the point," Verity said. "The girls and their families aren't witches. It's better that we don't even get involved."

"Better for whom?" I wanted to know. Not the girls, certainly. But I knew these weren't Verity's thoughts. They had come from her father, and the school's board of directors.

"She's right," Becca said. "It wouldn't do any good to tell the families that magic was the cause. They wouldn't believe it, anyway."

"And there's something else," Verity said. She looked from Becca to me. "By the way, you can't say anything about this."

Becca crossed her heart.

"You, too."

I dutifully complied, even though I didn't believe that crossing your heart meant anything.

Verity lowered her voice. "Apparently there were drugs involved."

"No way!" Becca shouted.

"Shh. They found a jar of some weird South American herb in Summer's room, and traces of the same thing in the girls' blood."

"A South American herb?" I asked.

"Apparently used for weight control," Verity said. "People make tea out of it and drink it."

"But . . . that's not a *drug*," I said.

"It's classified as one," Verity explained primly.

"But it doesn't count," I hissed. "Is that what they're saying caused four healthy people to lapse into comas? Drinking diet tea?"

"I guess it could happen," Becca reflected.

"Oh, for crying out loud." I stood up. "That's ridiculous."

"Maybe," Verity said. "But that's the position of the families. They've stopped the tests and blood analyses. And they're not going to sue the school."

So now Summer, A.J., Suzy Dusset, and Tiffany had been branded as drug fiends and abandoned by their own kind.

"That's cowen for you," Becca said.

Verity shrugged. "The board said it was up to them."

"So everyone's decided to let sleeping dogs lie."

"And let Summer live out her life as a vegetable," I said.

It wasn't fair. Those Muffy girls weren't my friends by any stretch of the imagination, but they deserved better than to be ignored and left to die. "I can't believe Miss P would let this happen," I said.

"Hey, it's better than when everyone was blaming you, isn't it?" Becca said.

"Don't you see, it's not just about me!" I turned to Verity. "You know how wrong this is," I said.

She refused to meet my eyes.

"Is it because they're cowen?" I asked. "What about that stuff about truth and justice?"

"But their own people won't help them," Becca said. "Why should we?"

"Because they're human beings," I said.

Verity stood up. "I have to get to class."

"Me too," Becca said. They picked up their trays. "We'll talk later," Becca mouthed.

I sat there with my thoughts for a while. I was exonerated. It was just a matter of time before it became public knowledge that Summer and the others had been ingesting foreign substances for recreational use and had suffered the consequences of their wrongdoing. By next year no one would even remember them very well. They weren't nice girls, after all. They didn't have many friends, except for one another. No one would miss them much.

My eyes filled with tears.

That night, while I was putting away my laundry, I came across the box that had contained the worthless "clues" to the Muffy incident that I'd collected from Summer's room. All that remained inside were the two broken pieces of brown plastic. When my fingers brushed against them, a feeling like lightning passed through me.

Taking a deep breath, I picked the pieces up slowly and, making sure whatever vibrations they carried wouldn't catch me unaware, I carried them to my bed. *I'm not going to see anything or feel anything unless I want to, and until I'm ready,* I reminded myself. That had been my mantra ever since I'd first learned to control my psychometry, and the reason why this ability hadn't driven me insane. Still, the vibes in these pieces were so strong that the plastic nearly jumped out of my hand.

Calm down, I told myself. *Breathe. Get ready. Okay.*

I concentrated on the smooth, lightweight fragments in my hand. I felt a sensation like movement flinging me through time and space. It was as if traces of light were shooting out behind me as I shot away at warp speed.

And then, abruptly, I was looking at the same green vista I'd seen in my earlier vision. The girl was there again too, but she was older this time, maybe thirteen or fourteen, and dressed in an elaborate costume of green brocade, although she paid no attention whatever to her odd clothing as she ran through the meadow laughing, her waist-length hair flying freely behind her.

In the background the doors of wattle-and-daub cottages opened slightly to reveal the awestruck faces of young girls, hardly breathing as they watched the exotic, beautiful creature among them, until their parents yanked them away and shut the doors.

Again vultures circled in the sky above her, but this time she seemed to be playing a game with them, although it was obviously not a game the vultures were enjoying. Every time the ungainly birds swooped down on her, she waited, poised, until the last possible moment, and then vanished from under their noses.

A moment later she reappeared, laughing, taunting the squawking birds of prey that had terrified her as a child. Again and again they swooped down with their long talons, only to lock onto thin air.

She's learned to amuse herself with her tormentors, I thought. And although I still didn't know who she was, where she was, or why I was seeing her, I couldn't help but give her a little silent cheer.

But those watching her from behind the almost-closed cottage doors did not cheer for her. *She'll be punished*, they said. *You wait and see. This girl's life will be short.*

CHAPTER

•

SEVENTEEN

I wasn't looking forward to working that night, because Bryce and Peter were both going to be at Hattie's—no doubt having a great time with each other while I did most of the work—but a job's a job. I had to go whether I was in the mood or not. Besides, I was hoping to talk to Hattie alone if I could, so I showed up a half hour early. Luckily, she was in the kitchen when I arrived, making the dough for her famous cheese biscuits.

"Can I help? I asked, putting on my apron.

"Just in time," she said cheerfully as she pulled out two big sheet pans. It made me almost pathetically happy that she'd accepted my offer of assistance. "Finish the biscuits while I write out the menu," she said. "Then we're going to need a couple of pies."

"My pleasure," I said.

"Now, what's on your mind?"

I didn't know how she could always tell. "Are you sure you want to hear?"

She sighed. "No, but go ahead."

I rolled out the biscuits. "It's about the girls at school who collapsed."

She nodded.

"They're Muffies . . . er, that is, non-adepts."

"I know."

"Well, from what I hear, their doctors have pretty much given up on them."

"And how would you hear anything?" she asked truculently. Hattie didn't exactly regard students as equals. Nevertheless, she was Whitfield's high priestess and I needed her help, so I barreled on.

"The school's position is to go along with the judgment of the girls' families and attorneys."

"Which is?"

"Which is that Summer and the others brought on their condition by drinking some South American tea."

The barest hint of a scowl played at the corners of Hattie's mouth.

"But that can't be it," I continued. "There was magic involved. Heavy magic. I watched them fall, Hattie."

"All right," she said. "Look what you're doing to the biscuits."

I guess I'd forgotten myself. I'd rolled the dough so hard that it was now paper thin and oozing over the edge of the counter. "Sorry," I said, gathering it up again.

"Now they'll be tough."

I ignored her. "Anyway, Verity Lloyd admits to being a scenter, and she thinks that someone took Summer's *soul*—"

"I know," Hattie said.

I was about to go on with my tirade, but her words stopped me short. "You do?"

"Penelope Bean—Miss P, your assistant headmistress—told me about it last night."

"Oh." I should have known. Miss P wouldn't let any of the students down, at least not without a fight. But the fact that they were Muffies made things a lot harder. "What are we going to do?" I whispered.

"*We?*" She arched her eyebrows disdainfully. "What do you think *you* could do?"

I took a deep breath. "Well, for one thing, I can walk through objects."

"I beg your pardon?"

"Into them, rather. I thought that maybe if I had something of Summer's—"

"You will do no such thing!" Hattie grabbed the rolling pin from me and held it up as if she were about to hit me with it. "This is not a matter for students. Do you understand?"

"Okay, okay," I said, holding out my hands to placate her.

"Get away from those biscuits before you kill them."

"Fine. Okay." I stepped away. "But about the girls . . ."

"Why, oh *why*, are you always sticking your nose into things that are none of your business?" she wailed.

"Hattie, there's no way those girls did that to themselves," I said. "No weight-loss tea would send all four of them into instant comas."

"Oh, so you're a medical expert now, are you?"

"No, but—"

"Well, people who *are* medical experts are saying that's exactly the case."

"They're cowen. They can't see—"

"And you can? Is that it? Katy Ainsworth, girl detective?"

"I'm not saying—"

"Leave it alone. I'm telling you—"

"No!" I shouted. "Look, I'm no medical expert, that's true, and I'm no detective, either. But I know there was Craft involved with those girls. And so do you."

We stood there for what seemed like a long time, staring each other down. To my amazement, Hattie looked away first.

"All right, all right," she said, and sighed. "If it makes you feel better, we're looking. We're looking as hard as we can. And it doesn't have anything to do with the cowen families. They'll never know, one way or the other. But we're trying to save the girls. I made a potion to get people to remember—"

"Was that the soup you made? That night you sent me home?"

She nodded. "It was an attempt. A failed attempt. But we're still trying."

"Then let me help," I said. "That's all I want. If we can just find out what happened to the Muffy girls—"

"We know what happened to them," Bryce said behind me.

I spun around. He was standing there, his head hanging. Peter was beside him. "Don't," Hattie began, but Bryce held up a hand.

"Katy has suffered sufficiently," he said. "I am honor-bound to tell her."

"Tell me what?" I asked.

Hattie rolled her eyes. "The question is, will we have to shoot her afterward, to keep her big mouth from blabbing all over town?"

"No," I said defensively. "I can keep a secret. You know that now," I said, sliding my eyes toward Bryce. I hadn't told a soul about him or where he came from. Hattie grunted reluctantly.

"Yes, we must tell her, Hattie," Bryce said. "Always Katy taketh the blame for everything that's happened to those girls."

"Oh, taketh off, Bryce," Hattie said.

"Forgive me, Mrs. Scott, but I cannot. We knew all along that Katy was innocent."

"What?" I gasped.

"I must tell her. Everything."

Hattie threw up her hands. "Fine. Don't say I didn't warn you. But don't just hang around jawing. Make the pies for dinner service, Katy. Two apple, three pecan."

"Yes, Hattie."

"Peter, you prepare salad for twenty-five. Bryce, pound fifteen chicken breasts for scaloppine."

"Yes, Hattie," they said in unison.

We all got busy until she left the kitchen. "Okay," I said, slapping the flour off my hands. "Talk."

Bryce put down the wooden mallet he was using to hammer a raft of chicken breasts. He looked small. Small and tired and scared. "It's my fault that those girls are in their unfortunate condition," he said.

"You?" What was he telling me? "You zapped them?"

"No. But because of me someone else did. Someone very dangerous."

"Who?"

"A sorceress," he said.

"Meaning what?"

"Meaning someone with a great deal more power than a witch. I cannot even mention her name, for fear that she might hear me."

I looked over at Peter, to see if this was some kind of a joke between them. "Are you serious?"

Bryce gave a rueful laugh. "I wish I were not. I was entrusted to transport her to a safe place, but I failed in my task," he said.

"Are you like a bounty hunter or something?" I asked.

"How'd she get away?" Peter interrupted.

"She did not 'get away,'" Bryce said. He cleared his throat. "Well, not exactly. She was trapped in a piece of amber, and I dropped it somewhere."

"Wait a second," I said, squinting. "Did you say 'trapped in amber'? Like, say, a fly?"

He nodded miserably.

"Er . . . Just how big was this person, exactly?" I asked.

"Small," he said. "That's how she came to be trapped."

"And you dropped her somewhere."

"Here, I think. In Whitfield." He sighed. "Those cowen girls must have found her and somehow released her from the amber."

"That's a big 'somehow,' Bryce," I said. "I don't know if Summer and her gang deserve that much credit."

"They needn't have known anything about witchcraft," he said. "The sorceress who was in the amber is very powerful. She could have communicated with them, told them how to break the spell that bound her. In fact, that is almost certainly what happened."

"And the potion—"

"It was a memory potion. Hattie and I were hoping that someone would remember seeing the sorceress. It might have given us an idea where she is."

"From your description, it sounds like she'd be pretty hard to forget," I said.

"Yes, but it yielded nothing. No one we've spoken to has seen her except for the four cowen girls, and they're . . ." He spread his hands in despair.

"Summer was trying to summon power the night I broke into her room," I remembered. "The girls were arguing about it. I got the feeling they'd done it before."

"Really?"

A lightbulb went off inside my head. "It *was* the Ouija!" I said. "I knew it! They were doing incantations over a Ouija board when they got into some kind of fight, and then—"

"And then she appeared?" he asked.

"No," I corrected. "And then they opened the door and saw me."

"And they collapsed?"

"Not right away. First they made fun of me for a while."

He shook his head. "That does not seem to be sensible," he muttered.

"So who is this tiny evil being you're chasing? Is she a fairy or something?"

He started seasoning the coating for the chicken. "Actually, she is a Traveler," he said. "Like me."

"A traveler?" Visions of Bryce lounging on a beach chair in the Caribbean while wearing a hair shirt swam into my head. "Where do you travel?"

"Anywhere I want." He grinned, then caught himself. "Of

course, I do not indulge in that sort of thing. I go only where I am told."

"Like here."

"Yes. Actually, that is the main thing a Traveler can do. Leave Avalon."

I smiled. "Avalon?"

To my surprise Peter caught on to what I was thinking. "Wasn't that where King Arthur ended up?" he asked.

"Yes, after he died. And only then because it had been the express wish of one of our greatest magicians, the Merlin."

"Merlin," I said, awestruck. "Merlin the magician was from Avalon?"

"You know of him?"

"A little." The witches of Whitfield practically revered the Merlin. Actually, "Merlin" was more of a title than a name. It meant "court magician" or something. According to legend the Merlin practically raised King Arthur. He was with him when Arthur became king by pulling the magical sword Excalibur from the stone, and was his mentor throughout Arthur's reign. With the Merlin's help Arthur brought peace to Britain by bringing all the local leaders together around the famous Round Table, where no one was considered more important than anyone else. That nearly changed the world.

Nearly.

"With Merlin's help Arthur nearly unified England," I said.

"Nearly," Bryce repeated. "They both died before their dream was realized. If they'd succeeded, there would have been no such thing as the Dark Ages. And by now the world would have been technologically ahead of where it is at present. Ahead by centuries."

"Because of one person," Peter said.

"Two," Bryce corrected. "King Arthur and the Merlin. It was the combination of the two of them that was so extraordinary."

I chewed on a slice of apple, unimpressed. "So what does that have to do with the fairy? Or with us?"

Bryce cocked his head. "Because that's where—and when—the sorceress I'm looking for is from," he said.

I frowned. "What do you mean 'when'?"

"Well . . . that was when she was captured. During the time of King Arthur."

"What?" Peter interjected. "Are you saying she's not only from a different plane of existence, but from a different *time* as well?"

"Yes," Bryce said, blinking innocently. "I thought you knew that. She was the Merlin's daughter."

Peter and I looked at each other. "And you guys trapped her in amber for a thousand years?" he asked incredulously.

"It was more like sixteen hundred years," Bryce said. "But it was necessary. She was a very wicked girl."

"But didn't you think the Merlin would be, well, extremely irritated that his daughter had been trapped for all time like an insect in amber?"

"The Merlin was already dead when that happened," Bryce said. He cleared his throat. "His daughter killed him," he added in a whisper.

I choked on my apple. "H—how?" I coughed.

"By summoning the Darkness," Bryce said.

I heard Peter suck in air. We'd all hoped that the Darkness would give us a rest for a while, but I guessed we were wrong.

CHAPTER

•

EIGHTEEN

"The Darkness" was our name for evil. That is, the distillation of evil. Most people—cowen, anyway—saw evil only through the terrible things they did to one another. But witches knew that it didn't work that way. Evil existed on its own. The Darkness, grown out of the evil in people's minds, was an entity unto itself, just waiting to infect whomever it could.

Cowen didn't have many defenses against the Darkness, although they had more than they knew—kindness, faith, loyalty, integrity, humor, gratitude, and love all kept the big D at bay. But a lot of people thought those things didn't matter. When the Darkness was overwhelming, they wanted supernatural help of some kind. So they started praying to gods that they'd ignored all their lives, or threw coins into wells, or they went to medicine men or wise women or anyone who they thought might be a witch. What they didn't realize was that the Darkness *preferred* magical people. We had more power to feed it. So we were the choice targets, if that made any sense.

"To keep the Darkness at bay, the elders among my people put a protective spell around Avalon," Bryce said.

That was certainly familiar. When my ancestor Serenity Ainsworth was living in Whitfield in the 1600s, the Darkness and its ensuing evil—meaning the bloodthirsty witch-hunting Puritans—got to be so much of a danger to the witches that they came up with a spell to protect a section of town, the Meadow, which sits right in the middle of downtown Whitfield.

It was Serenity's spell, actually. She and Hattie's ancestor Ola'ea Olokun, a West African shaman, created a barrier that would keep the Darkness forever out of the Meadow. It didn't work perfectly, though, as we all discovered some time ago. I guessed that was because the Darkness could be expelled but never destroyed. Still, the barrier was pretty effective most of the time. During every magical holiday, the whole Meadow moved to a different level of existence, so that while life went on as usual in the human world that we shared with cowen, the Meadow and every witch in it seemed to vanish.

"Is Avalon on the same plane as the Meadow, then?" I asked.

"The same, but deeper," Bryce said. "Your Meadow goes to an alternate plane only during Cross Quarters."

"Also equinoxes and solstices," Peter said.

Those words were witchspeak for the holidays of Beltane, Lammas, Samhain, and Imbolc, which occurred in May, August, October, and February, respectively. Those were the big ones, or Cross Quarter days. The equinoxes—times during the spring and fall when days and nights were of equal length—were known as Ostara and Mabon. Then there were the winter and summer solstices, Yule and Litha, which were the shortest and longest days of the year. Together they made up what we called the Wheel of the Year, since we viewed time—and life—as cyclical.

"In Avalon, the barrier is permanent," Bryce said. "The Darkness cannot touch it unless it is summoned by someone."

Suddenly things made sense. When the Darkness had come into our Meadow despite the witches' shield, it had been because someone—me, actually, if you must know—had inadvertently brought the Darkness into that sacred space. I'm sure our founding mothers had never even entertained such a possibility.

There was huge power in ineptitude.

"Is that what your fairy did?" I asked, mostly so I could stop thinking about my own stupidity.

"No. She summoned the Darkness from the human plane, where the Merlin was living at the time. Avalon is protected against all the ills of your world. We have no pollution, no industrial noise, no traffic, no skyscrapers."

Verity would love it there, I thought.

"There is no war," he said. "No dissent."

"No witch hunts," I said.

Bryce nodded. "Because nothing ever changes."

We were all silent for a long time. "Not ever?" Peter asked at last.

"Never," Bryce said. "Everything is exactly the way it was when the barrier was created. The way it's always been." He started pounding the chicken breasts again. It was too noisy to carry on the conversation, so I leaned close to Peter's ear.

"Is that why he sounded so strange when he first got here?" I asked. "Because he was speaking Old English, or whatever?"

He nodded. "You should have seen him the first time he watched TV."

It got suddenly quiet in the kitchen. "Your world has been full of surprises," Bryce said.

"I'll bet," I agreed. "Pollution, global warming, crime, drugs . . ."

"Yeah," Peter said. "Compared with this, Avalon must be paradise."

Bryce turned away. "Some would say so."

"Some?"

"At one time there were many who left. They were your ancestors. They turned away from the safety and security of our world to take their chances in this one."

"And ended up being burned at the stake," I said, trying to sound worldly.

"Their descendents, yes. Avalon was created a long time ago."

"How long?" I wanted to know.

"About the time of the earliest Roman incursions."

"Julius Caesar," Peter said.

"Two thousand years?" It seemed hard to believe.

"That was when it became clear that the Romans weren't going to leave until we either gave in or died fighting." He resumed his chicken pounding—in what I thought was a very intense way—so I put my hand on his, and he stopped.

"Sit down," I said.

He sighed and walked over to one of the folding chairs by the pantry. Peter and I pulled up two others.

"Avalon was a fairly big settlement then, from what I understand," Bryce said softly. "We thought we'd be able to keep the invaders at bay with magic, but the Romans had weapons and tactics we'd never imagined. It was the closest we'd ever come to seeing the Darkness in its pure form.

"Most of my people died. By the time the elders created the spell to take Avalon out of the human realm, there weren't many of us left. And even then more than half our number chose to remain in this world—your world—rather than vanish into the mists."

"What happened to them?" Peter asked.

"Not many of them survived, unfortunately. That's why true witches are rare in this plane. But our Seer predicted that after much tribulation, the traitors—" He blushed. "Forgive me, but that is what the ones who left are called. The traitors would once again form a community in a new land. Of course, the original witches of Avalon never dreamed it would take more than a millennium and a half to found Whitfield."

"Your Seer?" I asked. "You mentioned that before. Is he some kind of prophet or something?"

"The Seer is a woman," he said. "Like you, we have many different talents, but there is only one Seer, a witch who can read the future. This person is our leader."

"Oh," Peter said. "I guess that makes sense."

Bryce stood up, went to his station, and started pounding again. "Something's wrong," I mouthed to Peter. He went over to where Bryce was working and picked up one of the chicken breasts. It was so flattened that it had holes all over it.

"Hey, man, what's going on?" he asked. "You homesick? I mean, the modern world must seem pretty sucky at times. Katy and I get that."

Bryce laughed mirthlessly. "Right. You will not see any

overhead electrical wires in Avalon," he said, crushing another chicken breast to smithereens.

"Uh, cool," Peter said uncertainly. "Where do they put them? Underground?"

Bryce gave a bitter laugh. "There are no wires because there is no electricity," he said. "I told you, everything is the same as it was two thousand years ago. There is no running water. No cloth, except for what we spin and weave ourselves. No music except for our own singing. There are no books, no art, no movies."

"No Facebook," I said with a shiver.

"No phones," Peter added. "No TV. No Internet."

"No visitors." At that, Bryce met my gaze. "No one can come into Avalon," he said. "And very few can leave."

Peter and I looked at each other, bewildered. "Then why are you here?" I asked.

Bryce wiped his forehead with his sleeve. "I told you. I'm a Traveler. That means I have the ability to leave that plane, and permission from the Seer to leave Avalon. I may enter this world and travel wherever I need within it in the service of my mission."

"Right," I said. "The fairy."

"She is not a fairy," he said, irritated. "Just small. Small enough so that I could transport her." He shook his head. "But alas, I lost her through a hole in my pocket."

"Where were you taking her?" Peter asked.

Bryce looked abashed. "Here, I'm afraid."

"Wait a minute," I said. "You were bringing this dangerous-if-pint-size sorceress to *Whitfield*?"

Bryce nodded glumly. "To Hattie Scott," he said. "Your high priestess. Our Seer said she would know what to do."

"Like what, toss her in with the mashed potatoes?" I shouted. "We don't have demon jails here, Bryce. When witches go bad, we send them *away* from Whitfield. We don't invite them in."

"Calm down, Katy," Peter said, turning back to Bryce. "Why'd she—your Seer or whatever—send you here, of all places?"

"Because you are witches, like us," he said simply. "Your blood connections to us make Whitfield the closest place to Avalon on this plane."

"I don't see one peeled apple," Hattie boomed from the doorway.

"I'm on it, Hattie," I called back, running to my station.

Bryce picked up his mallet again. "Anyway, if I cannot find the sorceress, nothing else I do will matter a whit," he said.

"Why not?"

"Because Avalon will not exist. That's why the Seer sent me away with the amber. As long as the sorceress was trapped inside, our world was safe. But the Seer had a vision that the sorceress would one day destroy Avalon."

I swallowed. "And now she's escaped from the amber."

"She's escaped *here*," Peter said.

Bryce hung his head. "Because of me."

"Wait a minute," I said. "If your Seer sees everything, didn't she see this, too? That your little felon would escape?"

"Her vision was that the sorceress would destroy Avalon," Bryce went on doggedly. "By bringing her here, I was changing that future."

"Maybe," Peter said. "Or it might mean that the future can't be changed."

"Of course it can be changed," I said hotly. "That isn't the problem." I looked from one of them to the other, trying to wrap my head around what Bryce had told us. "The problem is that now she might destroy Whitfield instead."

"Have you three been jawing all this time?" Hattie growled. "After I told you how much there was to do?"

We all finally sprang into action. Within ten seconds the kitchen was running at full speed, a symphony of hisses, thumps, clicks, and the whoosh of running water.

"Anyway, that's why the witches here are dropping the investigation into the girls in the comas," Bryce said. "It all depends on my finding the sorceress before . . ." He shrugged hopelessly.

"Who knows about this?" I asked. "This whole thing."

"Hattie, of course. The Seer sent her a message. Miss P. Now you two. And honestly, I'd prefer it if the whole witch community didn't know how I'd failed." He looked pointedly at me. "With some luck I'll be able to capture her and make the whole thing go away. Those girls will revive. The amber will be with Hattie. And I'll go home," he added quietly.

"I won't tell, I promise," I said. "But you'll have to watch out for Peter." That was a joke. Peter wouldn't blab a secret if he were being tortured. That's a fact. Bryce and Peter both grinned.

"How many apples have you done?" Hattie yelled.

"Almost enough," I shouted.

"Is that chicken flat?"

"As a pancake," Bryce answered.

I smiled. "Your English is getting better," I said.

He smiled back. "My English is correct, if antiquated. Yours is the variant."

"How about mine?" Hattie interjected. "You understand my English?"

"Yes, ma'am," Bryce answered.

"What about when I say wrap those chicken parts in plastic and take them to the walk-in?"

"I understand clearly," Bryce said, abashed.

"Peter, are you done with the salad?"

"Yes, Hattie."

"Then help Katy pare her apples. She's slow."

That hurt. I'm normally a lightning-fast fruit parer, but I'd gotten absorbed in Bryce's story. To make up for lost time, I started moving faster than ever.

"Where's the other peeler?" Peter asked, rummaging through the utensil drawer.

"Use this," I said, handing over mine. "I'll use a knife." I could work even faster this way, paring and coring in one movement.

"Katy?" Peter's voice was soft.

"What?" When I was working at this speed, I really didn't want to be distracted.

"We need to talk," he said, looking over his shoulder to make sure that Bryce and Hattie were both out of earshot.

Oh, no, I thought. Not the "It's better if we're friends" talk. The "I need some space" talk. As if I'd even seen him outside of work lately. The "It's not you; it's me" talk. The—

"Katy, you're bleeding."

I looked down. My apples were covered with blood. My blood. While I'd been stressing about how Peter was going to break up with me, I'd sliced open my thumb.

"What's that blood doing on my apples?" Hattie shouted into my ear.

I jumped. I hadn't even seen her come in. I grabbed a towel. Cuts and burns didn't mean much in a professional kitchen. All of us were pretty familiar with the first aid cabinet in Hattie's upstairs bathroom.

"Go clean yourself up," she said. "Peter, go with her."

"It's not as bad as it looks," I said.

"Go!" Hattie pointed at the door. We left her griping as she threw into the garbage all the apples I'd cut.

"I hope I didn't freak you out," Peter said once we got to the bathroom.

That was such a guy thing to say. As if there were any possibility that I wouldn't be freaked out. "No, of course not," I lied as I ran cold water over my hand.

"Oh. Good. Because I thought . . . Well, you know . . ."

I wrapped my thumb in a paper towel and lifted it above my heart. "Just say it, Peter," I said wearily.

"Uh . . . Well, it's about the, uh, about Winter Frolic."

I knew it. My thumb throbbed in rhythm with the beating of my heart. "What is it this time?" I asked. "Some celebratory dinner? An awards ceremony? An emergency jaunt to South America with Uncle Jeremiah?" I'd heard all of these excuses before and they all meant the same thing: Peter wasn't going to be available.

"No. Actually, I can go."

"You can?" A spring of hope began to well up inside me.

He nodded, looking crestfallen. "Only I have to take someone else."

The towel dropped to the floor. "Someone else? *Someone else?*" I shouted. "*Who* else?"

"Some French girl," he said. "Her father's going into partnership with my uncle on some deal."

My thumb had started to bleed again, and was dripping onto the floor.

"Watch out," Peter said. "Hey, are you sure you're okay?"

"I'm fine."

He took my hand. I pulled away from him so hard that blood spattered all over both our faces. He grabbed it again and forced it under the water. "Jeez, Katy, the dance isn't that important, is it?"

"Yes, it is!" I shrieked. I heard my voice crack. "It *is* important, okay? To me, anyway."

"Okay, okay," he said conciliatorily. "I just thought—"

"Ever since Jeremiah Shaw came into your life, it's like you've become a different person."

"I have not," he protested, pulling the strips off a Band-Aid with his teeth.

"Well, I never see you." Ugh, what was I *saying*? I sounded like an insecure housewife.

"You're seeing me now."

"I want to see you at Winter Frolic," I whined.

"I wanted that too," he said, "but we can't always do what we want, can we?"

"Oh, stop being rational and mature," I spat. "I hate it when you're like that."

"I can't help the way I am, Katy. You must see—"

"Well, I don't!" I wailed. "I don't see at all why you're taking someone else to Winter Frolic, after we'd planned to go together."

"It wasn't exactly a *plan*," he said in his maddening, reasonable way. "As I remember, you said you hated those dress-up things. We were going to stop in for ten minutes and then go for pizza."

"Well, that was a plan, wasn't it?" I burst into tears. "Is she . . . Is she beautiful?"

Peter sighed. "Look, I don't even know this girl, Katy. I'm taking her as a favor for my uncle. Apparently this French guy thinks that American teenagers are all drunkards and sex fiends, so Jeremiah told him—"

"I don't care what he told him! I'm your girlfriend!" I shrilled.

"I know. And you always will be," he said, pulling me close to him. "But I have to listen to him, at least for now. He's my only hope of going to college. Do you know what that means to me?"

"That you have to do everything he wants?" I spat, pushing him away.

"You're not being fair," he said.

There was a long silence. I didn't want to admit it, but he was right. Before Uncle Jeremiah showed up, Peter had resigned himself to two years of community college and then a possible transfer to a four-year school that he could pay for with a bank loan and his savings from work. Now everything was different. He had a chance of going to Harvard, after all.

I knew how much that meant to him, because I knew how much it meant to me.

"All right," I said. "I guess it's not like it's prom or anything."

"Hold your thumb up."

I looked him over suspiciously. "You've never seen her?"

"Who?"

"Your *date*," I reminded him.

"No. She just started here. She's a freshman."

"So?"

"So she's fourteen. She'd probably rather be riding her bike."

I thought about that. At fourteen I was geeky and skinny and spent a week with my hand over my face because of a giant zit on the end of my nose.

"Besides, we can still see each other there."

"How?" I asked.

"Bring a date."

"A date?"

"Well, not a real date. But maybe someone . . . gay," he said, brightening. "That's it. Check out the guys in theater club."

"And what makes you think that anyone, gay, straight, or prone to necrophilia, is going to want to take the resident mass murderer to Winter Frolic?" I ranted.

"Oh, that. Yeah. Hmm. Well, that'll blow over before long."

"Never mind," I said. "Just have a good time."

"No, I want you to go, Katy."

"Right. Just not with you."

"I'll find you someone. How about Bryce?"

"You know he's taking Becca."

"Well, couldn't the three of you . . ."

"*Forget* it, Peter," I said. "Maybe I'll go alone."

He smiled. "Would you do that?"

"Maybe," I said, unable to resist a tiny smile. "For ten minutes. Then I'm going for a pizza."

He kissed my cheek. "Thank you," he said. Then he kissed my lips, and I forgot all about being mad at him. I knew that whatever stupid problems came into our lives, Peter and I would always be together. The dance didn't matter. The fourteen-year-old French girl was probably a beast, anyway, or she'd have been able to get her own date for Winter Frolic.

"I love you," Peter said.

"I know. I love you, too."

He kissed me again, this time stroking my hair with one hand while he held me close to him with the other. His tongue touched mine, and it was like an electric shock shooting through my body.

"Peter," I whispered.

"I hate being away from you," he breathed into my ear. "I wish I could spend my whole life touching you, loving you . . ." Then, once again, he pressed his lips against mine until I wanted to cry out with need.

"Is that what's taking you two so long in there?" Hattie bellowed from the hallway. "That had better be mouth-to-mouth resuscitation I'm seeing."

We scrambled to clean up the mountain of bloody paper towels around us.

"I thought by now either you'd be healed or your thumb would be amputated."

"We were just going back to the kitchen," I said.

"Oh? How were you planning to get there, on your lips? Because those were the only parts of you two that were moving," she shouted down the stairs after us.

She'd finished all the apples, so I looked around for something else to do while holding my thumb aloft. I must have looked like the Statue of Liberty, giving a big thumbs-up to all the world.

"You go home," Hattie said.

"No, really, I'm—"

"Go home and let your grandma see that cut. I won't have you bleeding on the food here."

Peter and I looked longingly at each other until Hattie spun him around. "Prepare two dozen artichokes," she said, pushing him toward the sink.

"I'll try to find you a date," Peter called.

"I don't even want to know what that's about," Hattie said as the double doors swung shut behind me.

After a brief visit to my great-grandmother, who bandaged my thumb, I called my father, the medievalist.

"Yes?" he muttered, preoccupied as usual. I think the only time he ever spoke to me without doing something else at the same time was when I was in the intensive care unit at the hospital last year. I guess that was what it took for him to pay attention to me. But I was calling about medieval history, so I figured he'd probably answer me.

"It's Katy, Dad. I need to know something about King Arthur. For a paper," I added.

He snorted. That was what he did when he thought something was too ridiculous to respond to. "Aside from the fact that he probably never existed, what specifically are you looking for?"

"He . . . Arthur never existed?"

"In all likelihood King Arthur is an amalgam of several tribal chieftains who attempted to unify Britain after the occupying Roman garrisons left the region to defend their own city, which was being invaded by Visigoths and other—"

"Er, what time frame are we talking about here?" I interrupted. I knew he could go on about Ancient Rome forever. Or until he got bored with me and hung up before answering my question.

"Well, the Romans left in 410, after having occupied—and modernized—Britain for nearly four centuries. The governor's last message to the Britons was 'Defend yourselves!' From that point on, Britain disintegrated."

"I thought they were modernized."

"By the *Romans*." Dad was warming up now. "They were the ones who built the roads, the aqueducts, the baths. The Romans supplied the architects, engineers, physicians, soldiers, and craftsmen. When the Romans left, they took their knowledge with them. Imagine a mansion that suddenly had no electricity, running water, replacement roof tiles, pipes to fix the plumbing, glass for the windows, or anyone who knew how to make or use these things. That was Britain, and it remained that way for several centuries.

"The warlords, including 'Arthur,' if that happened to be the name of one of them, made futile attempts at conquering one another. Had one succeeded, England might have been spared the worst of the so-called Dark Ages."

"So, er, when was it that he—they—Arthur—might have lived?"

"Oh, I'd say the most likely period within the sub-Roman catastrophe would have been about a hundred years after the Roman exodus. Everything the Romans built would have fallen into ruin by then. The cities would have been overrun by rats and disease. Tribal infighting would have been at a peak. That would have been between 475 and 535, generally."

"It sounds like unifying England would have been a pretty hard task."

"Virtually impossible, I'd say. Nothing short of magic could have helped, under the circumstances. And I mean *real* magic, not the sort of thing those silly women in Whitfield pretend to do."

I let that go. I always let it go.

"I can recommend several books about that era if you're interested," he offered hopefully. Dad would have liked for me to become a scholar like he was, even though we were both pretty sure that I wasn't cut out for academic life.

"Uh, sure," I said, and dutifully wrote down the titles. "So Arthur just . . . failed?"

"Obviously, they all did. Perhaps one or two of the chieftains managed to bring a few other strongholds under their purview before they died—"

"The Knights of the Round Table!" I said.

He sighed. "Katherine, why do you insist on speaking as if the legend were true?"

Because it is, I wanted to say. But I didn't. "It's an interesting story." That was the sort of nonanswer I'd perfected when talking with my father.

"I suppose," he said dismissively. "I wish you'd try to think a little more broadly, though, if you can. You tend to lack imagination."

That was a new one. "I do?"

"Well, all this speculating about legends and mystic things. It's a waste of time. And an embarrassment, really."

"Oh."

"But perhaps it's the best you can do, given your age and . . . inclinations."

He was talking about witchcraft again. He knew by now that it was real—in Whitfield, at least—but he still felt that the "gifts" we exhibited were trivial and unimportant, if not downright goofy. Nothing like the *real* work of analyzing ancient French poetry or tracing the circuits of traveling troubadours.

I heard papers rustling in the background. "Anything else?" he asked, sounding far away.

"No. Thank you."

"Good luck on your . . ." I could tell he was reading now.

"Paper," I finished. "Yes, I'll do my best."

"That's all one can expect, isn't it?"

I didn't answer right away. Dad must have gotten absorbed in what he was reading at that point, because during my silence he hung up.

"Yeah, I guess that's all you can expect," I said into the dead phone. I closed my eyes, counted to ten, and tried not to think about what a disappointment I was just by being me.

Love you too, Dad.

CHAPTER

•

TWENTY

Three days later Becca and I were in the library, studying for third-period geography. My hand, with its jumbo-size-bandaged thumb, lay on the table like a centerpiece. Actually, it wasn't as bad as it looked. Gram had taken me over to the hospital for stitches, but after a half hour in the Alternative Healing wing, I hadn't needed more than a butterfly bandage and some superglue, plus the big poufy gauze wrapping to keep it from splitting open again if I bumped it.

Becca pretended to busy herself with maps of the arctic circle while she leaned close to me. "What would you say if I told you I was falling in love with Bryce?" she whispered.

"I'd say it was a pretty bad idea," I said.

She gave me a squinty evil look. "Because he's not from around here?" she shrilled.

I rolled my eyes. "Actually, I was thinking more along the lines of him not being human," I said.

"What?"

Oh. My. God. She didn't know. This was why Hattie didn't trust me with secrets. Because blabbing was my middle name. Katy "B for 'Blab'" Ainsworth. "Er . . . I meant that he doesn't seem to treat *you* like a human being," I waffled.

"What are you talking about? He's the nicest guy I've ever dated."

Mrs. Miller, the librarian, gave us a look like a hawk eyeing mice.

"Sorry," I said. "I was thinking of someone else."

"Someone else named Bryce de Crewe?" Becca asked sarcastically.

"Girls!" Mrs. Miller admonished. We both sank deeper into our seats, our maps held in front of our faces.

"As if *your* boyfriend is so great," Becca said, and sniffed.

I looked over to her. "You know about Winter Frolic?" I asked. "Of course you do. Everybody knows, don't they?"

"Uh . . . " Now Becca had the *Oops* look on her face. "It doesn't mean anything," she said, trying to fix the suddenly awkward vibe between us. "Just because Fabienne— "

"*Fabienne?* Is that the name of Peter's date?"

"You didn't know?"

I sank down even lower. I knew my face was blazing red, but I was hoping no one would see. "She's only fourteen," I said. "A freshman."

"Really? I thought she was one of those exchange students who's already finished high school in her native country."

I blinked. "So she doesn't look like she's fourteen?"

Becca swallowed. "Well, not really."

"She's not covered in zits?"

"Huh?"

"Is she gorgeous?"

"Oh, I don't know if I'd say . . . Um, well . . . Oh. There she is now." Becca gestured with her chin toward Mrs. Miller's desk, where a tall blond girl who looked like a contestant in the Miss Universe pageant was standing.

I heard a sound like a dying antelope escape from me.

"She has a big butt," Becca said loyally.

The antelope moaned again.

"Miss Ainsworth!" Mrs. Miller hissed.

At the next table Verity was punching Cheswick's arm. He didn't seem to notice. He just kept staring openmouthed at the big-butted, underage French bombshell that my boyfriend was taking to Winter Frolic.

"You look weird," Becca said. "Are you going to puke or something?" She edged her chair away from me.

I crossed my arms on the table and buried my face in them. "It sucks to be me," I mumbled through my sweater.

"For sure," Becca said.

There was suddenly a lot of subtle activity in the library. Everyone seemed to be looking either at Fabienne (even her name was gorgeous) or at me. I gathered up my things. "I think I'm going to go jump off a bridge," I said, just as the door opened and the level of curiosity in the library leaped up about a thousand degrees.

It was Peter and Bryce, looking like models in a Prada ad. Peter was wearing a fleece-lined leather bomber jacket over a Missoni sweater and True Religion jeans. Bryce had on black chinos under a Burberry raincoat with a plaid lining that matched the scarf around his neck.

They were hot. I mean, watching them, you could almost

see them moving in slow motion with saxophone music in the background. I guess that's what a little confidence and a five-thousand-dollar wardrobe can do.

Out of the corner of my eye I saw Fabienne suck in her stomach and send a high-voltage smile in Peter's direction. Peter caught it and sent one back to her. If he'd stopped, I might have slit my wrists with Mrs. Miller's letter opener right then and there, but the boys kept moving toward us.

"Bryce!" Becca shouted, waving them over.

"My man!" Cheswick said, trying for a high five. God, but he could be embarrassing.

Mrs. Miller was listing from side to side, trying to wobble her way off her seat.

"Where have you *been*?" Becca squealed.

Peter put his arm around me. "Thailand," he said, grinning.

I blinked in response.

The librarian had finally pried herself off her chair and was waddling toward us. "This is a library!" she said, coming as near to shouting as she allowed herself. She pointed toward the door. "I'm afraid you people will have to leave."

"Certainly," Bryce said, bowing slightly. "Our apologies."

I let myself sort of float along with the group as we barreled into the hall. Verity and Cheswick ran to catch up with us, even though they hadn't really been invited. Through the library's glass panels I noticed that practically everyone inside was looking at us in an admiring way, as if we were the new IN crowd. Even Fabienne, who had probably never felt excluded from anything in her life, looked disappointed.

Nevertheless, I couldn't help feeling a little cranky. Why was Peter once again spending time with Bryce instead of with me? And why wasn't Bryce looking for his evil fairy, if finding her was as important as he'd said it was?

"Did you say you went to *Thailand*?" Verity gushed.

"Affirmative," Bryce said, evidently trying out his new vocabulary. "Check it out." Anxiously he turned toward Peter. "Check it out?" he repeated.

Peter nodded. *"Perfecto,"* he whispered.

Bryce grinned. "Check it out . . . dudes." He plucked at his shirt. "Thai silk."

"But how—" I began.

"Oh, didn't you know?" Verity said, a little too loudly. "Bryce is a Traveler."

"A . . ." I narrowed my eyes at Bryce. Who was the blabbermouth around here, exactly? "What's wrong with you?" I whispered. "I thought you said—"

Peter made a *Shut up* sign with his hand.

"I told you I could travel," Bryce said with a wink. "Thailand's no problem."

So that was it. It was only Avalon that was the secret.

Becca pouted. "You didn't take us."

"It was a spur-of-the-moment decision," Peter said. "Coach Levy subbed in gym. He made the whole class go for an eight-mile run."

"We made it back in time to cross the line," Bryce said.

"The finish line," Peter elaborated. "Coach didn't even notice that we weren't in sweats."

"Well, take us now," Becca said, linking her arm around Bryce's.

"Where, to Thailand?"

"Anywhere. Katy's never been. Have you, Katy?"

"No," I said, trying to stare Peter down. He knew I'd been languishing in my dorm, waiting for him to make some room in his schedule for me.

"It just came up," Peter said defensively, as if he could read my mind. Although I suppose my face might have given me away.

"Is she angry?" I heard Bryce whisper.

I hated that more than everything else, hearing them talk about me like I wasn't there. "No, she's not angry," I said between clenched teeth. "She has a geography class." I walked away.

"Hey, so do we!" Cheswick called after me. "It's not for forty minutes!" I ignored him.

Peter ran after me. When he tried to put his arm around me again, I squirmed away.

"Okay, what's with you?" he said levelly.

It was hard to keep my tears in check. "Nothing," I said. "Don't make a scene."

"You're the one making a scene," he said.

"This isn't a scene," I said. "I'm just not in the mood to hear about all your great adventures with *Bryce*." I managed to make the name sound like a curse.

"Oh, come on."

"*You* come on," I said inanely. "It's not enough that you expect me to go to Winter Frolic by myself while you take a date—"

"It's not like that, Katy. You know that."

"And now, instead of being with me . . ."

"We were in gym class. Be reasonable."

"I do not want to hear that again," I said, stomping away.

"Hear what?"

"About being reasonable," I shouted behind me.

He grabbed my arm. "Okay, then be unreasonable. But come with me." He steered me toward the exit.

"I don't want to go to Thailand," I said as he propelled me into the parking lot.

"I've got her," Peter called. The others swarmed out from behind an SUV, moving quickly so as not to be seen by Miss P or anyone else who might wonder what we were doing there.

Becca signaled behind her. "Hurry up, Bryce."

"Katy doesn't want to go to Thailand," Peter said.

"No problem." Bryce took my hand, careful of my bandaged thumb. "Very well, my friends. You must hold hands now, because you definitely do not want to get lost during this trip. Believe me."

Peter squeezed my other hand.

"Are you ready? Everybody got a coat on?"

"Hurry *up*," Becca said.

Bryce laughed. "Okay, then. We're off." He looked to Peter for reassurance. "Is that the right phrase? 'We're off'?"

"That's it, bro."

In the next second we were standing on an ice floe somewhere in the middle of a gray ocean. Freezing, blinding wind was blowing so hard that it threatened to sweep us off into the water. I could feel my eyelashes turning into icicles.

"What the—" Cheswick said. "Where are we?"

"Did you not complete your geography homework?" Bryce asked.

"It's the north pole!" Becca screeched.

"Very good," Bryce said approvingly.

"N-n-not really so good, babe," Becca said, her teeth chattering.

"Don't be so negative," Verity piped. "My allergies are gone."

"Seriously, dude," Peter said, cocking his head toward me. "Think about the ladies."

Bryce looked puzzled. "Very well. But we will probably be asked about the Arctic in our geography midterm examination."

"I'll take my chances," Becca said. "Get us out of here, Bryce."

Bryce checked our little circle. "Still holding hands?" he asked.

And then, just like that, all six of us were standing at the base of a sand dune, our shadows pooled like little puddles beside us. Overhead the sun beat down oppressively.

"Oh, come *on*," Becca complained.

"Sorry," Bryce said. "I overshot. Please forgive me."

"Oh, no. We're lost," Verity wailed.

I closed my eyes, imagining how depressing it would be to be trapped on a desert island with Verity.

"And we'll never . . . Oh."

In that instant we were standing in front of a beautiful church in a beautiful city.

"Notre Dame," I said. I recognized it from a picture in my French book.

"Alors." Bryce extended one hand, as if he were a stage magician drinking in applause. "Welcome to Paris, *mes amis*," he said.

• • •

A couple of passersby looked at us strangely, but I didn't know if it was because we'd suddenly appeared out of nowhere, or because Becca, Verity, and I were wearing heavy snow parkas and boots in a place that never got so cold that women had to abandon their high heels.

Becca actually screamed before throwing her arms around Bryce. Verity and Cheswick just sort of melted together until their heads touched.

"Feel better?" Peter said, squeezing my hand.

I didn't really know if I did or not. I mean, I still thought that Bryce was wasting precious time showing off for his friends, and that Peter's priorities weren't so right either. On the other hand, I was in Paris with the person I loved most in the world, a person who was looking at me with his beautiful gray eyes through his honey-gold hair.

"I guess," I said, and I couldn't help smiling a little.

"Shall we go somewhere for a *café au lait*?" Bryce suggested. Becca was hanging on to him so tightly that I didn't think it would have mattered to her if we'd gone on a tour of the Paris sewers, but before long we did find a place.

The French must have not been nearly as hardy as folks in Massachusetts, because we were the only people sitting outside at the café. After waiting for nearly twenty minutes for service, Peter finally went inside and persuaded a waiter to bring us coffee. When the waiter arrived, Peter gave him an American fifty-dollar bill and told him to keep the change.

"This is some pretty expensive coffee," I observed, reaching into my handbag to pay for my share.

Peter put his hand over mine. "My treat," he said.

"But—"

"It was worth it," he said. "Besides, we're only young once."

"And he has many dollars," Bryce said, slapping Peter on the back.

The two of them were making me sick. "Oh, right," I said. "Silly me. Who says that money can't buy happiness? Especially when it's someone else's money."

Cheswick started to laugh, then thought better of it. The others were just staring.

"Bryce is right," I went on. "There's always more where that came from, isn't there? As long as you suck up to the guy with the cash, that is. Then you can dress like a king and get all your friends to think you're some kind of—"

"Stop it." Peter set down his coffee cup with a clatter, spilling most of it in the saucer. "That was my money, Katy," he said. "It's money I earned at my job."

I looked away.

"I'm not my uncle's lapdog, whatever you may think."

It was a horrible moment. "All right. I'm sorry," I said, feeling as if I hadn't breathed in the past ten minutes. I wished there weren't so many other people around. "Let's drop it."

No one moved. The horrible moment didn't dissipate but hung in the air like a dark cloud for what seemed like forever.

"Ooo-kay," Bryce said finally, breaking the morbid silence. "Time to get back."

"But we just got here," Becca complained.

"Alas, world geography awaits," Bryce said, tapping his watch. "Library period is *over*."

We all moved to the side of the building so that our disappearance wouldn't seem so obvious. "Why'd she have to pick a fight here, of all places?" Verity whispered to Cheswick. He shushed her and smiled politely at me as he took my hand. Becca held my other hand. Peter had moved.

When we got back, the bell was ringing and the hall was packed. Once I got my bearings I tried to say something to Peter, but he was already walking away into the crowd.

"Wasn't that amazing?" Becca gushed, as if she hadn't noticed that I'd ruined everything.

I turned away and ran to my class.

CHAPTER

•

TWENTY-ONE

By the time I got back from dinner, it was already pitch-dark outside. Some of the dorm rooms were open, spilling light and music into the hallway, but most were closed and silent, their occupants studying for midterms. I'd done all right in world geography, but that was a cake course. The chemistry exam, which was coming up at eight o'clock the next morning, was another matter.

I was mentally going through the steps in Krebs cycle when I turned on the light to my room and saw an enormous black dog sitting on my bed. The remnants of a box of Cheez-Its lay around him in pieces, and my bedspread was stained orange. I recognized him: He was the same ugly mutt who'd bombed into the cafeteria the day my lunch had sprouted digits.

"How'd you get in here?" I griped. I was griping to myself, but the dog answered me with a loud "Woof!" and then leaped off the bed, knocking me to the ground. His big muddy paws were planted squarely on the middle of my chest, and there was a folded-up piece of paper in his mouth. His breath smelled of nondairy cheese product.

Gasping for air, I took the piece of paper away from him, wiping onto my rug the orange drool that coated it.

Come to the store. We'll play.
—M.

"I can't," I said out loud. I was practically failing chemistry as it was. Plus, after she'd taken off for six weeks without sending so much as a postcard, I didn't feel a tremendous obligation toward Morgan. I was looking up the Emporium of Remarkable Goods on the Internet so that I could get the phone number and tell her I was busy, but the dog knocked my laptop away with his huge tail. Diving across the room in a slide worthy of the World Series, I managed to catch it before it splintered against the floor in a fountain of sparks and plastic.

Actually, the sparks were in my head as my injured thumb crashed against the floor.

"Ow!" I yelled, tears springing to my eyes.

The dog came to me, smiling and wagging his tail so hard that his whole rear end swung from side to side. I set down the laptop and gritted my teeth as the throbbing in my thumb subsided. The dog grabbed the sleeve of my jacket in his mouth and pulled me toward the door.

I sighed. There was nothing to be done, I supposed, except to pop into the store, give my regards, return the dog, and leave. As I was zipping up my jacket, I noticed two matching mud blossoms on my sweater. "Cretin," I said. The dog grinned from ear to ear and then sneezed on my hand.

• • •

The emporium's front door was ajar. The dog nosed it open, sauntered in, and immediately transformed into Morgan, shaking out her dark waist-length hair. She was wearing a red cashmere sweater and leather pants.

"Are you kidding me?" I shouted. "It was you all along? Why didn't you just come over like a normal person?"

She shrugged. "I wanted you to come," she said. "You might have said no."

"I *would* have said no! I have a chemistry midterm tomorrow morning!"

"Blah, blah," she said, uncorking a bottle. "Champagne?"

"God, no. And . . . and why aren't you naked?"

She made a face. "What?"

"Whenever I see shape-shifters in movies or on TV, they come back naked."

"Yeah, I never understood that. I mean, they don't come back bald, or minus their fingernails, do they? If you're a bird, you don't come back without feathers. If you're a rhinoceros—"

"Okay, okay."

She poured herself a glassful and tasted it. "Ah. A good year," she said. "The point is, you go the way you are, and you come back the way you are. Easy." She gestured toward me with her chin. "So what'd you do to your hand?"

"Kitchen accident. No biggie."

"Ugh. Why do you have to *cook*? It's dangerous. And it makes you smelly."

I sighed. "Okay, I'm leaving."

"I didn't mean you were smelly *now*," Morgan amended, as if that made everything all right.

"Good to know. But I still have to go."

"No, you don't. It's hours till your midterm."

"That's right, *hours*. To learn months of material."

She waved me away. "Don't give me that, Katy. You're crazy smart." Actually, that was only half-true. My being in the store proved that I was indeed crazy, and not even a little bit smart. "Besides, there's something I want to show you." She crooked a finger at me as she sauntered to the back of the store.

"Where have you been, by the way?" I asked.

"Turkey. My aunt bought some artifacts that turned out to have been stolen from a museum in Ankara. I had to bribe twenty officials to get her out of jail."

"Wow," I said. "That sounds horrible."

"You have no idea," she said. "She was too grossed out to come back. She's at a spa in Switzerland now. But she gave me something as a reward for my help." Morgan stood back, pointing to a painting.

I supposed it was my ignorance about art, but it didn't look like a very interesting painting to me. It was a landscape, with lots of grass and trees, and not much else. There may have been a lake in the background, but it didn't show up as more than a sliver along the upper border. Worst of all, the painting appeared to be covered with dust and grit and other unsavory-looking crud.

"Er . . . nice," I said, resisting the urge to wipe it off with a tissue.

"You don't recognize it?" Morgan asked.

"Recognize? You mean the scene?"

"The type of painting. It's a versimka."

"Oh," I said, my mind a perfect blank. "Was he Turkish?"

"Who?"

"The artist. Ver . . ." I'd already forgotten the rest.

She laughed. "Versimka isn't an artist," she said. "It's a kind of magic, made especially for object-empaths like you." She smiled brightly.

"Object-empaths?"

"People who can enter objects at will," she said. "The Mistress of Real Things, remember?"

"Oh, that. Sure. I've been practicing."

"Awesome. See this grainy stuff at the bottom?" She ran her hand over the surface.

"I thought it was dirt," I said.

"It is. It's earth and crushed rock from the area that the painting depicts. Likewise with the green of the grass and the blue of the sky."

I blinked. "How did the grass stay green?" I asked. "And the *sky*?"

"I told you, it's magic," Morgan said. "Go ahead. Walk into it."

"Uh, I don't know," I said, waffling. "The last time—"

"This will be different. Your whole body goes through, not just your spirit."

I swallowed. "You mean I could die there?"

"You could die the other way too," she said matter-of-factly. "Anyway, trust me, it'll be easier."

"I can't, Morgan. My midterm—"

"Oh, for God's sake!" She sighed, exasperated. "Do you know how much trouble I went through to get this through customs, with the dirt and agricultural products and what all on it? Jeez. I thought you'd be excited."

"It's not that. I just don't have a lot of time."

"But it'll only take a minute!" she shouted. "You've already used up more time arguing with me than it would have taken for you to go and come back."

We stood there staring at each other for a few seconds, until finally she set the painting down. "Fine," she said. "It's not important, I guess. Not to you, anyway."

I blew air out my nose. It wasn't that I didn't want to see what was on the other side of the ver-whatsis, or that I was ungrateful to Morgan for thinking of me. I touched the rough surface of the painting. My ring, which I'd never taken off, suddenly glowed brightly for the first time since the night I'd gone into the tankard. Morgan was back in the main part of the store, with her back to me. I knew I'd let her down. And she had gone to a lot of trouble. . . .

"Okay, I'll go," I said glumly.

"You will?" She spun around, her face radiant. "That's wonderful. You're amazing," she said, downing her glass of wine. "Oh, I can't wait to hear what's inside the versimka!"

That surprised me. "Don't you know?"

"How would I? You're the psycho-whatsis."

"Psychometrist," I corrected. "But where is this place I'm going?"

"Does it matter?"

I studied the painting. "I guess not. Not if I'm just popping in and out again."

"That's all it'll be. Are you ready?"

I sighed. "I guess so."

"Don't knock yourself out with enthusiasm," she said.

"Look, I said I'd go."

"Okay, okay," she said placatingly. "Would you like some vino?" she asked, waving her empty glass.

"No, thanks," I said.

"Well, you'll need something." She set down her glass and ran to the back.

"I'm not thirsty," I called after her. "Besides, I'm only going to be gone for a minute—"

As usual, she paid no attention to me and sprinted back with a glass of pink liquid. "Lemonade," she said breathlessly as she handed it to me. "You never know."

"Never know what?" I almost choked on the drink. "I can get back, can't I?"

"Of course. This is even easier than the other way. Your whole body goes through. It's not virtual anything. That's what makes it magic."

I took a deep breath. "Well, okay. If you're sure it's safe."

"Trust me," Morgan said.

I got myself ready by concentrating on the glowing blue ring on my finger. Morgan had said that there was nothing supernatural about the ring, but I had to disagree. The question, though, was whether it glowed because the stone itself was magic or because it was responding to something I was generating—*conjuring*—inside myself. That was the thing about magic. It was hard to tell exactly where it came from.

Wherever the point of origin was, I began to feel the tingling sensation that I always got before I entered a solid object, and I knew it was time to stop thinking and go with it.

"Bon voyage," I heard Morgan say as I vaulted into the canvas.

I looked back. It was only for the most fleeting moment, but I saw her watching me. To my surprise her face looked inexplicably sad.

"Morgan . . . ," I began, but she was lost to me.

CHAPTER

•

TWENTY-TWO

It was beautiful. That was all I could think of when I found myself standing in the meadow where the painting had taken me. Wildflowers blossomed all around me. The sky was cloudless, and the sun cast a golden light over the distant green hills. . . .

Those hills.

They were oddly familiar. I looked around. *Everything* here was familiar to me.

Suddenly it came to me—my vision. When I'd held the pieces of plastic in my hand, I'd seen this same scene. Into it had walked a young girl with her magician father. She had changed daisies into butterflies, and then cried when he'd left her.

Why had I seen this? What was the connection?

"Hello?" I called. "Anybody here?" But my only answer was the faint, low hum of insects in the grass, droning in the warm sun.

"Oh," I said as I caught myself staggering. The sun was so *warm*. Sun, yes . . . It had been night when I'd left—night and winter. Had I really left, then, or was my body still back at the Emporium of Remarkable Goods? I took a deliberate step to see if my foot left an imprint. It did. The insects droned louder, as if in complaint for disturbing them.

I reached behind me, and could feel the faint thickness of the air where I'd crossed into this . . . what? Place? Dimension? Time? I had no idea where I was or what I should be doing here, and with every passing second, it seemed, my mind grew foggier. I must have had some purpose in coming here, but frankly, I was becoming too tired to care.

That was it. I was tired. I needed to rest. It had been a long day . . . Or was it night back where I'd come from? Which was . . . where, exactly? All I knew was that I had to lie down here, in this fragrant meadow, right now. Just for a minute.

A voice in the back of my mind was shrieking. The drink. *The drink!* Morgan had given me a lemonade. But of course it hadn't been lemonade; it had only looked like lemonade, the way those horrible moldy gingersnaps had looked like delicious cookies.

But why would Morgan do that? I was her friend. The Mistress of Real Things. Why would she poison me?

Poison.

Oh, God. She'd *poisoned* me! Blindly I reached out for the barrier, but I could no longer feel it. My fingers felt like bananas, no longer connected to my body, as I swiped at empty air.

My knees buckled beneath me. I fell into a thick patch of blossoming clover. It smelled wonderful. *Paradise*, I thought.

While part of my mind was panicking and struggling to make my spaghetti legs stand upright again, the other part was breathing in the scent of the clover and longing to stretch out in the warm sun. If I could only rest for a few minutes, I was sure I'd be able to think more clearly.

I remained there on all fours for what seemed like a very long time, nodding off but fighting it, trying to keep my eyes open while drool spilled out of my mouth.

Poison, I thought. But why? What had I done? Through the fog of my drugged vision I saw the blue ring on my finger. It was glowing brightly. *It's laughing*, I thought. *It's happy.*

The insects around me grew louder. They crawled up my arms and inside my jeans. Into my ears. Into the corners of my eyes. I shook my head like a cow trying to rid itself of flies, but the movement was slow and pointless. Then they started to bite.

I gasped, sucking in some of the creatures that were gathered around my mouth. Choking, I tried to crawl away. Where was the barrier? I could no longer remember. I swatted at the bugs, which were now swarming around me in clouds so dense that I could barely see through them to the vague shapes that were rising up from the grass.

They were like wraiths, these beings that floated just out of reach, ghouls with the faces of ancient women, dressed in rags that swirled around them like smoke.

Needing desperately to come out of my stupor, I pinched myself and tried to stand up, but I was so uncoordinated that I fell over. That was when I saw the birds. They were vultures, huge beasts that were heading toward me from the opposite direction as the wraiths, their wings so wide that they made shadows on the ground.

"Wait a minute," I said thickly. Shadows on the ground. Vultures.

I remembered. The little girl in my vision had been running from *vultures*. In this same place. And they had caught her.

As I watched, horrified, the giant birds turned into women— the same sort of ragged women that had risen out of the ground around me, their spectral garments waving in the wind, their faces twisted with malice as they surrounded me. One of them spoke:

"Poison."

I blinked hard. How did they know I'd been poisoned? I'd only figured it out myself a minute ago.

They came closer, reaching out for me with gnarled, claw-like fingers. I remembered how the little girl in my vision had screamed with fear and hopelessness when they'd descended on her, predators clutching at their prey. What had they done with her? Killed her, probably. Torn her apart like confetti while she cried out for help . . .

Well, that wasn't going to happen again. Not to me. Poisoned or not, I had no intention of making *anything* easy for these hags. If they were going to murder me, it was going to cost them.

Summoning more strength than I'd thought I possessed, I grabbed two handfuls of dirt and threw them in the direction of the ghouls. They backed away. I lunged for the bony hands that had been taunting me, and they withdrew with a shriek.

They don't want me to touch them, I realized. Oh, my God. Could it be? They were actually *afraid* of me. With a scream worthy of the coeds in the Freddy Krueger movies, I forced myself to stagger upright. The women—if that was what they were—flew out of my reach.

With my foot I felt for the barrier. Even with my adrenaline pumping, I still felt as if I were walking through molasses, but I thought I detected a slight change in pressure. As the hags regrouped, I backed toward what I hoped was the two-by-three-foot rectangle of space that would take me back to Morgan's store.

A tiny worm of worry intruded into my thoughts. *What if Morgan is waiting for me on the other side?* If she'd tried to poison me with the lemonade, what would she do to me if I showed up again? But I wasn't going to think about that now. The creatures—they couldn't really be called human—were pressed together in a tight mass and were moving forward again, their eyes glinting, their breath fouling the air. Together they raised their arms toward me.

As I felt desperately for the opening, I shielded my face with my hands. Suddenly the ring, with no help from me, flashed with a blue light so intense, it was as if the sun had fallen out of the sky.

The wraiths who had been directly in the path of the light fell to the ground, their rags floating behind them, while the others flew away. At that moment I leaped backward into the barrier.

The next thing I knew, I was crawling over the wooden frame of the painting, just me in the darkness, gasping for air.

I think I may have fallen asleep right there on the floor, without even knowing exactly where I was. It wasn't for very long, though, because when I woke up, there were still bugs in my shoes. Smacking my lips with residual sleep, I lumbered to my feet and looked around.

I was back in the store, but all the lights were out, and Morgan was nowhere in sight. Also, the painting had been moved to the back of the store, behind the curtain that separated the clean, inviting retail area that the customers saw from the squalid back room that housed all the broken stuff as well as new shipments and excess inventory.

Well, of course Morgan would have moved the painting over here, I thought. She'd probably assumed that I wouldn't be coming back, since she'd obviously sent me to die on the other side of her magic painting.

Some friend, I thought with a shiver of anger and, well, to be truthful, shame. I should have known that someone as cool as Morgan wouldn't have considered having me as a friend. I hadn't been anything more to her than a tool for her use. She must have sensed how pathetic I was, and had decided that I'd make a perfect dupe. *Way to go, Katy.*

I toyed seriously with the idea of stomping upstairs and punching her in the nose, but I knew that wouldn't do much good. Even if I managed to do it—and I probably couldn't, since she was a much stronger witch than I was—it would still take more time than I was willing to spare. At least she hadn't been waiting for me with a dagger to stab into my heart.

I could see that, outside, the sky was pitch-black. I checked my cell phone. Three forty-five a.m. My body was still shaking all over from the fear that had flooded through me. Still, that fear had probably saved my life. But now I was so tired, I was afraid to lean against anything because I knew I'd be out cold again within a minute. And the chemistry exam still loomed over me like a mushroom cloud. With a sigh I tried to shake myself awake. Time and Krebs cycle waited for no one. I stood there for a moment, waiting to work up enough strength to make it to the door.

That was when I heard it, a whisper, as soft as spring rain, coming from somewhere in the darkness behind me.

"Help me," it said.

A shiver ran down my spine. I listened. There was no sound. No traffic outside, no furnace noises. Just the faraway ticktock of an old grandfather clock that had stopped telling the right time years ago, and the whoosh of my own breath going in and out.

I don't know how long I stayed that way, immobile and listening.

Nothing.

Nothing.

Then: *"Kay-tee."*

I leaped up, my heart pounding in my chest.

"Okay, I know you're there," I called. As if that meant anything. If it was a burglar, he was probably armed. What was I going to fight him with, a porcelain figurine?

I gulped. I knew it wasn't a burglar. The voice that had spoken my name hadn't sounded human.

A ghost, then. A ghost who knew my name. *No big deal*, I told myself. You didn't hang out in Whitfield for long without encountering a few ectoplasmic entities. But this felt somehow different. Not ghostly, really. More like *trapped*. That was what it sounded like, as if someone were calling me from inside a box. A box, or a . . . I didn't even want to think the word "coffin," but that was what came to mind. The voice was so constrained, it was as if whoever was calling for help could barely move their lips.

Immediately I started rummaging through the inventory that was piled willy-nilly behind the curtain. I wished I could turn on the lights, but there'd be no way I could explain to the police—or the school—or Morgan, for that matter—what I was doing there at four in the morning.

With only the light from my cell phone to see by, I had to do most of my exploring by feel. A lot of the merchandise was old, and most of it was dirty. There were books, photographs, an old TV, a bamboo end table shaped like a monkey. Also a jack-in-the-box that almost gave me a heart attack when it boinged into my face. I tripped over a casserole dish that looked like a pumpkin, and I ended up on the floor facing a gizmo made of iron with a lot of evil-looking prongs sticking out of it.

The hardest part for me was maintaining a psychic distance from these things. I'd called myself the Mistress of Real Things, but the truth was that I still hadn't fully mastered my ability to feel their history. Most of the time I was all right. I only "read" objects when I concentrated on them. But sometimes I got taken by surprise, like when I'd held those broken pieces of plastic and gotten a preview of life behind the verplinko, or whatever it was called. In this place, surrounded by very old things with thousands of stories among them, I felt my control loosening.

There was a cup that an opera singer had drunk from before every performance. I could hear her singing in a corner of my mind. An oil lamp still stained with the blood of the man who'd shot himself in the circle of its light. A silver rattle that had been found lodged in the throat of a dead infant.

With a swift intake of air, I lifted my hands in a gesture of surrender. "I'm sorry," I said, "but this is too much for me." If a ghost were taking up residence in the Emporium of Remarkable Goods, it was going to have to stay there.

"Kay-tee . . ."

"Listen, I'll come back," I said, relenting, wiping my hand over my face. "In the morning. I'll bring real witches with me, Hattie or . . ."

My voice dried up in my throat. In the far corner of the room, I noticed two small yellowish lights. They glowed once, then dimmed to blackness again.

I pointed my cell phone toward where they had been. The jack-in-the-box I'd inadvertently opened was lying nearby, its long neck hanging limply like a dead turkey's, its painted clown face shining in the dim bluish light from my phone. Beside it was an antique teddy bear with no arms, a wooden wagon, a Victorian doll house, and an array of porcelain-headed dolls dressed in old lace.

"Here . . . I . . . am . . ." The voice sounded miserable, the despair in it so thick that it must have taken every iota of energy to speak those words.

Suddenly I was no longer afraid. Whoever, *whatever* was speaking to me wasn't going to hurt me. It was crying out for help. "Where?" I whispered. "Tell me how to find you."

And then I saw it. From the corner, among the dolls, the yellow eyes glowed once more.

Toys, I thought wildly. I remembered hearing something about . . . I closed my eyes and tried to remember. Toys. Souls. Summer.

Summer's soul.

I remembered. Verity had said the girls' souls had been placed among *toys*.

My thoughts were all jumbled inside my head as I scrambled over the pile to reach the dolls stacked against the far wall. Why would they be *here*?

"Summer?" I ventured.

The eyes blazed, almost bringing one of the doll's faces to life. Beside it, three other dolls glowed with dim light from their tortured eyes.

"Oh, God," I said. "Oh, God." I cast around wildly, trying to figure out what I should do. Briefly I touched the Summer doll, then pulled my hands away. This . . . this *thing* held Summer's living soul, and I didn't want some ham-handed action of mine to destroy it forever.

I swallowed, though my mouth was dry. "I don't know what to do, Summer," I whispered. "Maybe if we wait till morning—"

A chorus of tiny muffled shrieks rose up around me.

"Right," I agreed. Morning would probably be too late for all of us. "Did Morgan do this to you?"

All four pairs of eyes seemed to tremble in terror.

Of course it had been Morgan. I had no idea what she would want with four Muffies, but at this point I wouldn't put anything past her.

While I was frantically trying to figure out how best to help them, my cell phone made the blooping sound that told me a text was coming through. It was from Peter.

Where RU?

I wrote back: *Emporium of Curious Gds*. That way, if I didn't come back, at least the witches would know where to look.

"Please help," Summer whimpered.

I wanted to, more than anything. "Are you all right in there?" I asked.

There was a lot of muffled grunting. I didn't know if she just had difficulty talking through the doll, or if something was really wrong.

"I think I know some people who might be able to get you out, but I don't know if I should move you—er, I mean this thing you're in. This doll."

There was a long silence, followed by the unmistakable sound of someone crying.

I sighed. The last, and I mean the very last thing I wanted to do just then was take another trip through an object. But there were some things I had to find out before turning the dolls over to the Whitfield witches, like whether or not Summer was really inside, and what condition she was in.

"All right," I said, wishing with all my heart that I'd stayed in my dorm room studying chemistry. Under the circumstances, there was only one thing I could do. "It's now or never, I guess."

With that I hurled myself into the doll.

I landed with a thud on a bare white floor surrounded by four bare white walls. Summer was pressed against one of them, her face a mask of astonishment.

"Summer?" I ventured.

She hesitated for a moment, her eyes darting around wildly. "How'd you get in here?"

I shook my head. It was going to be very hard to explain to a Muffy. Fortunately, I didn't have to, because the next second she ran sobbing into my arms. "Oh, Katy, I'm sorry for all the mean things I did to you!" she whispered into my ear while gripping my neck in a desperate hammerlock.

"That's okay—," I began, but she was apparently in confessional mode.

"Like turning your lunch into slugs, and telling Miss P that you put the voodoo doll in Verity's locker."

"Yeah, I know," I said, struggling to pull her arms off me. "But how did you—"

"And for telling Peter that you hooked up with the track team."

"What?" I pushed her away. "You told him *what*?"

"I don't think he believed me, anyway."

"The *whole team*?" I was shouting.

"I know, crazy. Like they'd ever even consider—I mean . . ."

"Forget it," I said. I looked around at the sterile cube where we stood. "What is this place?" I asked.

"How should I know?" She tossed her hair, which was now unkempt and tangled, showing dark roots. "Backstabber," she said bitterly. "She said she'd give us power."

"Who? Morgan?"

"She said we could have whatever we wanted."

I made a face. "And what you wanted most was to turn my burger into slugs?"

"That was supposed to just be for practice. Besides, I was pissed. You did some kind of weird thing to me and my friends, and I wanted to pay you back. But I didn't think she'd do *this*."

"But why would she? With you? *How*—"

"Hey, do I look like Dick Tracy to you?" she snapped. "Anyway, I know she's not your buddy, not really. I thought so at first, though. I mean, how else would you be able to do that stuff to A.J. and Suzy and Tiff?"

She paused, waiting for an answer.

I cleared my throat. I couldn't very well tell Summer that I'd come up with a stink spell on my own. "That was, er, the um . . ." I thought hard. "The power of suggestion," I said in a flash of inspiration.

That seemed to do it for her. "Whatever," she said with a dismissive wave. Maybe she let it go so easily because, like most people confronting the impossible, she preferred not to think about it. Or it could have been that Summer just didn't think much about anything.

"Anyway, after a while I figured out that you were clueless." She gave me a beauty pageant smile. "I mean that in a good way. Now get me out of here."

"First you need to tell me how you got in here in the first place."

She rolled her eyes. "Oh, all right," she said. "Some girls were saying that you and Verity and some of the other geeks—I mean local students—" She gave me a guilty look.

"Go ahead," I said wearily.

"That you were pretending to have this magic mojo, so we put the doll in Verity's locker." She shrugged. "It was a joke, that's all."

"What about the Ouija board?" I asked. "Did anything happen when you used it?"

"Anything?" she asked pointedly. "How about *everything*?" She paced away from me. "Okay, after you did that stink thing or whatever it was—"

"A suggestion," I repeated.

She huffed with impatience at my interruption. "Anyway, A.J. and I went to Fred's Bargain Mart that night and picked up this funky old Ouija board so that we could get even with you."

"Ouijas don't do that."

"Who's talking here?" she said irritably, flashing me the mean-girl stare. When she was convinced that I was sufficiently cowed, she went on: "Only this Ouija didn't have the arrow thing."

"The arrow thing?"

"The thing that points to the letters. A.J. wanted to take it back, but Fred's was closed for the night. Anyway, I remembered I had this arrowhead thingy—"

"You used an arrowhead?"

"Well, it wasn't exactly an arrowhead. It was plastic. But it was kind of a triangle shape. You know, with a pointy end?"

I nodded inanely, trying to get into the spirit of this inane conversation.

"Actually, Tiff picked it up off the sidewalk right after Halloween. I remember we were out toilet-papering trees, and she found this thing, and I was like, 'Ewww. What migrant worker peed on that?' But she—"

"Huh?" I wondered if I'd begun to drift off. "Migrant whats?"

"You know. It's the reason why you should wash fruit before you eat it. Because you never know what migrant workers peed on it. So I always wash my fruit, even if it comes in a can."

I blinked. Summer's thought processes were too bizarre for me to follow.

"Maybe you didn't know that, being poor and everything," she went on breezily. "But anyway, I said, 'That's *too gross*, picking that thing up like that,' but Tiff said it looked like there was a lady inside, so—"

"A lady?" Something in the back of my mind was stirring back to consciousness.

"Swear to God. It looked *exactly* like Snow White Barbie, except for the puff sleeves on her dress. I mean, that would have just been too retro—"

"Okay, okay," I said. "What happened next?"

"Well, we all gathered around the Ouija board, you know,

asking for power and stuff, and the arrowhead was whizzing around the board like crazy—"

"What did it spell out?"

"Huh?"

"The message on the Ouija board. What was it?"

"There was a message?"

"There usually is," I said.

She held up her hands. "Hey, I can't keep track of everything, you know? Anyway, the thing was zipping around so fast, I could barely hold on to it. But then it . . . it sort of *exploded*, like *boom*, you know? Like a supersonic jet or something. The hall proctor even knocked on the door, but we said we were moving furniture."

"What was the explosion?"

"It was *her*. " She gestured around the area.

"Morgan?"

"*Snow White Barbie*. So anyway, one minute she's part of the plastic arrowhead, and the next minute she's standing, as big as life, in the middle of the room. I swear."

"I believe you."

"Well, okay, 'cause this is where it gets kind of weird. Because she says, like, 'I'm here to do your bidding' or whatever, like she's some genie or something, and she's going to grant our wishes, you know? Except she didn't say there was a limit on the wishes, so we think there's, like, unlimited wishes—"

"And you wished that my lunch would turn into slugs."

"But don't you see? I thought there'd be *multiple* wishes. I didn't think I'd be wasting my only wish on your stupid lunch! I mean A.J. and Tiff and Suzy Dusset didn't even get to make a wish at all, because as soon as I said I wanted to turn your french fries into fingers because you'd made us stink, Snow White Barbie says 'Okay, done. It'll happen at lunch tomorrow,' and then she walks out the *door!* Like without even asking what A.J. and Tiff want. I didn't care if Suzy Dusset got any wishes or not, but still, it was rude.

"So we all ran after her, but she was gone, like *poof*, and there was nothing in the hall except for this gigantic moth. So of course we ran back in and closed the door."

"And you never saw, er, Snow White Barbie again?"

Summer shook her head and crossed her arms over her chest. "*Supertramp* is more like it, the lying skank. We tried to bring her back—that's what we were doing the night you came into my dorm room. I mean, the lunch thing happened, but what about our other wishes? She owed us."

Something was gnawing at the corners of my mind. "What happened to the planchette?" I asked.

"What?"

"The plastic triangle thing that used to hold tiny Barbie?"

"I told you, it blew apart that first night. So we didn't use anything. I mean, there we are, invoking her and everything, really respectfully, and then splat, I'm in here. If I knew that was the price I'd have to pay for one stupid wish, believe me, I would've wished for diamonds or something. Or to be Lady Gaga."

"So it was still in your room?" The thought wouldn't leave me. "The planchette."

"What difference does it make where the thing was? She wasn't in it anymore. That's what matters. And the fact that I'm in here. Now get me out."

I scratched my head. "I guess I could try to take you out

with me," I said. "Is that where the doll's eyes are?" I walked over to one wall that seemed to have some vague markings on it. Up close, I could see the interior of the store. More precisely, I saw myself lying on the floor amid a jumble of old toys. "I guess we've left our bodies," I said, remembering my experience with the tankard.

"Really?" she asked, peering over my shoulder. "So where's mine? I only see you out there."

I hated to tell her. "It's in a hospital in Michigan, I think."

Her face crumpled. "Will I . . . you know, get back all right?"

"I don't know," I answered honestly. "That's why I'd rather ask someone who knows about these things."

"No!" Summer stamped her foot. "I'm not going to stay in here one second longer. Now do something!"

I gulped. "Okay," I said. "Take my hand."

"Hurry up!" Summer ordered as I walked through the doll's eyes.

"Summer?" I hauled myself up onto all fours. My head felt like it was splitting apart. The kind of magic I'd been doing was taking its toll on me. I could barely move without sending shooting pains into my head. "Summer, did you make it?"

But of course she wouldn't answer, I realized. If I'd managed to get Summer's soul—or whatever part of her I'd visited—out of the doll, it would have returned to her body back in Michigan.

Maybe the others went with her, I thought hopefully. The prospect of doing this three more times wasn't something I was looking forward to at all.

"A.J.? Suzy?" I whispered as I crawled toward the heap of antique dolls. "Tiffany?"

Then I saw it. The Summer doll, with its human eyes glaring at me.

"I guess it didn't work," I said, picking up the doll as if I could give it some comfort in my arms. "I'm sorry."

At first the eyes looked as if Summer wanted to strangle me, but within a few seconds her bravado abandoned her. The doll's expression softened until I thought the eyes were about to cry. I wondered if somewhere in a hospital far away, Summer's impassive face was covered with tears. "I'll find a way to get you out," I whispered, cradling her in my arms as I picked up the other three dolls. "I promise you."

Suddenly there was a loud pounding on the door. The little bell jingled furiously while a hundred delicate things in the store quivered and trembled in its wake.

Morgan, I thought, and then: *No.* Morgan wouldn't have to force open her own door. It had to be someone else, a drunk probably, or . . .

"Peter!" Hanging on to the four dolls in my arms, I lumbered to my feet and moved as quickly as I could toward the front door, where Peter was making urgent-looking faces through the glass. "Hey," I said, managing to get the door open. "Can you take a couple of these?" I handed him the dolls.

He looked at me like I was crazy. "What're you doing, robbing the place?"

"I'll explain later," I said. "Right now, we have to get them out of here." I shoved him away and closed the door behind us. "As fast as we can."

"Okay," he said dubiously. "Only . . ."

"What?" I pushed him with my shoulder. "Talk while we're moving. Go."

"It's just . . . I didn't think there was anything in that place anymore."

"What are you talking about?" I turned around. "The store just opened—"

My tongue stuck to the roof of my mouth, and my legs almost gave out beneath me.

In the soft early morning light I saw an abandoned storefront, its filthy windows revealing an empty space with a broken counter and a floor with half its tiles missing. Outside hung a broken sign that had fallen over the doorway:

Fr d's Barga

"What'd you call it?" Peter asked. "I walked up and down the street for more than an hour trying to find the place you texted me about. Finally I just looked in every store to see if there was any movement."

It was gone. The Emporium. The whole place.

Vanished.

Under my arm, Summer's horrified eyes stared out of the doll's porcelain face.

PART THREE
THE
KILLING GIFT

CHAPTER

·

TWENTY-FIVE

Peter didn't ask a lot of questions on the way to my great-grandmother's, although I think he wanted to.

"I'll tell you all about it afterward," I said. "Okay?"

"Sure." He tried not to look hurt. "I understand. I'm not much use when it comes to magic."

"It's not that . . ."

But it was, and we both knew it. There were some high-powered male witches in the world, but, in Whitfield at least, the women were definitely the prime movers.

"Hey, I don't mind," he said gently. "You've been left out of my life often enough."

"Like at Winter Frolic," I said, hoping to sound jolly and mature about it, even though I didn't really feel that way.

I think it was the opening Peter was waiting for. "So will you come to the dance?" he asked.

"With you and your date?" My good humor was beginning to sound forced.

"You know I have to take Fabienne."

I sighed. "I don't know," I said. "I can't think about it now."

"Okay," he said, giving me back the dolls. "I'll let you do what you need to do. Good luck." Then he kissed me.

Whoever had come up with the idea that only bad boys were interesting must have been crazy. I'd take my nice guy any day.

An hour later Gram, Hattie, Miss P, and I stood around Gram's kitchen with the four dolls propped up in the middle of us.

"Now, dears, there's no need for concern," Gram said, patting the Summer doll on its head. "This won't hurt a bit."

She hadn't blinked an eye when I'd bombed into her bedroom before dawn asking for her help. Gram was an empath. Her gift was compassion. She volunteered at the local hospital seven days a week, helping people get ready for surgery, or calming frightened children or soothing the grieving relatives of the dead. I knew that if I'd been one of the souls trapped inside those dolls, she would have been the person I'd want to have around me. When she touched them, I saw their terrified eyes soften inside their little china heads.

"We have to get them out before Morgan gets back to the store," I said. "Or what I thought was the store. Actually—"

"That's all right, Katy," she said, shushing me as she stood dialing the phone. I'd been babbling ever since I'd walked in. "We'll sort all that out later. The important thing is, you've found the girls. And you're right. There's no time to waste. . . . Hattie, dear?" she said into the mouthpiece.

Of course Hattie had to be notified. Then there was Miss P, the djinn. She could put ideas into people's heads, which meant she could start a revolution just by *thinking* if she wanted to. She could convince the guards at Fort Knox to turn over all the gold in their vaults to her, get the President to declare that the United States had become a territory of Switzerland, or make Justin Bieber fall in love with her, even though she's nearly thirty. If Miss P was going to be there, I knew that what was going on was a big deal.

And then there was me, but only because my aunt Agnes wasn't available. It felt strange to be in the company of these three witches. They represented the values of knowledge, strength, and compassion. Translated into witch ritual, that meant the elements air, fire, and water, or east, south, and west. I was positioned at north, signifying earth, the grounding influence. I didn't know what I could possibly contribute to the group, but I was willing to do my best. I just hoped I wouldn't screw things up.

"Katy, concentrate!" Gram snapped, nudging me with her wand.

Wands, which amplified whatever gifts you had, were called for only in extreme cases. This must have been one, because they all had their wands out, except for me. I used to own one, but I'd lost it somewhere in the middle of Whitfield Bay last year. So I held a hammer. It wasn't a very magical tool, but necessary all the same.

I set my mind on what I wanted to happen. In High Magic you didn't have to know exactly what to do. You just had to focus your intention clearly and open up a channel to let the forces of the universe do what needed to be done. All of the rituals and magic words that witches and sorcerers were supposed to use were just ways to get them into that state of pure focus, so that the channel would open. But these witches were too well trained to need those crutches. They just zeroed in on the dolls with so much intensity that the tips of their wands glowed.

I saw Miss P's wand out of the corner of my eye, but I made a point of not looking at her face. When she went into djinn mode, she became pretty scary-looking, with these luminescent not-of-this-earth eyes and a telepathic voice.

The energy we generated began to hum. It traveled in a circle around us, thin at first, then growing louder as the cone of power grew thicker around us. The dolls vibrated on the table. We all heard the faint, pitiful screams of the girls inside as the energy inside the cone became so strong that it was hard for me to hang on to my hammer.

Then, when everything threatened to fly apart and I didn't think I could hold on any longer, I smashed the hammer down onto Gram's wooden cutting board. It was the signal for the witches to shoot their power out through their wands.

The dolls exploded into a thousand pieces, leaving nothing but dust behind.

I stood there blinking for a long time afterward, afraid that the girls had been vaporized.

"Are they all right?" I finally whispered timidly.

"Shh." Gram nodded toward Miss P, who was gradually turning back into herself. She shook all over, as if throwing off the magic that had enveloped her, then patted her hair back into place. "I'll go find out," Miss P said in a breathy voice, and left the room.

Gram tucked her wand into the lacy sleeve of her dress. "Tea, anyone?" she warbled.

"I've got to be going," I said. "I've got an eight o'clock exam."

Hattie pointed at me. "Sit down," she said. I sat. "We released those girls without much information about what put them there because it was an emergency situation, but it's time you told us everything you learned from Summer."

I looked at my watch. "Can't this—"

"No."

I blew air out of my nose. "Okay," I said, "but Bryce has to be here too."

"Bryce?" Hattie raised an eyebrow. "What's he got to do with this?"

I gave her a level look. "I'll tell you everything I know, but he's got to answer some of my questions too," I said. "Like why he didn't warn me about Morgan, so that I might have suspected something before she poisoned me and sent me off to die."

"I was looking for someone *small*," Bryce said when he arrived ten minutes later. "That was the main thing about her, her size—"

"Hello, she's a *shape-shifter*," I reminded him acidly.

"All right, all right," he said, and sulked. "I had planned to bring the amber containing her to Whitfield and then go back. There were not supposed to be complications." He shook his head. "And now Morgan le Fay has eluded us forever—"

"Whoa," I said. "*Morgan le Fay*? As in King Arthur's nemesis?"

"And sister," he said.

"Sister?"

"Half sister," Bryce corrected. "At least according to legend."

"Wait a minute," I said. "What about Uther Pendragon, the king?" I argued. I hadn't spent the better part of a day looking up references to King Arthur online for nothing. "He was supposed to be Arthur's father, even though Queen Igraine was married to—"

Gram cleared her throat. "Fatherhood is never a certainty," she said delicately.

Miss P raised her eyebrows.

"Morgan the sorceress killed her father the Merlin because she was jealous of his love for his human son, Arthur, whom he helped to become king," Bryce recited.

I sat back. "Wow," I said. "So *that's* Morgan's story. And so the place she sent me to was . . ."

"Avalon," Bryce said grimly. "My home. And hers."

Suddenly I was able to see why Bryce hadn't seemed wholehearted in his appreciation of his native land, and why he wasn't knocking himself out to return there. "Those vulture women, then—"

"They're the Seer's security force," Bryce said. "They keep the rest of us . . . morally responsible."

"By killing you?" I asked.

Bryce didn't answer.

"Fine, dear," Gram said. "That's all terribly interesting, but the question we ought to be asking is not what this Morgan person did in the fifth century but how the cowen girls broke a sixteen-hundred-year-old spell six weeks ago."

"I've told you from the beginning," I said. "The Ouija board. They called her with that."

"But those girls didn't know the first thing about magic," Hattie said. "I'll bet they didn't even know who Morgan le Fay was."

"It didn't matter. Summer said the planchette was moving

all over the board. She didn't figure out that it was spelling out a message, but I'll bet it was. My guess is that the message was the spell to break the binding."

"That was how they released her," Bryce said, awed. "By writing a spell they themselves knew nothing about."

"Even while they were writing it," Miss P added.

Agnes, who had just materialized on the sofa, frowned. "Forgive me," she said. "I came as quickly as I could."

"Quite all right, Agnes, dear," Gram said before turning back to me. "But what about the amber?"

"The what?" I asked.

"The substance that encased Morgan le Fay. If the girls released her from it, then it had to have been nearby. Perhaps one of them had it in her possession."

"I'm afraid I'm not following this at all," Agnes said.

"Penelope's finding out about the girls now," Gram said, getting to her feet. "I'll ask her. Meanwhile, Katy, would you try to bring Agnes up to speed?"

"Okay," I said. "It'll probably help us all to put things in the right sequence." They all turned to look at me. "First, the Seer of Avalon sent Bryce de Crewe to Whitfield," I began.

Bryce nodded uncertainly.

"He was bringing a piece of amber to Hattie for safekeeping, because it contained Morgan le Fay, who the Seer said was destined to escape and destroy Avalon."

"It's all my fault," Bryce said, sounding wretched. "That's what we were trying to avoid. And now it's going to happen after all—"

"Just stay with me for a minute," I said. "At the time Morgan was captured, she'd shrunk down to the size of a mosquito because she can shape-shift, just like the Seer's army of ghouls."

"It's a pretty common gift," Bryce observed with a sniff.

"Morgan has another gift too, one that isn't so common. She's what's called a Traveler, meaning that she can travel between Avalon and the real world. Bryce has the same gift."

"I am not sure what you mean by 'real,'" Bryce said.

"Hush up," Hattie said.

"So Bryce made it to the so-called real world, at least as far as Whitfield. But then the amber containing Morgan fell out of his pocket and landed on the street."

"Where Summer and her friends picked it up," Agnes said with a *Let's get on with it* motion.

"Right. Then later Summer put the witch doll in Verity Lloyd's locker, and her boyfriend Cheswick got so mad that he threw out five fingers at Summer."

"For shame!" Gram said. "And in *school*."

"I didn't know what he was going to do to the girls, so I threw out another spell to knock his out."

"The one that made them stink," Bryce said, smirking. Hattie elbowed him.

"Right. After that I thought everything was okay because the school didn't punish anyone, but Summer was still angry about the stink spell. To get even with me, she bought a Ouija board at Fred's Bargain Mart."

"Fred's must have been going out of business at the time," Gram said.

"But a Ouija board?" Hattie looked skeptical. "Why would she do that? A Ouija can't do anything except call up the dead."

"She didn't know that," I explained. "Summer and her friends were totally clueless."

"Cowen," Gram stage-whispered behind her hand.

"Then how—" Hattie began.

I knew what she was going to ask. "The planchette that was supposed to come with the board was missing, so they used the piece of amber they'd found instead."

"The one I'd lost!" Bryce said excitedly.

Agnes nodded. "The amber with Morgan le Fay trapped inside."

Hattie's eyes widened. "And those idiot girls used it in a *board game?*"

I nodded. "After it wrote out the releasing spell, she burst out of the amber and promised to grant the girls a wish."

"Why?" Hattie asked. "She didn't have to do any such thing."

"I think it was so that they wouldn't talk to anyone about what had happened."

Everyone seemed to be in agreement about this. "And they really thought they had power," Hattie said, shaking her head. Gram *tsk*ed.

"They had enough to turn my burger and fries into slugs and severed fingers," I said.

"That must have been a terrible strain," Agnes said.

"No lie. It totally wrecked my lunch."

"On *them*," she explained. "Spellwork is demanding, even for trained and talented witches. For non-adepts . . ."

"Can you *imagine?*" Gram said, wincing.

"But they all collapsed at the same time," I said. "It happened the next night, in front of me. That didn't happen because they just got *tired*."

"You're right," Agnes said. "They didn't do anything. Morgan performed the magic that transmogrified your food."

"So why did they fall down then, just when I arrived? Was that a coincidence?"

Hattie laughed, a deep alto rumble. "Honey, nothing's a coincidence," she said. "That part of it seems clear to me." She looked over at Gram, and then back at me. "You were what she was after all along."

"Her?" Bryce stared at me. "Am I missing something? Why would Morgan want Katy?"

"Because she has power," Hattie said. "And your sorceress knew it as soon as Katy walked into the girls' dorm room. Maybe even before that."

Bryce frowned. "Excuse me, but this is Whitfield. There are many powerful people here."

I sucked in air. "But not many who can travel through objects."

"What?"

I told them about the tankard. "But then she gave me this painting—a versimka, she called it—that I could just walk through."

"To get to Avalon?"

I nodded.

There was a long silence. Finally Gram asked, "What did you do there?"

I shrugged. "I don't know. Nothing much. The first time, I fell into the lake. The second time, Morgan slipped me a roofie or something and I just wanted to sleep, but these witches chased me away. Well, first they bit me—"

"They bit you?"

"They turned into sand fleas or something," I said. "But then they shape-shifted into vultures and came after me."

Bryce nodded. "They're the price we pay for living in peace and security."

"But they didn't hurt me," I interrupted. "The vultures. Actually, I think I hurt *them*."

"It sounds as if they wanted you to leave," Agnes said.

"Oh, definitely."

"Because you hurt them?"

"No, I didn't do that until . . . I can't remember." I shook my head. "I'm sorry, but I was pretty groggy by then. I remember a bright light . . ." I tried to remember exactly what had driven them away, but I couldn't. "I guess they just don't like strangers," I finished.

Bryce swallowed, thinking. "No, it's more than that," he said. "Morgan *is* going to destroy Avalon, just as the Seer predicted. Only she's not going to do it herself." He narrowed his eyes at me. "That's why she wanted Katy. As an assassin."

There was a swift intake of air from everyone in the room.

"No!" I shouted. "That can't be! I didn't do anything!"

"Not yet," Agnes said cryptically.

"Summer and her three friends are all conscious and doing well." Miss P stood in the archway leading from the kitchen. There were sighs of relief all around. "They all came to at the same time. Not that the hospitals are likely to check with one another," she added.

"Then we shall all remain silent about the matter," Gram said.

I objected. "But what about Summer? I talked to her when she was inside the doll. I was *with* her. She's not just going to forget that."

"You'd be surprised the things people forget," Miss P said primly.

"Oh." I was getting it. "Right." Miss P had gone into Summer's mind and convinced her that our encounter had never taken place, that she'd never released Morgan le Fay from the piece of amber, that she and her friends had never asked for or received any unusual powers, and that none of them had ever been incarcerated inside antique dolls in a store that didn't exist. What those four believed, and would continue to believe for the rest of their lives, was that they had drunk some tainted diet tea that had knocked them out for a month and a half.

"I also urge you not to embarrass yourself by telling fantastic tales to your friends, Katy."

The others all squinted at me. "Er . . . okay," I said.

"Not even your best friends," Agnes reminded me. Hattie just rolled her eyes.

"All right. I know already." Jeez. Nobody trusted me with a secret as far as they could throw me.

"The best course of action would be to put this all behind us and move forward with our lives," Miss P said.

"Yes, but . . . ," Bryce waffled. "What about the amber?"

Gram looked earnestly at Miss P. "Penelope, dear, did any of those girls—"

"No," she answered. "None of them had any inkling about the importance of the amber."

"Then I guess it's gone forever," Bryce said morosely.

"Does it really matter?" I asked.

"Of course it matters!" he shouted. "Without the amber, Morgan can't be trapped again!"

I pressed my lips together, thinking. Something had been bothering me for a long time. "Er . . . ," I began.

Everyone sighed in exasperation. "What is it now, Katy?" Agnes asked, looking at her watch. "I have an eight o'clock class."

"Me too," I said. "But I need to ask . . . er . . . amber's a stone, right?

Bryce sighed. "You don't even know what it looks like?"

"Of course I do," I answered defensively. "Sort of." Which was to say, I knew it often had things like flies and bubbles in it, but I'd never actually seen a piece of amber, or touched one.

Hattie clucked irritably, but Gram was unperturbed. "Why, it's *amber*-colored, dear. Brownish-yellowish. Transparent. It's made from the resin of trees, so it's very lightweight—so much so that it's often mistaken for plastic—"

"Oh, God," I said, closing my eyes. The thing that had been lurking at the back of my mind burst forward. "I'll be right back."

"What on earth . . . " Gram squeaked behind me as I took the stairs to my bedroom three at a time.

They were still here, the two broken pieces of what I'd thought was brown plastic that I'd taken from Summer's room. I pressed the pieces together. Summer had been right: The hole in the middle was shaped like Snow White Barbie.

And as soon as I touched them, I saw Morgan's face.

It was the face of the young girl in my visions. She was younger and less glamorous than the real-life Morgan I'd known, but now that I'd made the connection, it was obvious that they were one and the same. The girl who had befriended me was the monster that Bryce had been hunting all along. And her whole life was contained in these pieces of amber.

I tossed them into the air and caught them again. This was where Morgan had spent the past sixteen hundred years. And where, once Bryce caught her again, she would spend eternity. *Sorry, Morgan*, I thought. *Wish things could have been different.*

"Is this what you're looking for?" I asked, handing the pieces to Bryce.

He leaped to his feet. "How long have you had these?"

"I got it from Summer's room after she was taken away,"

Hattie sputtered, putting down her teacup with a clatter. "Do you mean to tell us that you broke into that child's room *again*?"

"I was trying to find some evidence," I said, although it sounded more like a question. "And I didn't break in the first time. The girls opened the door—"

"Saints alive, will you *never* cease meddling—"

"It's not her fault," Miss P said, fatigue showing in blue patches under her eyes. Magic takes a lot out of you. "Summer's room had been cleared out. Everyone overlooked the pieces of amber. Even the police."

"They were stuck inside the heat register, I think," I explained. "They must have been blown there when the thing exploded. I didn't pay much attention to them either, until I started to see images from someone's—Morgan's—life."

"Morgan's?" Miss P asked, cocking her head curiously.

"I didn't put it together at the time, but yes, I'm sure now that it was Morgan. I caught glimpses of her childhood when I touched the amber pieces."

"Well, you can keep them," Bryce said, handing the fragments back to me. "We can't trap her now. The amber's broken."

He looked so forlorn that I hated to leave, but I had to get to my chem test. "I'm sorry, Bryce," I said putting on my parka. "Does this mean you'll have to go home?"

He looked stricken. "Home," he repeated woodenly. I felt sorry for him. I couldn't imagine anyone wanting to live in Avalon.

To my amazement I got to school on time, sliding into my seat in chemistry class seconds before the bell sounded. As I waited for the exam sheets to be passed out, I saw my ring glowing softly. I rubbed my cold hands together, once again feeling the wave of warmth and well-being that the ring exuded.

Suddenly I stopped and stared at my hands. The ring was large and ornate and—as if it needed anything to make it more conspicuous—*glowing*. So what went through my mind for a second before I became preoccupied with the midterm was this: Why hadn't any of those powerful witches who'd been grilling me for an hour or more ever mentioned—or even appeared to have noticed—my ring?

CHAPTER

•

TWENTY-EIGHT

Dead days.

Every time I walked into Old Town, my heart sank at the sight of the abandoned store with the broken sign swinging in the wind. No one had seen the Emporium of Remarkable Goods except me. It had all been a glamour—the store, the versimka, even Morgan herself, I supposed. Especially Morgan.

Funny, I'd really believed she was my friend.

Some friend, huh?

And what was it those harpies who'd come after me had said?

Poison.

Yes, that was it. But what did that mean? That they knew Morgan had poisoned me? How could they know that? Or were they going to poison me themselves? Didn't seem to be much point in that, since they were about to tear me limb from limb. Was the poisoning supposed to have come after the dismemberment, or during?

Oh, just let it go, I told myself.

I don't really know why, but it was strangely comforting to have the amber pieces back in my possession. I guess part of it was that, whatever Morgan had done, I didn't want to see her trapped forever in solidified resin. And because I'd known her.

Morgan had been the coolest girl I'd ever met. She was worldly and funny and cynical in a way I could never be. She was brimming with self-confidence. She was okay with being alone. She was fearless. She was magical, a *Traveler*, someone who could move between planes of existence as easily as the rest of us could walk out a door.

She'd been everything I'd ever wanted to be.

I know I should have hated her, especially after what she'd done to me, but even so, I couldn't. When I rolled the smooth stones between my fingers, all I knew was that I wanted to know more about her. *Give up your secrets*, I thought. *Show me who you are, Morgan le Fay.*

I didn't have to wait long to see her. She was a few years older than she'd been the last time—maybe my age. I could recognize her face now as the Morgan I knew. Again she was dressed in beautiful clothes, with a metal chain around her waist and soft cloth shoes. As she moved, I realized that she was in a large building with long, slender windows surrounded by a circle of water.

She crept silently up the length of a stone-lined corridor and listened outside a room with an open door. Inside was the same man I'd seen in the first vision, when he had made magic butterflies with his young daughter and then left her to the vultures as he'd disappeared from view. He had changed considerably since then. His hair had turned white, and he had grown a beard. He was speaking with a man who was around my father's age, who wore a gold coronet around his forehead. *The king*, I thought.

The old man put his hand on the younger man's shoulder. "Arthur," he began.

Arthur? I gasped. The man was the king, all right. The king himself. It had to be. King Arthur.

Out of their sight Morgan leaned against the stone wall that separated her from the men, her fingers splayed and trembling. Morgan shook with rage smarting from her father's rejection.

I felt it too. Suddenly I understood not just Morgan's jealousy, but the world that had caused it. Her father had chosen Arthur over Morgan because that had been the way of those times. Boys and men were valued. Girls and women were not.

This was the king her father had raised from a baby, though the Merlin had had to leave Avalon and his own family to be with him. He had lavished his love on the boy, had taught him the Craft even though Arthur had been born with almost no magic of his own, while Merlin's own daughter had been left to grow up alone, her extraordinary talents unrecognized.

Why? *Morgan asked herself, half choking on her unchecked tears. Why had her father ignored her to spend his life caring for another man's child?*

There were some who claimed that Arthur was the Merlin's own natural son, but Morgan would not—could not—believe that, no matter what the talk was that circulated around the castle. A magician of his stature would not have fallen so far into the human realm. No, the truth was much simpler than that. The Merlin loved Arthur because he'd wanted to make a king. And only a male child could become king.

Morgan's father had loved another child more than he had loved her, his firstborn, solely because the other was a boy. Had she been born male, would the Merlin have used his powers to make her *king of all England*? Would she have been the one to pull the magical sword Excalibur from the stone? Would the great Merlin have spent his life helping to achieve her *goals, fulfill* her *destiny*?

But that was not the way of the world, of any world. Morgan had taught herself how to use her considerable talents. She had learned how to shape-shift by watching the Seer's guards, those hags who enforced Avalon's cruel laws by turning into beasts that tore apart the flesh of anyone who dared to defy them. She had learned that she was a Traveler when she'd decided to follow her father through the mists that surrounded Avalon into this other world, this realm where Arthur, the child of Merlin's heart, dwelled.

In time Morgan refined her gifts. Not only was she able to move between Avalon and the world beyond the mist, but she was also able to move within that world. She discovered that there were places far beyond the borders of England, Arthur's domain—exotic places inhabited by strange-looking peoples, places that had their own magic. She learned from all of these. Though she was young, she was becoming powerful beyond her own reckoning. Perhaps, she hoped, powerful enough for her father to notice her.

Her tears burned as she leaned against the cool stone wall, feeling the camaraderie between the two men inside *the chamber.* Love me! *Morgan wanted to scream.* Love me!

Her helpless rage sparked out the tips of her fingers. Her father would never love her, not while Arthur was alive. Arthur was important, she thought bitterly. He was the king, the one person who, with the Merlin's help, could save the world from the shambles it had become.

And who was she, Morgan le Fay? Only another unwanted female child, destined to become someone's wife, nothing more. Given a choice, the Merlin had chosen Arthur. Of course. It was the way of the world. And there was nothing she could do about it.

I didn't want to see any more. I put the pieces away, thinking about my dad.

According to Miss P, Summer and her friends were doing so well that three of the four were planning to return to Ainsworth after the holidays. Suzy Dusset, who had been an even worse student than Summer, was going to attend a fashionable prep school in Manhattan. None of them remembered anything out of the ordinary. They all believed that they'd gotten sick from drinking some South American diet tea that Summer had bought at a Boston rave. All of them vowed never to experiment with drugs again.

No one at school even mentioned Summer and the other Muffies to me. I suppose that was a kind of apology. After the story got out about the tainted tea, I stopped being the prime suspect in what became known as the "killer weed" incident. I no longer got anonymous gifts of doggie doo, or even any insulting Facebook messages.

By the week of winter frolic, the whole episode seemed to be over. Bryce was gone a lot of the time. He said he was searching for Morgan, but since he usually took Becca with him, I suspected that he had given up his search and now was just trying not to go back to Avalon.

Most of my midterms were over by then, and Peter's uncle kept him busy almost every night of the week, so I occupied myself with the fragments of amber that had held Morgan le Fay prisoner for so long. I hoped that I might be able to discover something that would lead Bryce to her, although I doubted that he'd be able to catch her even if he managed to find her. Besides, it was sort of fun. I'd never "read" a person as old as Morgan was. Even though she appeared to be not much older than I was, she'd actually lived around the beginning of what we knew as the Dark Ages.

Speaking of which, just as I was beginning to settle in with the amber fragments, the phone rang. I saw on the caller ID that it was my father.

During my first year at Ainsworth, he'd come to Whitfield only once, and that was only because his corporate barracuda girlfriend had had business there. Since then, Madam Mim—that was what I'd called her, after a wicked animated Disney villainess—had been fired from her million-dollar-a-year job and broken up with my dad, so I hadn't counted on seeing him at all.

But then late last summer Dad showed up to inspect a medieval artifact called a *botte*, or magic box, that had been uncovered in the Meadow. He wrote an article for *Medieval Times Quarterly*, and the article turned out to be the seminal source for information about magic boxes, since a month after its discovery the *botte* disappeared into a sinkhole and was never seen again. Of course, the Whitfield witches had arranged that, and they certainly knew how to make it reappear again if it was needed, but it wasn't necessary to inform outsiders about that. Anyway, because of the article, Dad had become a major star in the Columbia University English Department. This term he taught a course on medieval *bottes* and their relation to literature, and was considered one of the leading authorities on mechanical devices of the Dark Ages. He also had a standing lunch appointment with the chairman of the department on Tuesdays. Things like that were important to my father.

"Hello?" I answered tentatively.

"Hello!" It was his hearty-but-clueless voice, the one he used when he'd forgotten who he was calling. "Er . . ."

"Katy," I reminded him. "Katherine. Your daughter."

"Oh. Right you are! Sorry. I was a little preoccupied."

"Umm," I said. I'd learned that there wasn't much point in actually *talking* with Dad, since he usually wasn't listening anyway. "What's up?"

"Beg your pardon?"

"You called me, Dad."

"I did?" There was a brief silence while he shuffled through whichever papers he'd been reading when he'd decided to call me. "Oh, yes. It seems I'll be coming to Whitfield this Saturday. A colleague at Boston College wants to see the site of the *botte*." He just threw that out as if sharing his knowledge about the *botte* were nothing more than a minor annoyance, but I knew he totally got off on it. "I thought that perhaps afterward you'd like to join me for dinner."

"I work on Saturdays."

"I see." More shuffling of papers. He was already losing interest. "Well, then, I'll meet you at your place of work. Henry's, isn't it?"

"Hattie's," I said. "But come early if you can. Once it starts getting busy, I won't be able to stop and talk."

"Quite understandable," he said.

Well, that was going to be a pain in the butt, I knew, juggling Hattie and the customers and my father all at the same time, but I supposed it couldn't be helped.

I ought to mention that Peter—or rather, the missing person formerly known as Peter—chose this time to move yet again, this time into the Shaw mansion.

"Why?" I shouted after I'd found out by way of a text message he'd sent me. A *text*! I stomped over to the house—well, *palace*, really—and pounded on the door until the butler answered. "Did you move away from school just so you can cater to your uncle's every whim, day or night?"

"You're missing the point," he said, leading me to his room somewhere at the back of the mansion. "This is the best way to introduce myself to the business."

"You mean *immerse* yourself," I groused. "As in forgetting about everything and everyone else."

He frowned. "That's not going to happen, Katy."

"Then why don't you just work at the lab, or wherever? Shaw Enterprises owns most of the buildings in this town. You don't have to *live* here."

"I think I do," he said simply. "A lot of research goes on at the house."

"Like what?" I asked in my sharpest double-dog-dare-you voice. "French lessons?"

"Huh?"

"Forget it."

Peter sighed. "There are a lot of projects that are too experimental to keep in the Shaw laboratories."

"What are you saying?" I was instantly hurled out of any obnoxiousness by an overwhelming feeling of anxiety. "Are they dangerous?"

"No, just . . . Well, some ideas can get stolen or leaked."

"So of course you'd have full access to them," I said. "Because Jeremiah Shaw has made his fortune by trusting high school boys with industrial secrets."

Two dots of red appeared on Peter's cheeks, a sure sign that he was wildly angry. But of course he would never admit that. "He's only trusting me with one," he said patiently.

"As a test?"

He shrugged. "Maybe. Sort of. I made a suggestion about a program, and that led to . . . something else."

Here was a fact about Peter Shaw: Although he had never been any great shakes as far as magic went, he was not stupid. In fact, he was so knowledgeable about computer science that he'd tested out of Ainsworth School's two computer courses and had taken classes at the local community college since the beginning of junior year. "It's a cool idea," he said. "I wish I could tell you about it."

"Which of course you can't."

His head bobbed slightly. "Not yet. But maybe soon. And you'll see—"

"Fine."

"Really, it's not that big a deal," he said. "The secrecy, I mean. Anyway, I doubt if you'd even understand it."

"Is that so?" Shades of my father.

"I didn't mean it that way, Katy."

I wanted to ask just how he had meant it, but I was already tired of this conversation. "Great," I said, standing up. "So you'll be working on this new thing twenty-four–seven, right?"

"I don't . . ." His voice trailed off. "Okay, yeah. Pretty much. For a while."

"So I guess I'll see you even less than I already do."

His shoulders slumped. "Working on a major project for Shaw Enterprises might change a lot of things," he said quietly.

"Like getting you into Harvard," I said. "And we all know how important that is to you."

"It *is* important to me, Katy." He swallowed. "But it's more than that."

"Oh?"

He looked at his feet. "It's Eric," he said quietly. "My brother may have a lot of talent, but he'll never be able to take care of himself. In time he may not even be able to live outside of a hospital setting. And once Hattie's gone . . ." He closed his eyes, his face a mask of misery. "I've got to be able to give him what he needs, Katy. Do you understand that?"

I nodded, chastened.

"And yeah, I want to go to Harvard, too. That's part of what'll help me get what I want for Eric. And for myself."

"At least you're admitting it."

"Look, you don't have to think about things like college. You ace every class, and your father's been planning to send you to the Ivy Leagues since you were born. I don't have any of that, not the grades or the connections or the money—"

"You have Jeremiah Shaw!"

"Do you think he'd lift a finger for me if I didn't give him something equally important in return?" Peter shouted back.

"Okay, I get it," I said.

So there it was, Peter's very good reasons for seeing me even less than he already was. I understood. But all the same, there was nothing left to say.

"Th-thanks for showing me your new place," I stammered. "It's awesome."

"Katy, please don't—"

"Got to run. Work at four." I was almost at the front door. "I don't suppose you're going . . ." I gestured toward the outside world, meaning Hattie's Kitchen, where Peter had worked for most of his life. He stared at the floor. "Right," I finished for myself. "I'll tell Hattie."

"I've already told her," he said. "It'll just be for . . . a while. Then I'll be back."

"Sure, okay," I said, hearing how phony my voice sounded.

Suddenly the butler who'd opened the door for me appeared, seemingly from out of nowhere. "May I be of some assistance, sir?" he asked.

Peter, who had been standing with his hands in his pockets, looked up with obvious embarrassment. "No, thank you, Aldritch," he said.

No, thank you, Aldritch. I almost laughed out loud. Peter

looked every inch the young scion at home in his ancestral mansion. I glanced at the embossed wood on the walls of the entryway, the silk-covered antique furniture, the paintings by artists whose work I'd read about in books.

I can't compete with this, I thought. I wasn't losing Peter to another girl, even one as beautiful as Fabienne. My rival was a whole way of life that could never include me.

I blinked, conscious that this might be the last time I was ever alone with Peter. Peter, with his honey-blond hair and gray eyes and his mouth that I could still feel touching mine. I wanted to run back to him and wrap him in my arms, to hold him one last time, to erase everything that had kept us apart and start over, just him and me, handfasted. . . .

Handfasted. We had pledged ourselves to each other once, in what now seemed like an alternate universe. Of course, it hadn't been official, so I didn't suppose it really meant anything.

Except that I would love him until the day I died.

"See you later," I said. The butler held open the door for me.

CHAPTER

•

THIRTY

There was just Hattie and me in the kitchen that evening. She was going over the prep work I'd have to do to get ready for the dinner service.

"I've already made the desserts and breads, so you'll just have to do the vegetables." She read from a list: "Ten onions, diced. Ten tomatoes diced, ten sliced. Put sixteen potatoes in the oven right now." She stared at me. "Right now?" she repeated. "If that's all right with you."

"Oh." I scrambled over to the potato bin. "Sorry."

"How many potatoes?" she demanded, testing. I tried to remember. I couldn't. "That's what I thought," she snapped. "You came in here looking all moony, and you've gotten worse."

"I'm not all moony," I said.

Hattie put the list on the counter. "Is it Peter?" She rolled her eyes. "What am I saying? Of course it is. I guess you found out about him moving into the Shaw mansion."

"I just came from there," I answered glumly.

"And you're jealous."

I spat out a little puff of irritation. "Of course not. What would I do with a butler?"

"I didn't mean you were jealous of Peter's money. He doesn't have any, anyway."

I put my hands on my hips. "Okay. What, then? What am I so jealous of?"

She looked at me sideways. "His time, maybe?"

She'd hit the mother lode. I bit my lip, but my eyes welled up just the same.

Hattie clucked unsympathetically. "You young girls are ridiculous," she said. "Everything has to be so dramatic."

"Well, how am I supposed to feel?" I whined.

"How about *happy*," she shot back.

I gaped at her.

"Yes, happy. The Shaws are Peter's people, and it's a damn good thing that Jeremiah's finally welcoming him into the family." Hattie smacked a piece of chicken with a spoon. "Oh, take that look off your face. This is Peter's chance to make something of himself. Shoot, do you think I could send him to Harvard?" Her voice cracked. She swiped the back of her hand across her eyes. "Shoot."

"Is Harvard so important?"

"What are you saying, is it important!" She came up beside me like a freight train. "Don't you two ever *talk*? It's the most important thing in the world to him. So don't you dare make him choose between you and Harvard, you hear me?"

"All right," I said unenthusiastically.

"Because he'd choose you."

"That's what you think," I muttered.

"Yes, it is, more's the pity. That night when you found Summer Hayworth and her friends bound up in those old dolls, Peter was out of his mind with worry. He must have called everyone in Old Town looking for you. When no one knew where you were, he went out searching for you in the middle of the night."

"I know," I said, remembering. "I was glad when he showed up."

"Well, that's what Peter does. He shows up. Now I hope you'll give him the same consideration."

I made a face. "What are you talking about?"

"The dance. That frolic thing. He's afraid you won't go."

I sighed. "He's taking another *date*, Hattie," I said.

"Now, surely you don't think that little French girl means anything to him, do you?"

My eyes scanned the room.

"Well, she doesn't. She's an obligation. That's all. But you . . . well, you'd better go, and that's all I'm going to say about it. You understand me?"

"I guess so," I said. I recognized a threat when I heard one. "I'll go. I said I would."

"Good. Now get to work. Sixteen chicken breasts stuffed with red quinoa dressing. That's mushrooms, shallots—"

Just then Bryce burst through the kitchen's double doors, seething. "Do I have your permission to throw someone's haunch out?" he shouted.

"Haunch?" I asked.

"Butt," Hattie translated. "He means 'butt.' And no, you don't. That is a privilege reserved for me. What's wrong?"

"Some horrible woman who's demanding bulgogi."

"Bull what?" I couldn't help laughing out loud.

"It's some Korean dish. She says Korean food is the rage now, and if I don't know that, I must be an idiot." With a growl he kicked the counter island so hard that all the overhanging pots and pans clanked together. Then from upstairs we heard a piercing wail.

"Now you've gone and woken Eric up!" Hattie scolded, although I doubted if Peter's little brother could have heard Bryce's tantrum from the apartment above.

"She demands to see the chef," Bryce groused.

"Fine," Hattie said. "Katy, take her a bowl of chicken and dumplings."

"Right," Bryce said sarcastically. "That will make her happy, the butt."

Hattie pointed a bony finger at Bryce. "You go cool off in the walk-in," she commanded. "Lord, sometimes I wish that boy'd go back to being a foreigner," she said as Bryce cursed his way to the refrigerator.

I ladled some chicken and dumplings into a bowl. "Does this taste like bul . . . bul . . . whatever it was she wanted?" I asked.

"Oh, who knows," Hattie said as Eric shrieked again. "But no kind of bull parts are coming out of this kitchen as long as I'm in charge. Go."

I always got stuck with the irate customers. I put the bowl onto a tray with a hot buttered biscuit and an endive and radish salad. On my way I stuck my head into the walk-in cooler, where Bryce was sitting on a bench, grinning at me. "Give her hell," he cheered, fist in air. Despite mistaking a butt for a haunch, his use of the vernacular had improved dramatically.

"Right," I said. "Thanks a lot, Haunchhead."

The woman was seated facing the glass wall with her back to me. At first all I saw was a cascade of blond hair flowing over a full-length saffron robe draped elaborately over one shoulder. It wasn't until I set the tray down that I recognized her face: Madison Mimson, aka Mad Madam Mim, my father's ex-girlfriend. She had painted a yellow stripe down her forehead, accented by a ruby-red bindi dot between her eyes.

"Kathy!" she squealed, leaping up and grabbing me in a bear hug.

"Katy," I grunted, trying to balance the tray in my left hand while struggling to breathe. "Hi, Mim."

"I *love* it when you call me that!" She giggled, finally releasing me. "In fact, I'm going to insist that everyone at the ashram refer to me as *Mim*, rather than Ms. Mimson."

Or Godzilla, I thought.

"It sounds kind of Indian and spiritual, don't you think?"

"You're living in an ashram?"

"Next week. In a remote village in Punjab," she said wistfully. "I'm trying on outfits now. There's an Indian dressmaker in Whitfield." She held out her arms. "What do you think?"

"Er . . ."

"I've decided to eschew corporate America for the contemplative life of a seeker." She sighed eloquently. She probably didn't know that I'd heard about her being fired from her job.

"Ah," I said.

"My refined sensibilities require . . ." She poked at the chicken and dumplings. "What's this slop?"

"It's . . . er . . ."

"I wanted bulgogi, damn it."

"I know, but we thought—"

"What kind of place is this?" she screeched. "There isn't even a menu."

"Madison—Mim—please . . ." People were turning around to stare. "I'm sure that if you tried these dumplings—"

"*Dumplings?* Do I look like someone who eats *dumplings*? You must be out of . . . Oh."

Mim was like a rhinoceros. If she got distracted for three seconds, she'd forget why she was charging at you. In this case her attention shifted from the dumplings to a man coming through the door.

Admittedly, a handsome man. A man who most of my friends thought looked like a movie star.

"Dad," I moaned. If Hattie thought Bryce was unreasonable, she had no idea what was in store once these two started fighting with each other. Which they would, momentarily.

"Hello, Katherine," my father said. He kissed my cheek, then instantly forgot that I existed. "Madison," he whispered breathlessly, seeing her. As if it were the first time he had ever seen her. As if he didn't know what a nutcase she was. "What are you doing here?"

"I just came to try out the . . ." She peered down at her plate. "Dumplings," she said, her mouth twitching sensuously. "Will you join me?"

The two of them slowly melted into their seats, their eyes locked on to one another. Licking her lips, Mim speared a dumpling and fed it to my father.

"Ambrosia," he said.

I sighed. "I'll fix you a steak," I said.

"No." He sucked another dumpling off Mim's fork. "This." Their fingers touched. "Only this."

Oh, please. Didn't they ever learn?

Well, there was an expression in Whitfield that at Hattie's you always got what you needed. Apparently what my father and Madam Mim needed was each other, because five days later I got an e-mail from Dad saying that he would be spending a few weeks at an ashram in India.

There was no accounting for taste.

When I got back to the kitchen, Hattie was carrying Eric in her arms. "Everything go all right?" she asked.

"I think so," I said.

"Next time you tell them we serve only USDA Choice or better. No bull."

"Got it," I said.

"Kaaay!" Eric squealed. He was eleven now, but brain damaged from an incident a long time ago, and still a baby in a lot of ways.

"Who's a good boy?" I asked, walking into his open arms. He smeared his face against my cheek, and I felt all my problems fall away, the way they did every time I was around Eric.

I used to think it was just love I was feeling. I did love the little guy, and I think he loved me too, but it was more than that. Because Eric was more than a lovable special-needs kid.

He was also the most unusual being in Whitfield, which is saying a lot. For one thing, he could draw like Michelangelo, maybe better, even though he couldn't spell his own name or count to five.

He could also heal with a touch of his hand.

Not many people knew that about him, which was how Hattie wanted to keep things. "A gift like that would bring nothing but harm to this little boy," she had said when Gram had suggested that Eric volunteer at the hospital. The thing was, Eric's gift was so great that none of the other hospital volunteers would be necessary. In fact, no one else in the entire medical profession would be necessary. Eric could heal the whole world, one person at a time, until he dropped dead from exhaustion. And then there would still be people getting sick, people dying. In the end it would be as if he'd never come along at all.

Hattie had been right. Eric's gift, as extraordinary as it was, ultimately would mean nothing. And so all of us who were close to Eric agreed to shelter him from the demands of the world as much as we could.

I never told them that I believed Eric could do more than heal, but I knew that he could. Last year he had actually brought me back from death. But that would have been too great a secret for any of them to keep or even know.

There was something else he could do that even Hattie's inner circle of friends didn't know about, something Hattie herself didn't like to think about. He could predict the future.

Maybe. This wasn't something I knew for sure either.

"Kaaay!" He flailed his arms at me. When I walked back to him, he pounded on my head and shoulders with his bony little fists.

"Hey!" I yelled, laughing. "Are you trying to beat me up?"

"Kaaay!" He showed me a balled-up paper place mat in

his hand, then threw it at me, giggling wildly.

I went along with it. "For me?" I gushed. Eric was always giving me beautiful crayon drawings. "Why, it's . . ."

My words stuck in my throat. The drawing showed a country meadow, which resembled the park in the middle of Whitfield, being torn apart by what looked like a tornado. Bodies were flying through the air, while the earth beneath crawled with rats and snakes.

"Hattie," I whispered, my mouth dry.

She was putting Eric in his special high chair. "We don't have time for . . ." she began, until she saw my face. "What is it?"

I gave her the drawing.

"What on earth," she said, shaking her head.

"It's the Darkness."

I saw her swallow. But she came back in a second as if the drawing hadn't scared her senseless. "Don't be silly," she said.

"You know what his drawings mean."

"I do not!" she snapped. "And neither do you. Eric makes dozens of drawings every day."

"Erc!" Eric shouted.

"And some of them are prophecies."

"Just stop it, Katy," she snapped. "The Darkness doesn't just appear like a puff of smoke. There are always harbingers, signs—"

"Always?"

"Yes."

"Okay, then," I relented.

"Unless someone were to call it, of course," she added.

"Which no one in Whitfield would ever do."

"Even by accident?"

"You don't call the Darkness by accident," Hattie said.

I looked back at the drawing. "But this shows the Meadow."

"It does not. This"—she slapped the drawing with the back of her hand—"is nothing but some grassy place. And besides, if it *is* the Meadow, then you know it couldn't happen, because the Meadow is the most protected area in Whitfield. It must have more than a thousand charms around it. You know that."

It was true. The last time the Darkness had gotten near the Meadow, it had been expelled. If ever there was a Darkness-free zone, it was the Meadow.

And yet . . .

"What is it now?" Hattie asked as she opened a jar of baby food.

I shook my head. "I'm just remembering something Eric once told Peter," I said quietly.

"Erc!" Eric bounced in his seat and kicked his legs.

Hattie knew what I was talking about. Last year Eric had said that one day Peter would destroy Whitfield.

"Just listen to yourself," Hattie said. "Eric *told* Peter. In case you haven't noticed, this child can't *tell* anybody anything."

"But he—"

"He was *possessed*," she hissed. "Those words weren't his. The voice wasn't his. And that stupid prediction sure 'nuff wasn't his."

"All right," I said. There was no point in arguing. Either the prophecy would come true or it wouldn't, and there wasn't much I could do about it either way.

"And don't go talking about it either. Nobody even remembers that, anyway."

Except for me. Because there was a second part to the prophecy that apparently even Hattie hadn't remembered. Eric had said that Peter would destroy our world.

And also that I would help him.

CHAPTER

·

THIRTY-TWO

Such was the makeup of my winter: Peter, lost to Shaw Enterprises; Gram and Aunt Agnes, lost to wedding preparations; Morgan, lost to evil. Plus the slight possibility of imminent apocalypse.

In other words, everything was back to normal.

I tried to ignore the fact that I was alone and dateless as I prepared to take myself to Winter Frolic. I would rather have spent the evening having root canal work, but I'd promised Hattie, and she'd find out if I reneged.

"What the hell am I doing?" I muttered as I tried to figure out what to do with my hair.

Verity and Becca stopped in my room on their way back from the showers. Verity showed me a drawing of the bizarre upsweep she'd designed, complete with tulle butterflies to match the ones on her dress. It was a good thing that Cheswick was as strange as she was.

Becca, on the other hand, always looked fashion-model perfect. Her gold-blond hair naturally had the kind of bounce and curl that cost a fortune to achieve in a salon, and all she did was fluff it with her fingers. As for me . . . Well, I just wanted to get this evening over with. I'd promised I'd go, even though Peter was taking someone else. What was worse, I was probably going to be the only unescorted human being there.

"This all sucks," I muttered.

"I guess it would . . . for you," Verity said. Becca jabbed her with her elbow. "Ow." Verity rubbed her ribs. "Well, it's true."

"No, it isn't," Becca argued. "Besides, it's just one stupid night." She twirled my hair experimentally. "And you know Peter loves you."

"Yeah. That's why he's taking Fabienne."

"Oh, get real, Katy. She's a *child*."

"She's French, though," Verity said. "I think they mature faster than we do."

"Good to know, Verity," I said.

"So you'll show her up by looking gorgeous," Becca said, smoothing her hands over my dress that hung in the closet. "How could you not, in this?"

True, the dress was pretty spectacular, a navy blue satin Albert Nipon with a lot of crisscrossing straps across the low-cut back. It was a castoff from Madam Mim, but I had to admit, it still looked pretty fabulous.

"I'll do your hair," Becca volunteered. This was okay, because Becca never overdid things.

"My mom's hairdresser is doing mine," Verity said, "so I'd better be going. Toodles."

"Toodles," I repeated, deadpan.

Becca waited for the door to close behind Verity. "How much do you want to bet she ends up looking like RuPaul?" she asked.

"No takers on that," I said.

The style Becca chose for me was pretty simple, pulled back on the sides and held in place by a clip made of pearls. The rest of my hair hung straight over my shoulders. The only jewelry I had on, aside from the hair clip, was the blue ring on my finger.

It still made me wonder. I mean, you'd have thought that would be the first thing that Gram and the other witches would have noticed, especially since Morgan had given it to me, but they hadn't said anything about it. *No one* had ever said anything about it.

But let's be honest, that wasn't the real issue. The question I had to ask myself was, why hadn't *I* said anything about it? Why did I make a point of wearing it wrong way out, so that the stone didn't show? Why had it become a habit to keep my other hand held over it?

It didn't have anything to do with Morgan. I'd gotten over being hurt that she'd used me the way she had. Morgan was just one of those people who didn't value friendship. Actually, I was glad that she'd turned out to be the way she was, because now I wouldn't feel bad for her when Bryce did whatever he had to do to her.

No, that wasn't true. I would feel bad. I *did* feel bad. I'd liked Morgan, even if she didn't care a thing about me. But there was nothing I could do for either of us. At least I knew that she wouldn't be imprisoned in amber again.

But she wasn't the reason I still wore the ring. It was because of how it made me feel. Whole. Strong. Confident. But then why . . .

"Whoa," Becca said. I'd jumped in the chair. She stepped back, holding the comb aloft. "Did I pull your hair?"

"No. No, it's not that. I just wanted to know . . ." I turned the ring face out and held up my hand. "Can you see this?"

"Your ring?"

"Oh." For a moment I'd thought that maybe it was invisible.

"Sure," she said. "Nice. Did Peter give it to you?"

"Uh . . . yes," I lied.

"Cute."

Cute? That seemed like an odd word to describe a dime-size glowing blue stone in a gold rococo setting.

"You're not going to wear it with that dress, though, are you?"

I frowned. "Why not?" Nothing, I knew, could possibly be more appropriate. Nothing. In the fading light from my window, the stone began to glow.

"No reason," Becca said. "Just different tastes. I'm sure it'll look great. Well, I've got to get myself together." She waved to me at the door. "See you."

"Thanks, Becca," I said.

I turned off the lamp on my vanity. It was dark outside, and my ring suffused the room with its eldritch blue light.

Perfect, I thought.

The Winter Frolic decorations committee had done a good job, considering that no magic had been used. All of Ainsworth's dances were held in the theater, since it had been designed to have no permanent chairs. This was far preferable to the gym, with its basketball hoops and foul lines painted on the floors. The result was a pretty good illusion of a snowy fantasyland. The stage, where the band played, was done up like Santa's workshop. The musicians—who, I understand, had objected strenuously—were dressed and made up to look like mechanical toys. Drink stations resembling ice floes were scattered around the walls, and white snowlike confetti dropped languidly from a silk aurora borealis that stretched across the ceiling.

The only awkward thing was the entryway, where Mr. Levy, the football coach, was announcing everyone who came in. He was dressed up like Santa Claus. On either side of him two freshman girls in elf outfits handed out decorated candy cane favors, while a photographer from Snappy Shots took pictures of the couples as they strolled in, arm in arm.

When I saw what was going on, I was tempted to get out of line and go home, but I figured that a sudden flight would brand me as a coward in addition to being a loser who'd had to go to the dance alone. So I gritted my teeth and climbed the three steps to the platform that had been erected to ensure that everyone at the dance could witness my solitary entrance.

"Miss Katy Ainsworth," Santa intoned, while a giggling elf handed me a candy cane and a flashbulb popped in my face.

"I'll come by later," the photographer said, "to show you the picture."

"Don't bother," I answered as I climbed down the steps onto the dance floor, where I hoped I'd be swallowed up by the crowd.

Becca, resplendent in a white one-shoulder silk dress that looked as if it were made of rain, made her way over to me and basically forced me to dance with her, even though I felt weird about it. Bryce caught up to her a minute later. I felt jealous watching the two of them together, but at least I wasn't sitting by myself in a corner.

We all danced together, along with a few other people who felt more comfortable dancing in a group. Verity and Cheswick came over too, doing their unrhythmical version of the dance in Beyonce's "Single Ladies" video. And Becca had been right: Verity's hair looked like an ad for Dairy Queen.

Soon a whole bunch of us, witches and Muffies alike, were dancing together. Even Miss P joined in, dancing with Mr. Dominic, the geography teacher. He was short and fat and sweaty, and was hauling Miss P around the floor like she was a sack of potatoes.

"Go, Dominator!" one of the boys shouted. That was their sarcastic name for Mr. Dominic. I don't think he could have cared less what his students were thinking about him at the moment. He just seemed to be enraptured with Miss P, who had this frozen smile plastered on her face as the Dominator squashed her closer to his sweaty chest.

"We need to find her a boyfriend," Becca said, shaking her head.

Santa Claus struck a giant candy cane on the floor. "Mr. Peter Shaw," he announced from the platform. "And Miss Fabienne de la Soubise." An audible "Ooh" rose up from the crowd like a vapor. I glanced over, my heart racing involuntarily.

She was about a hundred times more gorgeous than she'd been that day in the library, and she'd looked pretty good then. And by "gorgeous," I mean fabulously, indescribably, makes-me-look-like-I'm-wearing-a-feed-bag gorgeous. Worse yet, Peter was grinning like an idiot beside her.

"Like I said, she's got a big butt," Becca said.

"Oh, shut up," I told her.

CHAPTER

•

THIRTY-THREE

That was when the nightmare began.

It wasn't Fabienne's fault, really, although I thought so at the time. Despite her great beauty, she was just kind of scared, the way any fourteen-year-old who didn't speak English would be. I tried out my third-year French with her, which helped a little, although it wasn't easy to make conversation at a dance, in any language. But before long some younger girls came over to our table with their dates. The dates were freshmen—the sort of freshman boys who leered at all the girls, even though they didn't have the nerve to talk to any of them. Instead they shared private jokes with one another, leaving the girls they'd escorted to fend for themselves. No wonder Fabienne's dad had insisted that Peter take his daughter to the dance, I thought. I wouldn't trust those fools with a day-old sandwich.

Then the band took a break, and recorded music came through the speakers. An old song was playing, Whitney Houston singing "I Will Always Love You." I didn't want to look at Peter—our arrangement at the dance was, to say the least, awkward—but my eyes sort of wandered his way. He was looking straight at me.

We both blushed. Then Peter said something to Fabienne, and she nodded, giving me a wink. Peter came over to me and held out his hand. "Dance?" he asked.

And I floated into his arms, as if that were where I belonged. The music rose around us like a shield. Inside it nothing in the universe existed except for the two of us, holding on to each other.

"I've missed you," he whispered.

"It won't be forever."

He pulled me closer to him and pressed his lips against my forehead while the song expressed the real words that were in my heart.

Then the freshman boys started making a scene over something stupid—cars, I think. Anyway, there was a lot of shoving and shouting, and then one guy grabbed another, and a pint bottle of Wild Turkey fell out of his jacket and smashed onto the floor.

Across the room Coach Levy must have seen all the action from his perch near the door, because he blew a whistle as if he were calling a penalty at the ten-yard line, but the freshman boys weren't paying any attention to him because it was pretty clear by that time that they'd all been drinking, apparently for some time before the dance had even started. The one who'd been carrying the bottle was the worst. Whenever someone tried to get him to quiet down, he'd slap them away, cursing loudly.

Still dressed like Santa Claus, Coach Levy climbed down

the stairs and was walking purposefully toward our table, where the boys were skidding on the spilled whiskey and broken glass as they argued among themselves. Then one of them—the drunkest one—lurched over to Fabienne and latched on to her arm. She gave a little shriek and tried to pull away, but the little creep just hung on tighter, grabbing her hair for good measure.

"I've got to stop him," Peter said, disengaging from me.

"Mr. Levy's . . ." I began, but Peter was already walking into the fray. He came up behind the drunken freshman and forced the guy's arms behind his back. This probably wasn't that hard to do, since Peter was at least a foot taller than the freshman.

What neither of them seemed to notice was that they were sliding around in a rapidly widening smear of liquor. On rubber legs the drunken freshman managed to twist around enough to throw Peter off balance. At the same time one of the freshman's buddies shoved Peter, and all three of them fell to the floor.

Things happened fast after that. Fabienne screamed. Mr. Levy slipped on the wet floor just as he approached the scene, and went down. Drunk Freshman's buddy scrambled to his feet and ran with his friends toward the exits, leaving Drunk Freshman to fend for himself. Peter sat up on the floor, his tuxedo studded with pieces of broken glass. A gash across his forehead was pouring blood over his eyes.

"Peter!" I ran over to him.

"Stay where you are, Katy!" Peter shouted. He was probably afraid I'd fall too, but I didn't care about that. I just needed to get to him. I wasn't giving a thought to the drunken freshman, who chose that moment to use my dress like a rope to hoist himself to a standing position.

The dress tore right above the knee, where I could still feel the imprint of Drunk Freshman's hot little wet hand. "Get away from me!" I yelled, pushing him straight into Mr. Levy, who dragged him by the collar toward the exits.

Peter was getting to his feet and wiping the blood from his eyes. I was walking toward him when Fabienne scampered up and flung her arms around his neck. "Oh, Pee-*tair*," she gushed, dabbing at his face with a dainty lace handkerchief. "How brave you are!" She burst into tears. "You *deed* this for me, I know."

"Yeah, dude. Awesome!" Cheswick shouted, offering Peter a high five. Other guys gathered around, slapping him on the back and congratulating him. Peter was drinking it in like lemonade on a hot day.

Then, in a moment of abandon—maybe—Fabienne lifted her head, gave Peter her finest imitation of a French deer, and *kissed him on the mouth*.

Oh, God, yes. That really happened.

While my world crumbled, the guys around him cheered. Someone yelled "Score!"

I couldn't believe it. I felt my fingernails cutting half-moons into the palms of my hands while my knees shook beneath my torn Albert Nipon dress like leaves in the wind.

Out of the corner of my eye I saw Verity pull away from Cheswick and move toward me. She looked as if she wanted to ask me something, but by then it was already too late. I was no longer seeing anything except a fiery red vista that enveloped everything. Hot air rushed out of my nose. My tongue felt parched. My throat constricted.

And my ring began to glow.

Every second it grew brighter until it was too bright to look at directly. All the other lights in the place flickered and went out. The music wound down into silence. Then, with a flash that was like a white-hot sun, it was over.

The music whirred back to life and the lights came back on. Everyone was walking around in a daze, blinking. It had all happened so fast that I don't think anyone even knew I'd had anything to do with it.

Well, one person knew. Verity was standing exactly where she'd been when I'd . . . I guess "given in" would best describe what I'd done. Yes, I'd given in to some force that was a lot bigger than me. And to tell the truth, I didn't care. I felt good now, the way I'd felt when I'd first put on the ring—buoyant, powerful, happy. All of the coldness and loneliness of that cold, lonely winter seemed to fall away like confetti. All of the rejection, indifference, betrayal, abandonment, and self-pity that I'd been wallowing in for months was suddenly gone. This was my time, my moment.

Verity was staring at me, looking accusing, as usual.

"What?" I mouthed.

She cut her eyes toward Peter, who was stumbling toward me. "Katy?" he shouted, squinting in the electric light that seemed strangely dim after the blinding brightness of my ring. "Are you all right?"

"Wonderful," I whispered, although I knew he couldn't hear me. To tell the truth, I didn't know what I was feeling anymore. It was all so confusing. I didn't know if I even wanted Peter near me. I didn't need him. I knew that. I didn't need anyone. I was complete just the way I was. Complete. Strong. Perfect.

"Bryce!" Becca shrieked, bumping into me as she sprinted past. Bryce was staggering and ashen. As soon as Becca reached him, he fainted in her arms.

He was the first to go down, his face sheened with sweat. Becca was struggling to hold him up. Peter grabbed him before he fell.

"Hey, buddy," Peter said, dragging Bryce to a chair.

"He must have gotten hold of some of Summer's tea," Cheswick said, chortling. It wasn't very funny, but I think it was sort of a hysterical comment, since within a few seconds Cheswick's legs buckled too.

Then I saw Miss P sink right through Mr. Dominic's arms onto the dance floor. The Dominator was right behind her. The two of them lay in a heap in front of the bandstand while Fabienne threw up all over our table. That was truly horrible. I looked to Becca, because she always knew what to do in an emergency, but she was panting and turning green next to Bryce's unconscious body. A knot of people was stamped-ing through the fire doors to get outside, while another bunch raced toward the bathrooms.

The strange thing was, about half the people at the dance seemed totally unaffected, blinking in bewilderment at the scene unfolding before them. I overheard two teachers hyster-ically going over the cafeteria dinner menu. The band gamely played on, but there was so much barf on the floor that nobody wanted to dance.

Then it dawned on me. *Only witches were sick.* The cowen were fine. Coach Levy, still dressed like Santa Claus, was shouting orders to members of the football team—cowen to a man—who had assembled as a kind of emergency task force to haul the sick and infirm outside.

I turned toward Peter, pulling myself out of the cocoon of well-being I'd been feeling. "Maybe I should take you home," I said.

He put a finger under his collar. "Okay. Just give me a minute to . . ." His eyes rolled back in his head.

"Leave him alone!" someone shrilled. It was Verity, looking like one of the zombies in *Night of the Living Dead*. Her face was pasty white. Dark circles under her eyes made her look like an old woman under her beehive hairdo. She was crawling— literally *crawling*—toward me. Whatever she wanted to tell me must have been pretty important, since Verity never left Cheswick's side for anything, and there he was passed out on the floor alone.

"Get out," she rasped.

At that moment Peter crashed to the floor. I started toward him, but Verity grabbed what was left of my dress. "Don't touch him," she rasped, retching. "Don't touch anyone."

I tried to disentangle her fingers from my dress, but they were like claws. "You did this," she said, her thin arms trembling. "I see it. There's a dark nimbus around you."

"A what?"

"Katy." It was Peter, coming to. Verity tried to wave him away, but she was too weak. "You must be . . ." Peter closed his eyes. "God, it's hot in here," he said.

"Go," Verity repeated, panting desperately. "You're poison."

I backed away.

Verity's head hit the floor. Peter tried to get to his feet, but he kept falling. That was the last thing I remember seeing, because my eyes were flooded with tears. I ran out of the building, past Peter's truck in the parking lot, past the string of ambulances that were already pulling into the entrance, into the welcome anonymity of my dorm.

The hallway was busy, as girls in various states of undress beat a path to the bathroom and showers. Whatever they'd come down with, I hoped they weren't going to blame me for it this time. I hadn't cooked the food. I hadn't been near the sodas at the dance. I hadn't done anything, no matter what Verity thought. . . .

"Oh," I said aloud. I knew as soon as I opened my door that something was wrong. Whatever it was—a slight shift in the space, maybe—it was clear that someone had been here. *Someone beautiful,* I thought as I tried to place the fragrance. *Someone I liked.*

The blue stone glowed suddenly bright in the darkness of the room. And then I saw it, propped up against my bed—the versimka.

But it was different from how it had been. The mist that had suffused the scene with a soft veil was gone, replaced by a harsh unworldly light. The water in the distance—the lake that surrounded the isle of Avalon—had turned a sickly green color. And across the whole canvas, written in what looked like blood, was one word:

POISON.

CHAPTER

·

THIRTY-FOUR

Poison?

That's what Verity had called me. It was the same word the witches of Avalon had used. But that hadn't been about me, had it? I mean, I'd *been* poisoned back then. Morgan had given me the lemonade so that I'd fall asleep. Or die. And then the witches had come.

And you killed them, a voice inside my head said.

"No!" I protested out loud. "I don't know what happened—"

Of course you do.

I felt myself shaking. *This doesn't have anything to do with what happened at the dance*, I told myself. *Pull yourself together. Do you hear me, Katy? Pull—*

Tears trickled down my face. I heard myself sobbing, saw my shoulders heaving. But I understood nothing except that Morgan le Fay had come into my room and left a message, the same message Verity Lloyd had croaked out with the last of her strength:

That I was poison.

Every witch at the dance had gotten sick. Every one except me.

I stood in front of the mirror, trying to undo my dress with shaking fingers. They weren't the only part of me that was shaking. In the dim light from the lamp on my dresser, I saw the gown shimmering down the length of my body, to my now-exposed knees. But there was something else, too. On my right hand, a ring. Not a glowing blue ring, but . . .

I leaned in closer. I turned up the brightness on my lamp. "*What?*" I whispered. I looked down. The ring was as beautiful and luminescent as ever. But when I saw its reflection in the mirror, what I saw was a plastic cat face on a pink elastic band.

Cute, Becca had said.

Was this what everyone besides me had seen instead of the glowing blue stone? A kittycat face? Was that why no one had thought to mention the ring that Morgan had given me—because it looked like a harmless trinket?

"Oh, God. It's the ring," I whispered. The ring that had given me such a feeling of well-being and goodwill. The ring that I wanted to keep so much that I hadn't said anything about it to the only people who might have helped me.

I wasn't poison; the ring was.

I grabbed it with my other hand. No matter how good it made me feel, the sooner I was rid of it, the better. I would throw it away, or bury it, or—

It didn't come off.

I struggled with it until my finger was raw and bleeding, but the ring wouldn't budge. I tried to calm down, breathing deeply and evenly. Then I soaked my hand in cold water. I rubbed lotion all over my fingers. Nothing. In the mirror the face of kittycat laughed at me slyly.

The poison in the ring had been slowly growing stronger every day, but it hadn't affected anyone until . . . until what? What had made it suddenly deadly?

You have a dark nimbus . . .

And Verity has an overactive imagination, I thought. I didn't even know what a nimbus was, for crying out loud. Was it like a nimrod, in which case it was definitely a product of Verity's mind?

I looked it up. "A luminous cloud or halo," quoth Wikipedia. Well, okay, that wasn't so bad.

Except that Verity was a scenter.

You're poison.

It was me. That's what Verity had seen. I had given the ring its power at the dance, just as I'd activated it in Avalon. The witches had been coming for me, and I'd . . . made them disappear.

You killed them.

"No! I didn't kill anyone. I never intended—"

And you would have killed Fabienne, too, wouldn't you?

"No!" I shouted again.

Because she kissed Peter.

"Oh, God," I sobbed. "I'm not like that! I wouldn't do that!"

But you did. And you know it.

Already the ring was powerful enough to make everyone around me sick. I thought of Miss P and Bryce, the most adept witches at the dance. They had been the first to be affected. Then eventually it had reached everyone else, even Peter.

Of course. That was why the Muffies hadn't felt anything. The poison had gone to the most sensitive witches first. The stronger their magic, the sicker they got. And the more powerful the ring became.

I looked back at the painting, at the sickly green water of the lake where I had gone when I'd entered the tankard in Morgan's shop. Had I done that, too? Just by falling into the water for a few minutes, had I polluted the lake that surrounded Avalon?

I groaned. "Oh, Morgan," I whispered. "How could you do this?"

Don't you mean we? the voice inside my head corrected. *How could* we *do this?*

I took the blanket off my bed and covered the painting with it so that I wouldn't have to look at it.

About an hour later I decided to take out the amber. It was the only thing I could think of that would take my mind off the horrible events of the night, and the even more horrible decisions I would have to make come morning.

Besides, I told myself, it was always a good idea to know your enemy, even if she was a million times stronger than you. Even if more than anything, you wished she would just leave you alone.

Holding the pieces in my hand, I inhaled sharply as I hurtled back to a forest clearing in a far distant time and place.

• • •

A woman wearing a cape and a hood pulled low over her face knelt on the bare earth a hundred feet or so in front of me.

I watched from behind a tree, my heart knocking in my chest and my hands trembling with fear. For what I saw was enough, I knew, to bring about my death.

What? Who said that? Who thought it? I wasn't behind any tree. And how would seeing anything, particularly a vision of someone else's life, bring about my death?

I felt strange, amorphous. Was I watching the witch in the clearing, or was I watching the watcher?

"Come to me, you who can do all things," *the witch in my vision intoned. As the image grew clearer, I could see that she was kneeling in the middle of a pentagram drawn in the dirt with ash. The pentagram was upside down, a sign of black magic.*

"Give me a gift to kill at will. A killing gift, a killing gift," *she chanted in a singsong voice that sounded like she was a hundred years old.*

A hundred years old? Morgan? Who was I seeing, exactly? I shook my head. But of course it was Morgan I was watching. It had to be. Who else would be in the vision brought about by the amber? Who else would be casting a spell to kill someone?

"A killing gift," *she repeated, raising her arms into the air.*

And then, with a gasp, I realized exactly what she—whoever she was—was doing. The woman I was observing wasn't just casting a spell. She was calling the Darkness.

"Don't," I heard myself whispering. Nobody who made a deal with the Darkness ever came away whole. What had she asked for? A gift to kill . . . Who? Her father? King Arthur? Had that been what had earned Morgan sixteen hundred years of captivity?

But then again, it was far too late for second thoughts. The evil had been done long, long ago, the price already paid.

CHAPTER

•

THIRTY-FIVE

"Katy?" someone whispered outside my door.

I jumped. It occurred to me—too late—that I hadn't locked it. As I was stashing the pieces of amber under my pillow, the door swung open.

It was Peter. "Can I come in?" he asked.

I was too horrified to speak. Spying on Morgan's past had temporarily blotted out the horrible memory of the dance, but now everything came crashing back. What if I made Peter sick all over again? "I—I don't . . . ," I finally managed to stammer. "I mean . . ."

"Still got the heaves?" he asked gently. "Can I get you anything?"

I shook my head, expecting him to fall over at any moment, but instead he brought a bunch of flowers from behind his back. They were orange roses, wrapped in cellophane. "Maybe these will make you feel a little better," he said. "They were the best I could do, considering the only place open was an all-night gas station."

The flowers were such a sweet gesture. I wanted to put my arms around him, hang on to him for all I was worth, but I didn't dare touch him.

He held the bouquet out to me again. "Don't you want them?" he asked. "I'm sorry they're orange, but—"

"I love them," I said, snatching them out of his hand.

"Great," he said. It was an awkward moment. "Um, mind if I sit down?" He pointed to my room's one chair.

I wrung my hands. Of all the people in the world, this was the last person I wanted to hurt. "Peter . . ."

He nodded, frowning. "Yes?"

"Are you . . . That is . . ." I cleared my throat. "How is everyone?" I asked finally.

He shrugged. "Good, I think. A few people went to the hospital—Bryce, Miss P, Verity and Cheswick, of course—but everybody's symptoms seemed to clear up in twenty minutes or so. I was taking Fabienne to the emergency room, but she got better. We passed Becca and Bryce on the way out of the hospital. They were fine too."

I blew a tendril of hair off my face. "So everybody made it?"

"I think so," he said. "Although Becca said that Verity was delirious."

"What'd she say?" I asked cautiously. "Verity, I mean."

He spread his hands. "Don't know. The usual Verity stuff, probably."

"So it was just a passing thing," I whispered.

"Looks that way. I'm sorry, though."

My head snapped up.

"For how things turned out. With Fabienne. You know what I'm talking about."

I turned away.

Peter stood up and walked toward me. "Come here," he said, taking my hands.

"No!" I fought him as he pulled me to a standing position. "Peter, there's something—"

He kissed me. Deeply, passionately, thrillingly, perfectly. I was terrified.

"Relax," Peter said, massaging my shoulders. "You've had a rough night."

After a moment I realized that whatever horrifying power had come through me at the dance was no longer working. Peter was safe from me. "You have no idea," I muttered.

"Well, everything's okay now." He kissed me again. This time I allowed myself to melt into his arms. "Please don't think that kiss—the other kiss, with Fabienne—meant anything. It didn't to me, and probably not to Fabienne, either. She was just scared, and—"

"Shh. I know," I said, burying my face in his neck. "I know."

"I've never loved anyone except you."

"I love you, too, Peter." Inwardly I felt a huge weight lifting off me. If Peter could be this close to me and not get sick, then maybe I wasn't the problem, after all. Maybe what happened at the dance was just some freak occurrence—

"Dude!" Cheswick stood in the open doorway as my door bonged against the wall. "I thought I heard your voice. Some night, huh?"

"What do you want, Cheswick?" Peter pulled away from me, frowning in annoyance.

Cheswick put up his hands, palms out. "Hey, busting in on you guys was definitely not my idea, man."

"Huh?"

"It's Verity," I said flatly. I should have known the little snitch would do something, although I didn't yet know what that would be.

"What's she look like?" Verity's voice came from somewhere down the hall.

"She looks *normal*, babe. I told you—"

Verity's face appeared. Not her body, just her face peeking into the open doorway as if it were growing out of the frame. "It's gone," she said with some surprise. "The nimbus."

"The what?" Cheswick asked.

Verity just kept staring at me.

"Okay, what's this about?" Peter asked.

"I believed you the last time you said you didn't use magic," Verity said, not paying any attention to either of the boys. "You lied then, and you're probably going to lie again."

"I *didn't* lie!" I protested. "And I'm not—"

"You know I'm obligated to tell my father what you did." Her voice was quiet and even. "And he's going to have to take it to the board. You shouldn't be at Ainsworth, Katy. You're too dangerous."

"Will someone please tell me what she did?" Cheswick pressed.

No one answered him. In the silence that followed I saw that they were all looking at me, even Peter, and I realized there was no point in deluding myself anymore. "It's this," I said, holding up my hand. I thought about what Verity had said, and how irritating she was. The ring on my finger glowed a dull blue.

"It's coming back," Verity said, squinting her eyes. "The

nimbus. I can see it forming around you like a dark cloud."

I closed my eyes. As miserable as I should have been—Verity hadn't been kidding about telling her father, the school's attorney—I nevertheless couldn't help but feel the ring's strength as it filled me with its power. With its poison, which felt so good.

With a little shriek Verity retreated into the hall, where I heard her retching. Cheswick ran after her.

"Katy—" Peter began.

"Get out."

"But—"

"Get out now." I heard the rising note of panic in my voice. "Please." It was happening all over again. "Go!" I screamed, slamming the door behind him.

It didn't feel good now. It just felt like I'd lost the person I loved most in the world.

I stood for a long time with my back against the door, crying silent tears. Verity had been right. I was dangerous. I couldn't control the ring. I never had been able to. I couldn't even control how I felt about it. I'd known when the power had started to grow just now. It was when Verity had called me a liar. And it wasn't even what she'd said that had set things off. It had just been something in the whiny, weaselly sound of her voice. I didn't like it. I didn't like *her*. And when the ring had started to glow, I'd been glad. I'd felt powerful. I'd felt *right*. So right that, at that moment, I could have killed her.

It was the Darkness coming into me, just as it had come into Morgan le Fay. I knew it, and—God help me—I welcomed it.

As I stood there trembling, hating myself, the orange roses Peter brought me withered and died inside their paper cone.

CHAPTER

•

THIRTY-SIX

Calm. Stay calm. Think.

Being alone during those early-morning hours gave me a chance to assess my situation. As horrible as it was, there were two things that offered some hope. One was that apparently I wasn't always the bringer of doom. Peter hadn't keeled over when he'd come to my room. Neither had Verity, until she'd started threatening me. I knew she was going to say that I'd zapped her out of spite, but that wasn't the case. I couldn't help it.

I supposed that made things worse, the fact that I couldn't control the ring's power. It seemed to be tied in with my emotions. I was like the Incredible Hulk, except that instead of turning green and beefy when I got angry, I became evil.

Great. That was just swell. I could picture my entry in the yearbook: Serenity Katherine Ainsworth, honor roll, French club, pawn of the Darkness.

Okay, it wasn't funny. Which was what made me cling like

crazy to the other slender possibility—that maybe someone could unmake this curse Morgan had saddled me with. Only one person had ever bested her—the Seer of Avalon. Unfortunately, from everything I'd heard, she wasn't exactly Glinda the Good Witch, but I was desperate. The Seer was my last hope.

When the first streaks of daylight cut through the dark of night, I picked up the phone and called Bryce. "I need to see you," I said.

"What? Who is this?"

"Katy. Can you meet me right away?"

A snort. "Dream on, girl." His modern English wasn't giving him any trouble now, the little creep.

"Please."

"I just stopped heaving an hour ago," he said crankily.

"Believe me, I wouldn't call you if it wasn't important."

"Jeez," he complained. There was some scuffling, yawning, water running, throat clearing. "All right. I'm up now. What do you want?"

I told him about the versimka. "It's the same scene as before, but there are things about the picture that are different. The lake is . . . Well, the picture's just different."

There was a long pause before he said, "You woke me up at the crack of dawn to tell me about a painting?"

"A painting that Morgan le Fay brought to my room, Bryce." I heard him exhaling. "There was something else. Written across it was the word 'poison.'"

"Meaning what?"

"Meaning that . . . well, I might have caused what happened at the dance last night."

"What?" He yawned. "Are you telling me that *you're* what made everyone get sick?"

"I think so. And not just here but in Avalon, too." I told him about the ring Morgan had given me. "I was wearing it when I fell into the lake. I think when that happened, I may have poisoned it."

"The lake?"

"Yes."

"So take the ring off," he said irritably.

"I can't."

I could picture him rubbing his head and examining his teeth in the mirror. "Have you tried butter?"

"It's not that the ring is *tight*," I said irritably. "It's bonded to me somehow, by magic. I need to know how to break that bond."

"And you're asking me how to do that?"

"Not you," I said. "The Seer of Avalon."

He coughed. "Are you insane? You're lucky she didn't kill you the last time you decided to pay a visit."

"I know, but I can't think of anyone else who'd be able to help me."

"Yeah, well . . ."

"Please, Bryce," I pleaded. "You could convince the Seer to listen to me."

"Why should she?" he shouted into the phone. "Look, Morgan gave you a poison ring that won't come off, and then this painting thing to get you back to Avalon. She *wants* you to go there, Katy."

"I know."

"Do you know why?"

"To destroy it, I think."

"But the lake . . ."

"I don't know. Maybe that wasn't enough. Maybe that's why she sent me back a second time."

"That makes sense." The line was quiet for a few seconds. "Still, I think your plan is hobbling."

"Hobbling?" I thought about it. "You mean 'lame.'"

"I do. As lame as it can be."

"Well, I can't go to Avalon by myself. Those witches will kill me if you're not there to protect me."

"Protect you? What do you think they'll do to me?" he sputtered. "I'm the one who lost Morgan in the first place. They're not exactly going to greet me with a brass band, either. Besides, if you're right about being poisonous or whatever, I don't really want to come near you. No offense."

"I'm okay now. It won't happen again, I swear." I crossed my fingers. "Just meet me at my gram's house. And don't tell Peter."

"Listen, I don't know about any of this—"

"Bryce?" It was Peter's voice.

"What are you doing here?" Bryce asked, away from the phone.

"Don't say anything to him!" I hissed.

"Why not?"

"Because he'll try to stop me from going."

"That might be a good idea," Bryce said. "Listen, Katy—"

"Shut *up*!"

"Give me that." Peter again. "Katy?"

Oh, hell.

"Katy?"

I hung up. So much for Bryce's help.

Plan B.

It must have been the coldest day of the entire winter, with winds so fast that the bits of snow that blew off the trees and rooftops felt like icy daggers. Clutching the versimka under my arm, I made my way to Gram's.

She was waiting for me, along with the others I'd asked her to invite: Miss P, Agnes, and Hattie Scott. They were standing on Gram's porch, bundled up in their parkas. "Katy, dear, let's do go inside," Gram entreated.

"I can't, Gram. I need to be out here while I talk." I knew I was probably safe to be around, but I'd seen how quickly things could change, and I didn't want to take any chances with my eighty-six-year-old great-grandmother.

"Well, this better be damn good," Hattie said, red-eyed and looking at her watch. Saturday was always a late night at the restaurant, and she'd been alone in the kitchen while Bryce, Peter, and I had been at the dance.

"I'm sorry, Hattie. I won't take long." I moved the versimka in front of me. "I guess I'd better start with this." I explained that it was the painting that I'd gone through to get to Avalon. "They called me poison," I said. "And they were right. I think I've poisoned their water supply."

"You what?"

"I didn't mean to, Gram. It happened because of this." I held out my hand.

"Your kitty cat ring?" Gram squinted at it. "You've had that for weeks."

Hattie put her hands on her hips. "If you brought us out here for some kind of engagement announcement—"

"Gracious me!" Gram exclaimed. "It's not even gold."

"Are you pregnant?" Hattie demanded.

"Is it Peter?" Agnes ventured.

"No, no, no!" I shouted. "It's a lot worse than that, believe me."

"I see it," Miss P said. Her eyes were slits, partially concealing a greenish glowing light behind them. "Yes . . . there's a blue stone," she said slowly.

"Morgan le Fay gave it to me, and now I can't take it off," I nearly sobbed. "That's why I asked you here. Can you help me?

"Land sakes," Hattie said, trundling off the porch. "Hold out your hand."

"No, stay back!" I warned, but it was too late. Hattie lunged at me in an attempt to grab my arm. She never made it. It was as if she had run headlong into an electric fence. With a cry of pain she recoiled backward and fell into a snowbank.

I screamed too. Nothing like this had ever happened before.

As Gram and Agnes scrambled to help Hattie, Miss P looked directly at me.

"I don't understand," I babbled. "I thought it made people sick, but it never—"

"It knew," Miss P said quietly.

"What?" I asked, bewildered.

"It hides itself," she said. "The ring. It won't allow itself to be removed." She blinked once, slowly. "And it's getting stronger."

I felt cold tears trickling down my face. "Is there anything you can do?" I squeaked. The witches looked at me, their faces caricatures of worry. "I need to get rid of it before . . . before . . ."

"Katy!" It was Peter, coming around the side of the house with Bryce.

"He forced me to tell him," Bryce said.

Yeah, right. Bryce was a wuss, plain and simple. "You didn't have to bring him here," I snapped.

"Yes, he did." Peter pushed past him, striding toward me.

"Keep away from her!" Hattie shouted.

Bryce grabbed Peter's arm. Peter shook it off.

"Listen to them!" I shouted, wiping my nose on my sleeve. "There's something wrong. With me. You saw what I can do!"

"There's nothing wrong with you," Peter growled. Bryce looked at me and shrugged. "And if there is, we'll fix it," Peter went on. "All of us, together, okay?" He helped Hattie back onto the porch. "Okay?" he repeated.

"Of course, dear," Gram said. "And we will. We'll fix it." Her gaze wandered toward the others. "We just have to find out how."

The older women all looked blankly at one another. Finally Bryce sighed. "There may be someone who already knows how," he said.

I closed my eyes in relief. "Thank you, Bryce," I whispered. Wuss or not, he was coming through for me after all.

Peter glowered at him.

"What are you talking about?" Hattie demanded.

"I'm going to take Katy back to Avalon," Bryce said. "To the Seer."

"Oh, no, you aren't," Hattie said. "This girl's poison, like she said. You're not going to go near her."

"If I don't, she'll eventually poison Whitfield, too," he countered miserably. "But they're not going to care about that in Avalon. They'll want vengeance for what she's already done to their lake. And I'm the only one who can protect her."

"No, you're not," Peter said. "I will." Our eyes met. That was Peter all over, willing to go up against forces that he had no idea how to fight.

"You can't go," I said.

"Oh, no? Watch me."

"Peter, don't—," I warned, but he wasn't listening to me. He stepped through the painting, feet first.

And tore it.

"Oh, man," Bryce said.

"I'm sorry." Peter knelt down beside me as I tried to pull the ripped canvas together.

"That was my last chance," I said, choking.

"I can fix this. I know I can," he countered. "I've been working on something—"

"This may be a bigger problem than we thought," Gram

said. Everyone looked over at her. "From what you've said, the witches of Avalon are already doomed."

"What?"

"If their water supply has been poisoned, their world will end, and they will have nowhere else to go."

"Except for here," Hattie said, gesturing toward the torn versimka. "Through that."

Gram nodded. "That's the real problem."

"No, it isn't!" I shrieked. "The problem is getting this stupid ring off me!"

Gram gave me a pitying look. "We're talking about a whole community, Katy. A community that you were sent to destroy."

"But it's all tied together. If I can get rid of the ring—"

"It may already be too late to save Avalon," Gram said. "We have to find a way to bring the residents here."

"But what about me?" I said in a small voice.

Gram shook her head. "I think it would be best if you waited," she said.

"She's right," Peter said. "Let's give ourselves some time to—"

"I don't *have* any more time! Don't you see? I already can't go to school anymore. I can't be around anyone. I can't live anywhere near other people. Every day I get more poisonous."

"And you want to expose the people in Avalon to you?" Gram shook her head, clucking. "Not good form, I'm afraid."

"Help me," I mouthed to Bryce. He nodded slightly. He understood.

"I'm telling you, I can help," Peter was saying. "I've been working on something that's very close to this. . . ." He nodded toward the versimka. "It's touch-screen technology, only any sort of picture can be adapted—"

"Dude, can't you see she's cold?" Bryce asked.

Peter hesitated.

"She's your girlfriend. The least you could do would be to get her a blanket."

Peter looked at me, bewildered. I shivered in response. "Okay," he said at last. "I'll be right back."

"Peter—"

"Just wait, okay? Don't do anything."

I expelled a puff of air as he ran toward the steps leading to Gram's porch. I was going to say good-bye, but that would have defeated my purpose.

"If you're going to go," Bryce whispered, "go now."

"But the versimka—"

"It might still work." Bryce pushed me toward the painting. At that moment Peter, who was at the top of the steps with his hand on the doorjamb, turned around, looking as if he'd just been stabbed. He knew.

"Hurry!" Bryce said.

"Come back!" Peter shouted as he ran down the stairs, his breath making hot clouds around him.

I turned around. My eyes met Peter's. "Katy, stay," he whispered hopelessly.

"I can't," I whispered back.

Then in one anguished movement, I fell backward into the painting.

"I love you," I added, but I didn't think he heard me.

CHAPTER

•

THIRTY-EIGHT

I found myself rolling down a grassy hill, scrambling to find my feet. Once I finally righted myself, I looked around for Bryce. He wasn't there. For a moment I thought about going back, but I knew that wasn't really an option. Gram and the other women, not to mention Peter, would never allow me to leave again. I guessed that I would have to face the Seer alone, until I noticed someone cresting a hill up ahead. I tried to slink unobtrusively into the woods, but he waved at me, and I realized that it was Bryce.

"Why'd you go way over there?" I asked, stripping off my coat and mittens.

"Traveling is a lot harder than walking through a painting," he bristled. "I wouldn't be here at all, except that your crazy boyfriend was ready to strangle me."

"I know the feeling. My relatives aren't going to be that happy about our coming here either."

"Yeah, well, I have a feeling we'll be wishing we'd stayed with them."

I swallowed. "Is the Seer really that bad?"

"Does it matter?" he said. "We need her to help us. And the only way she'll do that is if we can offer some alternative to their world being obliterated."

"Easy," I said. "If I can get rid of this ring, her problem is solved too."

"Mm," he replied. "Maybe. On the other hand, she could just chop off your finger."

I gulped. "In that case we'd better talk fast."

"Preferably while running away."

"Great," I said. "You know, I've got to wonder why you stayed here in the first place."

He didn't answer.

"I mean, you said it yourself, nothing ever changes."

"Why do you think I haven't left Whitfield since I got there?" he mumbled.

"I thought you were just— I thought . . . You *wanted* to leave Avalon?"

"Of course. Who wouldn't? Do you think it's fun living in a cave and cooking over a fire?"

"Sometimes it is."

"Try impressing a date over a dinner of turnips and deer meat."

I laughed. "I thought you were their darling. That's why they sent you, isn't it?"

He shrugged. "I guess. I've worked as a servant to . . . the Seer my whole life, almost since I was born."

He looked dejected. "I didn't know there was anything else until I came to Whitfield."

"I'm with you there," I said. "I come from a long line of cowen. I grew up thinking I was some kind of freak."

"At least cowen can be forgiven for being ignorant. They don't deliberately choose to live like Neanderthals." He shook his head. "What started out as protection against attack has turned into a prison for everyone here. But nobody can say anything, because there's nowhere else to go."

"I just can't imagine Morgan le Fay accepting this life."

Bryce laughed. "I'm pretty sure she didn't do anything she didn't want to do," he said. "From the stories I've heard, she was pure evil."

I had to think about that. Morgan had disappointed me, yes, but I wouldn't have called her *evil*.

"She did kill her father, after all," he added.

I tried to remember the details of the King Arthur legend, and if it was common knowledge that the Merlin was Morgan's—if not Arthur's—father. "Wasn't he walled up in a cave or something?"

Bryce shrugged. "Maybe. All I know is, Morgan brought his body back here."

"She brought back his body? Why? I mean, it doesn't exactly sound like something a cold-blooded killer would do."

"Hey, don't ask me. That was way before my time."

"Then how do you know?"

"We all know the stories. This is the place where nothing ever changes, remember? All we have are stories."

I was still thinking about something he'd said earlier. "Did Morgan have a trial?" I asked.

"A trial? Here?" Bryce laughed.

I stopped in my tracks. "Are you saying that Morgan was turned into a bug in amber as punishment for something she might never have done?"

He ruffled my hair. "Peter told me you were dramatic," he said. "It happened a millennium and a half ago. Let it be, Katy."

"Listen to yourself! Your Seer wants to lock Morgan up again. And that's right now, not a millennium ago. If she was never guilty, that changes everything!"

"Okay, okay!" He held his hands up in front of him. "So what do you want to do, arrest the Seer?"

"I don't know, but it makes a difference. Because Morgan's still alive."

"So is the Seer," he said.

I blinked at him stupidly. "What do you mean?"

He shrugged. "I told you. Nothing ever changes."

"Are you saying that no one here ever dies?"

He chuckled. "Oh, we do. But the Seer doesn't. She's immortal."

I reeled backward. "You mean you've had the same leader since the beginning of time?"

"I told you, we all have different gifts," he said with a sigh. "I guess immortality is hers."

"Man," I said, running my fingers through my hair. "Talk about absolute rulers. She can do anything she wants."

"Yep."

"And she's got that army of vultures to carry out her commands."

"They're not always vultures," he said. "Shape-shifters, remember? Sometimes they're worse than vultures."

I was feeling nauseated. "I'm starting to think maybe this wasn't such a good idea."

"I agree. Let's go back." He tugged at my arm.

"No," I said, pulling away from him. "This is the only hope I have, now that the Whitfield witches are stumped. If I don't find a way to lose this ring, I'll probably cause the destruction of everything I know. Not to mention my own life."

"And mine," Bryce said expressionlessly. "Incidentally, it'll take us hours to get to get where we're going."

I moaned, dismayed.

"Unless you're willing to try something new."

"New? Here?"

"It's not new to us," he said. "Just you. Don't freak."

And then it happened, the slight shift from Avalon into crazyland. It started with Bryce's hands, which changed into *hooves*—yes, that's right, *hooves*—before my eyes. His body became covered with coarse brown hair, and his head elongated as a rack of antlers sprouted from his skull. "Are you cool with this?" he asked casually. "It's pretty far. This'll be faster."

"You're a deer," I observed.

"Yes," he said pleasantly. "Now you, if you would."

"If I would what?"

"Shape-shift," he said. "Go ahead."

"That's not something I can do," I said.

"Of course you can. You're in Avalon."

"If I went to Southern California, would it mean I could surf?" I shouted.

"Shape-shifting is a skill that you can master, Katy. Even if you've never done it before. At least try."

It was very strange, to say the least, seeing Bryce's expressions on the face of this woodland creature. And stranger still to watch him talk. It was as if I'd walked right into the middle of a cartoon. I expected dancing bunnies and birds carrying garlands of flowers to come out and start singing to us.

"Are you feeling well?" he asked.

I shook my head to get my bearings. "What should I do?" I asked.

"Just think like a deer."

Oh, was that all? "Er . . ."

He touched my forehead with his cold wet nose. "Does that help?"

I looked down. With a gasp I noticed that my hands and feet had morphed. And my mouth felt odd. I chomped experimentally. Big teeth. Really big. The grass around me looked suddenly delicious. I craned my long neck and snipped off a few buttercups. Ambrosia.

I was headed for some clover when Bryce called me back. "You're liking this too much," he said, laughing.

Well, not *said*, exactly. There were no words. These Avalon witches, trapped for so long in their protected, unchanging home, had developed all sorts of magic as a way of life. Telepathy, shape-shifting . . . What else were they capable of?

I started to run. That was it, running from a dead stop, and running like the wind. "Look at me!" I shouted, twitching my ears.

Bryce was right beside me, his long body sleek with sweat. The breeze brought my own scent to me, rank and female, and my knees nearly buckled. I *stank*. "Not much farther," he said.

Good, I thought. *Because I'm in desperate need of deodorant.* "You can change me back, can't you?" I asked nervously, my mind now completely separate from my running, powerful legs.

"I didn't change you in the first place," he said.

"You did so! When you—"

"I made a glamour. An illusion that caused you to think you looked like a deer. Then your own magic took over, and you became what you believed yourself to be."

That made sense. I'd known anorexic girls who'd thought they were fat, and smart ones who'd thought they were stupid. And they hadn't even been witches.

"It all comes down to belief," he said with a wink of his big, long-lashed Bambi eye.

Then he was off, pounding across the field toward an outcropping of rock and a copse of trees in the distance. I followed him, moving faster, feeling myself almost leaving the earth, my hooves touching down only for the briefest instant before propelling me into the air again.

I never want to forget this feeling, I thought.

CHAPTER

•

THIRTY-NINE

My deer companion stopped in front of the rocks, rearing on his heels like a stallion. And then, in a shimmering instant, he turned into Bryce again.

"Oh," I said, feeling my deer-ness drop off me like a suit of armor in reverse. That is, as my deer shape fell away, I felt heavier and thicker. I saw color, but my vision was not as clear as it had been. My hearing dropped so low that for a moment I thought I was deaf. And I could smell virtually nothing. I clasped my hands together. They were trembling, remembering the joy of being hooves springing off the ground.

"It's hard to come back," he said, touching my arm.

"Have you always been able to do this?"

He made a vague gesture. "Anyone can do anything, given enough time," he said. "The witches here have been . . . " I sensed that he was trying not to use the word "trapped."

". . . encased in the magic of Avalon for so long that we've all developed certain skills." He grinned. "On the other hand we've lost some abilities too."

"Like what?"

"Astral projection, for one. Since we're not permitted to travel beyond Avalon, we don't need that particular talent." He shrugged. "And of course we can't do anything destructive, like fire-starting."

"But the Seer—"

"Shh!" He looked around in panic. I guessed she was nearby. "Be careful what you say," he whispered, taking me by the hand.

He led me through the small grove of trees to an area that was covered by huge, flat rocks. The biggest of them, at least ten feet higher than the rest, was the size of the gym floor at school. Once we climbed it, I could see that it was cleaved in the center by a long fissure spewing out a constant jet of hissing steam. "This is where she speaks," he whispered.

"From inside the rock?"

"Be as quiet as you can." He gestured for me to stay where I was, on the far side of the big rock, as he ventured forward toward the fissure. Bryce looked back at me once, then spoke.

"Great Seer who knows all things," he began, "I bring to you—"

"Poison!" a voice rasped from the depths. The sound was so loud and strange, I nearly swallowed my tongue. It seemed to come from the rocks themselves, a deep, breathy groan like a cry of pain from inside the earth as the steam from the crevasse gusted upward in a geyser. *"You have brought poison to Avalon."*

Bryce licked his lips nervously. "It is the ring she wears," he said. "She was tricked into putting it on, and now she cannot take it off."

Steam covered him like a curtain. *"Send her elsewhere!"* A witch sitting on the limb of a tree chattered her teeth at me like a monkey. Beyond her were figures that I now noticed for the first time, kneeling or crouching among the rocks. I guessed I hadn't seen them before because they were all dressed in hooded gray robes that blended in with the surrounding stone. The first thing that came to mind was that they looked like "real" witches—that is, the kind of witches you read about in fairy tales or saw in amusement park fun houses. Hags in rags, living in the valley of the shadow of death. Very creepy.

They didn't look up, although I'm sure they saw me. I raised my index finger as a way of asking permission to speak. "Actually—"

Bryce shot me a warning glance. "The witches of Whitfield ask for your advice and help in this matter," he went on. "They are prepared to compensate you handsomely for your assistance."

I glared at him. The witches of Whitfield had said no such thing! Bryce gave me a little shrug, a *What else could I do?* gesture.

Steam rose again from the bank of rocks. *"The poison serves the evil one,"* the Seer said.

"She is an agent of the Darkness," monkey-woman said. Others joined her. *"Darkness,"* they muttered. *"Darkness . . ."*

"I am not!" I interrupted, suddenly too angry to feel afraid. "Hey, what kind of Seer are you, anyway, if you can't even see—"

"Kill her."

I gasped. It hadn't taken her long to bring out the big guns, that was for sure.

The steam rose up again, whiting out everything in sight.

"Bryce!" I called, aware of the shrill sound of my voice.

"Run!" he called back. "They have me."

"What?" My mouth went dry.

As the air cleared, I could see Bryce surrounded by the hags. They were turning into vultures that raised him into the air as he flailed and struggled against them. "It's too late!" he shouted. "Just run! Go!"

Then with a scream he disappeared among them and they flew away, birds of prey after the hunt had ended.

CHAPTER

•

FORTY

The gray women who remained rose up like wraiths around me, their tattered garments billowing in the breeze like the clothes on scarecrows. One picked up a rock at her feet and curled her bony fingers around it.

There were more of them than I'd thought, and they were all getting to their feet now. A wild murmur spread among them like electricity. More and more of them armed themselves with rocks and sticks. Some filled the skirts of their robes.

Then one of them let out a wild shriek and threw the rock in her hand. It hit me square on my arm and knocked me down.

I sucked in my breath with the pain and shock of it, then scrambled to my feet. Some of the women were crawling up onto the big rock where I stood. "Stop!" I yelled, skittering backward. "Let me talk!" I shouted. "If you understood—"

I got a face full of dirt. As I sputtered and tried to wipe the debris out of my eyes, another rock hit me, this time on the side of my head. And another. And another.

Reeling, not sure if I could even stay upright, I turned and ran, sliding off the rock on my back and landing in a heap. A shower of stones pelted me from above, where the witch women stood, grinning like ghouls, throwing at me whatever they could grab. I skittered to my feet and ran blindly away as stones smacked against my legs.

Halfway across the meadow, staggering and panting, I ventured a glance back toward the Seer's rock. To my relief I could still see the silhouettes of the women. I'd been afraid that they might turn into some kind of predators and finish me off, but it seemed they'd only wanted me to go away. They reminded me of ghosts. That's what they were, really, wraiths, the useless remnants of what used to be human beings.

I felt like I wanted to vomit, but my panic was too strong to allow me to stop for even a moment. The problem was, I didn't know where I was or how to get back to Whitfield. For a moment a lightning bolt of panic swept through my veins. If I didn't find my way back to the scene in the painting, I'd never get back to Whitfield. The prospect of spending the rest of my life in this horrible place was too gruesome to think about for long. A one-dress wardrobe in classic gray, perfect for lounging on rocks, hanging from trees, or strutting in my choice of caves.

While I was trying to figure out where I was, something like a fly started buzzing around me. I say "something like" because even when the thing was flying around really fast, I knew it wasn't a fly, since it was the size of a softball. Within seconds, other softball-size insects joined it.

So the witches had come after me after all, I thought. They were shape-shifters. The last time I'd been here, they'd morphed themselves into biting flies. This time they'd become giant mosquitoes.

That gave me an idea. In the near distance was a cave, where I could see a couple of bats just inside the entrance. I remembered reading in science class that mosquitoes were the favorite food of bats, so I hoped that loping toward the two sleepy-looking creatures hanging upside down in the mouth of the cave would be enough to scare off the mega-bugs that were following me.

Wrong. Well, not about the bats, only the number of them. Within seconds there were hundreds of thousands of them, screeching and dive-bombing me. I tried to bolt, but my feet got tangled up in the roots and undergrowth, and I went down with a crash while the bats flowed around me like black water.

Through it all the mosquitoes never budged. While I lay crouching on the ground with my arms over my head, I heard them beneath the swooshing movement of the bats, beating their wings near me as if they wanted to get my attention. I peeked underneath my elbow to see . . .

Omigod. It was a human face. These creatures weren't insects at all, and they weren't the hag women, either. They were girls around my age, who could have been in high school if they hadn't been four inches tall.

"Help us," one of them squeaked, holding out her hands in supplication.

I raised my head. "What?"

"Take us out of this place," she begged.

"But I—"

"You have come here, though you are not one of us," she said, peering anxiously over her shoulder. "There are many of us. We will serve you all our days if only you will take us with you when you go." She reached out to touch my face.

"Stop!" I rolled away from her. These little beings didn't stand a chance against me, I knew. "Don't come any closer."

"Please, we beseech you."

"You don't understand—"

"Please . . ."

"Go away!" I shouted. Then I picked up a handful of dirt and threw it at her. "I'll kill you if you touch me, don't you understand? I'm poison!"

She backed away, frowning. Then she staggered backward a few steps, her wings beating more and more slowly, making marks in the dry earth.

"Oh, God," I said, looking at my hands. I'd *killed* her! But how? With the dirt I'd thrown at her? I hadn't even been angry. I'd just been frightened. And I hadn't touched her.

But then, she'd been so small. . . .

A sound filled the air. I couldn't recognize it until the moment when I realized it was me, screaming. The sound seemed to go on and on while everything around me blurred into a visual soup that I was drowning in.

Then the fairy—the *girl*, I realized, a girl just like me who had shape-shifted into something small with wings—lay still as a swarm of other creatures like her carried her away from me. Some distance away they shifted back into normal girls, carrying their lifeless friend in their arms. A couple of them looked back at me, their eyes filled with bitterness.

"Please. I didn't mean . . ." I began, but I knew that what I was saying was so foolish, so useless. *I hadn't meant to kill her*. As if that made everything all right. As if anything would ever be right again.

I staggered away from them, looking from the lifeless girl who had begged for my help to the rocks where Bryce had been carried off, and my heart was so heavy with grief and shame that I felt as if it were going to fall out of my chest. I had destroyed them both.

My knees buckled, but before I hit the ground, someone grabbed me by the collar of my sweater and shoved me toward the cave where the bats had come from.

Over my shoulder I saw her face. "You," I whispered, meeting Morgan's eyes.

CHAPTER

•

FORTY-ONE

"Relax," Morgan said. "She's not dead. They're just sensitive here. She only had to be close to you to get knocked out by your mojo."

I blinked in astonishment.

"Move." Her rudeness seemed to wake me out of my guilty torpor. "Into the bat cave, Robin."

I stared at her in shock and disgust. "How . . . How . . ."

She sighed. "Just get inside."

I noticed that she was dressed in rags, like the other witches of Avalon. Without her sophisticated clothes and perfect makeup, Morgan looked ordinary, almost pitiful. She reminded me of what I thought mountain people who lived a hundred years ago might look like. Her pathetic appearance made me feel less afraid of her as I let her lead me deeper into the cave.

It was obviously a home, despite its primitive structure. There was a fire burning inside an earthen pit, beneath an opening that let out the smoke and let in a single shaft of bright sunlight. Nearby were a few cratelike blocks made of wood that served as chairs and a rickety table on which burned a smelly candle that popped and spewed black smoke.

"Not much like the Emporium of Remarkable Goods, is it," Morgan said bitterly.

"What are you doing here?" I asked, completely flummoxed. She was the last person I thought I'd find in this place.

"Waiting for you," she said with a smile.

I shook my head, trying to hold myself together. "Look, Morgan, if there's an antidote to what I've got, what I did to that girl—"

"I told you, she'll be fine," she said. "For a while anyway. They're all dying, though. It's just a matter of time."

"From . . . the water?"

She shrugged. "I didn't want it to drag on like this. I thought you'd just come in with guns blazing. It was a mistake to put you into the lake. That lessened the effect of the poison. I didn't plan it that way." She leaned against one of the uneven damp walls. A spider crawled beside her. "But then, in the end, I suppose it doesn't make much difference how it happens."

"It happened because of me," I said hotly, before I remembered who had started all this. "Because of *you*."

She waved me away. "Don't be stupid. It's because of *her*." She gestured with her head.

"Who? The Seer?"

"She's the one who's kept us all in the Stone Age, and it's killing us. Killed us already," she said. "There's no hope here. No future. And anyone who tries to make one is killed."

I couldn't believe what I was hearing. "She didn't pollute the lake," I said levelly. "I did."

Morgan laughed. She *laughed*. "Okay, fine," she said. "You want the prize for wallowing in guilt, you got it."

I opened my mouth to speak a couple of times, but closed it again. She was beyond unbelievable. "You make me sick," I said finally. "They're all going to die here, Morgan, and you're laughing about it."

She looked at her nails. "That was the point."

I buried my face in my hands.

"Oh, stop being boring."

That was it. If killing off an entire civilization was boring, Morgan was about to get very bored. Bored to death. I lunged at her, claws out.

She caught me by both wrists. "Hey, you were trying to kill me, you little turd," she said.

I took a long look at her hands, enclosing my wrists. "You're not . . ."

"Poisoned? No." She pushed me away. "I gave the ring to you, so I'm immune. Too bad, huh?"

"I . . ." I felt my eyes filling with tears. What was I becoming? In the end was I any better than she was? "I'm sorry," I whispered. I really was. It had been a terrible thing for me to do, no matter what.

"Oh, for pity's sake," she said. "Is there anything you're *not* sorry for?"

I turned away from her.

"Sooner or later, babe, you've got to accept that you're not perfect."

I whirled around to face her. *"Not perfect?"* I shouted. "I kill people by touching them, Morgan!" Angrily I wiped my eyes. "Oh, what do you care? As soon as you met me, you sent me into a lake to drown."

Her eyebrows raised. "I beg your pardon?"

"Get off it, Morgan. You know that you wanted—expected—me to die there."

"You mean when you went through the tankard?" She gave a disgusted sigh. "I hardly think I tried to kill you, especially since I was the one who pulled you out."

"What are you talking about?"

"Your precious Peter," Morgan said, morphing in front of my eyes into an exact duplicate of Peter Shaw. "Do you still believe after all this time that he rescued you?"

For a moment all I could do was gape. She looked *exactly* like Peter, except for the expression on his face. Peter would never have looked at me with such disdain. "No one rescued me," I muttered, trying to remember what had happened. I'd been in the water, I remembered that. And then Peter . . . well, he'd just sort of *appeared*. "He told me how to get back," I recalled. Morgan nodded. "Are you saying that was you?"

"Do you really think your boyfriend would have told you to find the tankard?"

I was confused. "But then why . . ."

"Would you have listened if it had been anyone besides Peter telling you what to do?"

I guessed she knew me better than I'd thought.

"What about being your own hero, Katy?"

She was just so *harsh*. "Whatever," I said. "What are you doing here, anyway?"

"Came to watch," she said, smiling. "Those bird-women

are *old*. They're dropping already." She held out her hands, palms up. "Can't live without water."

"What about the others?" I shouted. "The innocent ones."

"I'm the innocent one," she said. "And I've already been punished. Now it's their turn."

"Oh, for pity's sake." I stood up. "You're insane."

"Why? Because I want to get rid of this place, this place that's so poisonous it makes you look like cotton candy?"

"Because you're destroying people who had nothing to do with what happened to you!" But it was pointless to talk to her. "Fine, do whatever you want. I only want to get rid of this stupid ring."

"Then you came to the wrong place. Or haven't you noticed that our so-called Seer isn't interested in helping you . . . or anyone else?"

I swallowed.

"It's getting stronger, isn't it," she said. "The poison."

"Do you care?"

She shrugged again.

"Yeah, that's what I thought," I said. "But for the record, destroying Avalon isn't going to kill the Seer. She's immortal, in case you didn't know."

"Oh, I know," she said. "Once everyone's gone, she'll have this whole world to herself. A master without slaves. A queen whose subjects are all ghosts."

I headed toward the mouth of the cave. "Great. Enjoy yourself, Morgan."

"Don't go out there," she said. "Those hags are looking for you, waiting for you. If they see you, you're dead."

I looked back at her for what I hoped was the last time. "Then they'll save everyone a lot of trouble," I said.

. . .

As I walked out of the cave, I saw the witches on the rock outcropping begin to stir. They had spotted me. Now they were coming for me, sliding down the rock or leaping off it, transforming into animals and other things I didn't ever want to see up close. Two of them changed in midair into the huge vultures I recognized, their tattered robes morphing into wings, their voices rising in a wild scream as they sped toward me over the meadow.

I ran blindly, without any idea which way the versimka was. I could hear the witch creatures behind me now, their shrieks and cries growing louder as their wings made shadows over my head. When I felt the first talon's scratch on my back, I whirled around.

"Get away!" I spat, and light poured out of me. One of the witches fell to the ground before I could close my eyes. I heard the others dropping behind me as I ran, ablaze like a torch with my own dangerous power.

Poison. You are poison, a voice inside me said. *You are death.*

"No!" I screamed. I tried to cover my face with my hands, but the light emanating from them was too bright.

Then a voice, familiar, close. "Katy!"

"Who . . . Where . . ."

"Over here!"

I stumbled, squinting. "Peter?" I called. "Is it really you, this time?"

"What?"

"Don't come near me. I'm—"

"Katy!" Before I could see past my poisonous light, Peter

caught me in his arms. "I've found a way inside," he said as he pulled me through what felt like a membrane of thick air. Those were the last words he spoke.

I screamed as we fell to the floor together in a room filled with electronic equipment. Against the oddly ornate nineteenth-century walls stood my great-grandmother, Hattie Scott, and Miss P. All of them looked shocked, their faces frozen into masks of horrified surprise.

Before I even saw him, I knew what I had done.

Peter wasn't breathing. He lay on the floor like a rag doll, dead.

He was dead.

I skittered away, blinking, trying to hold my poison in, trying to retract it, take it back.

Miss P fainted. Hattie ran up to Peter and held him, rocking and wailing. By the time Gram knelt beside them, the nimbus around me had dimmed to nearly nothing.

"He's gone," Gram said, looking at me.

I felt myself shaking all over. Sparks were flying out my fingers, and my throat opened to let out a moan that would have poured out of me like a river, but I didn't let that happen.

"Take him to Eric," I said in a hoarse whisper, using every ounce of control I could muster to keep my voice steady.

"Can't you see!" Hattie shouted in a burst of anger. "Can't you see it's too late for that?"

"Hattie, please. She's only trying to help."

"I don't want her help!" she shrieked. "I want her out of here! Do you understand?"

"Shh," Gram said, placing her hand on Hattie's arm.

"Eric can help him," I said levelly. "He helped me."

"Were you *dead*?" Hattie growled.

I had to tell her. "Yes," I said quietly. "I was."

Both Hattie and Gram swiveled their heads to face me. Miss P was just coming to, bewildered.

"It happened last year," I said. "I died and Eric brought me back."

Gram and Hattie exchanged glances.

"Take him, Gram," I said. "Take him to Eric."

Gram blinked for a moment, then nodded her head. "All right." She stood up. When Hattie kept rocking with Peter in her arms, Gram pried her hands away. "Come on, Hattie," she said gently.

"Why should we listen to her?" Hattie choked, weeping.

Gram sighed. "Because it's the only hope we have. Take his arms, Hattie."

As the three women were struggling with Peter's weight, Gram turned to me again. "Where is Bryce?" she asked.

The word seemed to roll in the pit of my stomach before clawing its way up my throat and bursting from my mouth: "Gone."

Everything hung still for a moment, as if all the air had left the room. Then a low moan escaped from Hattie. "Steady," Gram said.

I took a step forward. "Maybe I can—"

"No," Hattie said.

"I think perhaps you'd better go for now," Miss P said, coughing softly. "If you're all right."

"Yes," I said. "I'm—" I began, but "sorry" wouldn't begin to express what I felt.

And it wouldn't matter anyway.

So I slunk away like a thief, staying close to the walls, while the women pushed and pulled at Peter's lifeless body.

I followed Hattie's car on foot. Aunt Agnes's fiancé, Jonathan, met the women at Hattie's house and carried Peter inside.

From a window I watched as the boy I loved was laid on his bed, on top of a quilt my great-grandmother had made. Near the bed was a desk with a few books on it—not many, since recently Peter had been living at the Shaw mansion— and a framed photograph of the two of us that Becca had taken the previous September during the car wash fund-raiser for Winter Frolic. In the picture we're both blasting each other with hoses. Our eyes are closed, our mouths are open, there's a pouf of soap on his head, and my legs are slick with water.

I leaned my head against the window as snow began to fall. All I could think about was that I wanted to turn back time. If only I'd listened to Peter when he'd asked me not to go through the painting . . . If only I hadn't called Bryce, hadn't asked him to go with me . . . If only I hadn't accepted the ring, Morgan's gift of death . . . If only, if only, if only . . .

If only it took more than a second to change your life.

By the time Hattie carried Eric into the room, I could barely see through my tears. With shaking hands I wiped a place where my breath had fogged the window. Eric must have been sleeping, because he was yawning and digging his fists into his eyes. Then, when he saw Peter, he held out his arms enthusiastically, a big smile on his face, as if he expected a response. When there was none, his expression changed to one of puzzlement. He flapped his thin arms and kicked out his legs, wanting to be set down. I had carried him myself so many times that I could almost feel him squirming against my side, snuffling and whimpering.

Hattie lay him gently beside his brother. Eric cooed and patted Peter's face as the adults in the room held their breath.

"Buh," Eric said.

Do it, I thought, willing his power. *Nownownownownow.*

For a long time Peter just lay there, his face impassive as a stone.

Oh, God, no.

"Buh!" Eric said, thumping on Peter's chest.

Hattie came over and put her arms around him. "It's all right, baby," she said softly. "You did your best."

But Eric squirmed away from her. "Buh! Buh!"

Hattie sobbed into her hands. Gram sat down on Peter's desk chair. Miss P leaned against the wall.

"Peter!" I screamed, so loudly that they all looked over at the window. Hattie's haggard face turned toward me. "Peter!" I banged on the window with my fists. Silently Hattie stood up and, without ever meeting my eyes, pulled down the shade.

"No!" I screamed. "Please, Hattie! Let me see him! Oh, God, please!"

But no one else came to the window, and I didn't hear another sound.

I crouched down in the snow for a while, trying to make myself stop shivering.

Peter was dead. Like the bird women in Avalon. Like Bryce. I had killed them all.

Numbly I walked to Gram's, scribbled a note saying where I was headed, then took the keys to her car and started driving.

I drove until I reached New York City. It snowed the whole way.

And all I could think of were three words:

Peter is dead.

Peter is dead.

Peter is dead.

PART FOUR
THE TRAVELERS
FROM AVALON

Chapter

•

Forty-three

Now that I look back on it, I must have been out of my mind to drive to Manhattan during a snowstorm, especially since I didn't even have a license. Gram had been teaching me—that was how I knew the basics of handling her '58 Cadillac—but I was a long way from being a proficient driver. Fortunately, the streets were nearly deserted. My dad had told me that when it snowed in Manhattan, no one drove. That certainly seemed to be the case when I arrived that evening, and probably the reason why I didn't get pulled over or crash.

The truth was, though, I didn't care. The way I was thinking at the time, it would probably have been best all around if I'd just gone up in a ball of flame on the highway. But that didn't happen. Luck, I guess. Lucky, lucky me.

On the street where my father lived, cars were scattered willy-nilly, having been abandoned in snowdrifts by their owners, but a car pulled out of a parking spot right in front of Dad's building just as I drove up. I locked Gram's Caddie and went inside the first set of doors to Dad's intercom.

This building was a lot different from Madam Mim's, where he'd lived previous to their breakup. Her building was on Sutton Place, with a uniformed doorman and a marble-floored lobby dotted with potted palm trees and a sculpture by Picasso. Dad's current entryway was a drafty area between two sets of doors with dirty glass, adorned only by a wall of mailboxes, and smelling of stale cigarette smoke.

I didn't think he was home—he'd written that he was going to India with Madam Mim—but I rang anyway. No one answered, so I used my key to get in. At least I had this place to come to—for a while, anyway, until he got back. After that I didn't know where I would go.

The apartment was dark. The kitchen was clean, with no dishes in the sink. His bed was made. The papers on the desk in his office were neat. His answering machine had sixteen messages on it. For a while I just wandered from room to room, listening to the quiet. It felt like a professor's home, spare and utilitarian, with no frills except for hundreds of books, most of them old, lining shelves in every room and smelling musty and comfortable. Plus it was quiet. That was undoubtedly due to the snowstorm and would change as soon as the roads got cleared, but for that night, anyway, it felt safe. Almost. I knew I'd never really be safe again.

I plopped down on a wing chair—a Salvation Army special, from the looks of it—and closed my eyes. My life had become a horrible dream, so frightening that I couldn't bear to think of it. *Later*, I told myself. *Later I'll go over everything that has happened. Later, when I can picture Peter's face without dying inside, when I can speak Bryce's name without tears, when I can think of the young girl from Avalon who withered just by being near me, I will remember.*

I ran into the bathroom and threw up, again and again, until I was weak and shaking and sobbing again.

Later, I reminded myself. Think of something else. Anything.

Something was pressing against my hip. In the pocket of my jeans were the two pieces of Morgan's amber.

Yes, I thought. *I can go there, to her world, sixteen hundred years in the past.* Whatever she had done, I would rather be in her skin than mine.

Morgan is in the center of the reverse pentagram, where I left her, casting her spell. She walks widdershins, or counterclockwise—another sign that the magic she is performing is black. It will bring harm.

She calls on the elements of fire, water, air, and earth, and their compass points—north for the great powers of earth; south for fire and passion; east for air and its provenance, thought; and west for water, comfort, and healing. The homage she pays to the lords of air and water is perfunctory; she does not need them. Her driving force is her passion, and her ultimate goal is an object forged from earth things.

During the ritual the air stills around her as the earth inside her magic circle heats and trembles. The moon is new, invisible, and there is no light. She has chosen a place far removed from human habitation, where thunderclouds obscure the moon and stars.

"Be with me, Darkness, thou who art the center of the world, the perfection of the universe," she says in her peculiar old-woman voice.

How aged she has become!

What? My own thought startles me. Aged? How could Morgan be so old? It is Morgan I'm seeing, isn't it?

Isn't it?

I am biting my fingernails. Again, odd. I never do that. In fact, I feel completely different again, in the same weird way I felt the last time I'd picked up the amber pieces. And again, an insistent question burns through my brain: Who am I watching—the witch, or the watcher?

And then I realize, understand, grasp at last what has happened. I am no longer Katy Ainsworth, but *Morgan herself.* It is Morgan who is standing behind the tree, holding her breath, biting her nails. And I am inside with her, feeling her fear, hearing the sound that has been bothering me since I came upon this evil sight.

The sound is a cry of wretched terror, uttered by a child. The cloaked figure inside the reverse pentagram reaches out bony arms to pick up the toddler—a boy no more than two years old—screaming through the gag in his mouth, struggling against the ropes that bind him.

"For you, my Sire, a sacrifice," the old woman says. The child squirms wildly; he kicks off the woman's head covering.

I almost scream as I recognize the rheumy eyes, the mouth filled with brown teeth, the thin white hair plastered against the pink spotted head.

It is the Seer and *I* know her for I am fully Morgan now.

The Seer . . . the Seer . . . I remember her from an incident in my childhood. My father had left me in a meadow and had

*vanished into the worldly realm. I called for him to come back.
I ran after his shadow, already gone.*

"Da!" I screamed. "Da, come back!"

*But he did not come back to me. He had gone to his child of
preference, the boy, Arthur. The boy my father would one day
make into a king, while I was left as a plaything for the vultures
who served the Seer.*

*They picked me up with their talons and carried me to the
rock where she lived within the deepest crevasse, away from all
light. I caught only a glimpse of her in that dank, dark place,
but the image of her face never left me. She was as pale as a
worm's belly, almost iridescent in the gloom.*

*"I have seen your future," she whispered, dragging a long
fingernail lightly across my cheek. "One day you will be me."*

*I was too frightened to answer, but in my heart I knew that
she was wrong. I would never be one of her ugly birds. I would
never serve her or whatever Master she answered to, because I
would not remain in Avalon for one moment longer than I had
to. One day my father would teach me how to enter that other,
better realm, and when I got there, I would never return.*

Or so I thought. I was very young then.

*The Seer looks around now, watchful, her movements those of a
small bird. She knows she has been seen. She senses me.*

*She swallows, afraid, guilty. "Who is it?" she asks, slipping
her hand over the child's mouth. The boy tries to scream again.*

*"Stop it!" I rasp, stepping out from my hiding place. "Let
him go! He's a baby!"*

*For a moment the hag hesitates. Her grip loosens. But then
her eyes narrow, thinking, calculating. "I know you," she*

says. "You are Merlin's wild and unloved daughter."

This hurts. The Seer's gift is that she is able to look into your heart and find your weakness. This is what has enabled her to be our leader. We all fear her. We do not question her, because she is immortal. She will outlive all of us, no matter what we do. But she will outlive us far longer if we dare to criticize her.

"Why have you returned to Avalon, child?" *she asks sweetly.* "Ah, but of course. You have come for some magic, haven't you? Do you think I do not know your dark dreams?"

I know that I will not be forgiven for my intrusion. I should have let her kill the child. But I could not. I have not yet lost all of my humanity.

Is it worth my life? *I ask myself. Because I know that will be the price I will have to pay.*

Ah, but I do not have to decide to end my life as a hero. This evil woman is the Seer. She sees me, the black heart of me. She knows I would never save anyone but myself.

"A gift," *she says, extending her skeletal hand. In it is a ring, blue as ice, shimmering with beauty and evil. She adds in a whisper:* "A gift to kill a king."

I fall back. How did she know? Even I myself . . .

A gift to kill a king.

Oh, my. How extreme! And how exactly right.

I reach out to touch the blinking, inviting jewel. It smiles, in its cold way, like an impossibly beautiful woman or an unattainable man who knows the power of his charm.

But would that solve anything? Would it make my father love me?

It would make him sorry.

Would that be enough? For such a crime . . .

Perhaps he would notice you again. Turn flowers into butterflies for you. Walk through open fields with your hand in his,
teach you the Merlin's magic, talk with you the way he talks
with Arthur, easy, comfortable, caring.

"Da," I whisper aloud. "Oh, Da, don't leave me. Don't go."

The hag gestures curtly for me to take the ring. My hand
closes over it, trembling, lovingly.

Oh, Morgan, think what you're doing!

I feel its warmth pour through me like warm syrup. All is
well. All shall be well. All manner of things shall be . . .

There is a sharp, sickening crack as the Seer breaks the boy's
neck and the child goes limp in her arms.

I gasp as she shudders, holding the dead child close. As I
watch, the tiny corpse turns to ash and disintegrates in her arms
while, at the same time, the Seer's face becomes relaxed, calm
again, alive. The skin of her hands fleshes out. She breathes
deeply, relieved, whole again.

She has not taken her eyes off me. They flash now, teasing,
sparkling, cold.

I look at the ring in my hand. It is the seal of the covenant
I have made with the Darkness, the seal that has bound me to
this creature of death forever.

"No," I moan. "I didn't know what I was doing. I wasn't in
my right mind. I didn't mean . . ."

But we both know that all that is of no importance anymore.

The Seer, now serene and in control, turns away from me
with a sneer.

I have become her servant, and I am sick with grief.

CHAPTER

•

FORTY-FOUR

The next day dawned clean and sunny, with the sound of snow-plows coming from everywhere in the city. I'd fallen asleep in the wing chair, and woke up squinting into the sunlight streaming through the window.

After a quick look in the refrigerator, which contained a dried-up piece of smoked mozzarella, a jar of mustard, and two bottles of Dos Equis, I decided to venture outside to search for food. It was the last thing I wanted to do. I felt guilty about everything, even eating, but even though I may have wanted to die from shame and regret, my belly was still rumbling ferociously.

Outside, I felt as if I were in the middle of a gigantic maze. Most of the streets had been plowed, but they were all flanked on either side by snow walls four feet high. On some corners where the plows had deposited their loads, the snow reached eight or nine feet. Already at eight in the morning, little kids were hanging on to those snow mountains like monkeys while cars zipped around below.

I found an open deli near my dad's apartment and bought a bagel with cream cheese. There didn't seem to be much point in taking it back to the apartment, so I kept walking until I reached Central Park a few blocks later.

It was like fairyland there, the sparkling snow reflecting so much light that it was hard to look at anything without my eyes watering. All sorts of people were in the park—runners jogging along the roads, cross-country skiers, lots of kids sliding down hills on sleds and saucers, and even a few snowboarders, plus old people who walked down the lanes wearing overcoats and hats, as if this were just another winter morning instead of the weird, rare, citywide snow day it was.

I found a bench that I knew no one had sat on since before the snowstorm because at least a foot of snow had accumulated on the slats and an equal amount rose up from the ground beneath it. After sweeping the snow away with my arm, I sat down and bit into my bagel, feeling like I was a part of this phenomenon, this scene, an instant New Yorker. For once I felt like there was nothing dangerous or horrible about me. I was just another face in the crowd.

Like I was before I went to Whitfield. All those years when I struggled to fit in, so that my freakish abilities wouldn't be noticed. Until last year, when I'd moved to Whitfield and discovered that there were others like me, my life had been nothing but lies and hiding and shame.

Pretty much what it was now.

I'd been really hungry, but suddenly the bagel seemed to turn to raw dough in my mouth. I put the rest of it back into the bag and leaned back on the bench.

At about the same moment a man sat down next to me. He

looked like he was homeless, with a scraggly black beard shot with gray, and long hair and a filthy ski jacket full of holes where the stuffing stuck out. He smelled like a sewer. The first thing he did was take a bottle from inside the jacket and glug it so that his Adam's apple bobbed up and down.

"Ahh," he said. Then he turned to face me. He had turquoise-colored eyes, but they weren't looking at me. They were fixated on the paper bag in my hand. Hesitantly I offered it to him. He grabbed it, tore open the bag, and gobbled what was left of the bagel. Then he threw the bag onto the ground. Passersby gave us both dirty looks as he quaffed some more from the bottle that had been nestled against his chest.

The blue eyes fastened on my face this time. "Wine?" he croaked, holding out the bottle to me. I shook my head, thinking that the last thing I ever wanted to do was drink from that bottle.

He shrugged, then took another slug. "Ahh," he said again. I stood up. "The feast of Christmas," he said.

"I beg your pardon?" I asked, immediately regretting saying anything at all to him.

"Bread and wine. It brings us all together. We are one."

I started backing away.

"Just do what you can," he said, the blue eyes boring into me like lasers.

"Okay," I whispered.

He belched. I ran away, out of the park, down the mazelike streets. I was thinking that I should have gone in the other direction so that I could have picked up the paper bag. I kept thinking about the homeless man's piercing turquoise blue eyes. In other circumstances he might have been considered good-looking. Handsome, even. I wondered what made people give up their whole lives and live the way he did, eating someone's old discarded bagel. Drinking rotgut wine from a bottle.

The feast of Christmas.

I checked my cell phone. It was December 21, the eve of the winter solstice. I guessed that was as much of a Yuletide celebration as I was going to get, me and the homeless guy offering to swap spit on a public bench. With a little littering thrown in for excitement.

Just do what you can.

Yeah, dude. If you only knew what I can do. A human hydrogen bomb, that was me. The next deadly plague, artfully packaged in a school uniform. Miss Teen Death.

We are one.

But we weren't. *Even being you would be better than being me.* Wiping my eyes, I walked as fast as I could toward the apartment, where I once again sprawled across the big wing chair.

I don't know why I picked up the amber pieces again.

Yes, I do. I was lonely. It was almost Yule, the solstice—a date that didn't mean much to anyone except witches. And even for us Yule wasn't a big holiday, at least not compared to times of huge Wiccan celebrations like Imbolc or Samhain, but it was still important. Yule was for family. For seeing old friends. For having a quiet day in a warm place by a fire. None of which I had.

Just do what you can.

And join hands and sing "Kumbaya" and hug the trees and pray for world peace. Oh, yes, what a big difference each one of us can make.

Right. Excuse me while I barf. Or cry. My tears are for myself, and also for Morgan, whose face, as I see it in my vision, is also wet with tears.

They stream down Morgan's face. She knows the magnitude of the step she has taken, and it frightens her.

She has forgotten the dead child and the evil, satisfied face of the Seer. She must forget, or she will lose her footing on the slippery slope she has chosen to walk.

I will kill the king, *she thinks,* and then my father will love me. *He would understand how she had loved him, waited for him all these years, how she had tolerated living in the prison that was Avalon until he showed her how to leave it.*

She had listened to the Merlin, her father, who was filled with greatness. She had stepped aside like a good girl while he'd lavished his love on the boy he had painstakingly raised in her place. He had used his powerful magic to place a sword in a stone—a sword that only Arthur's hand could remove, ensuring that the boy, the Merlin's new "son," would one day rule all of Britain.

I gripped the amber harder and allowed myself to be pulled into Morgan's mind. Waves of bitterness and anger washed over me as I let Morgan bare her very soul.

It's not that I want to rule Britain, or even live here, particularly. I just want my life to be more than scrambling for food in a place where the future doesn't exist. And I want my father to see me for who I am—witch, magus, Traveler, mind—and not just a potential helper for some man who'll think I'm lucky to have been chosen to serve him.

I have more talent than anyone I know. That includes all the boys I've met and all the men, including Arthur, king of Britain. The Merlin loves him because he has a pinch of magical blood. Arthur's mother, Igraine, was Welsh, descended from the original Travelers, the witches who left Avalon before it was sealed against the world. The concentration of Arthur's magic isn't much, but it's enough for the Merlin to accept him as the son he never had. Enough to replace the daughter he never wanted.

The force of Morgan's fury shook me from my intense concentration. I held fast to the amber, but I had lost hold of Morgan's mind. Suddenly I was just watching again.

"Give me justice!" Morgan demands, and the demand is answered. The starless sky bursts into sudden blinding light. A hundred miles away on the open sea, a crew of Italian sailors looks up in wonder at the blazing star. Some, the Christians among them, fall to their knees, crossing themselves. Others tremble in fear that the end of the world has come.

But the light vanishes as quickly as it came, leaving the sea engulfed in darkness once again. And in that darkness gleams a stone of unearthly blue, the seal of her pact with the Darkness.

She touches it, feels the stone's magnificent power coursing through her like sunlight, like love. It hums through her blood. She has never felt so well.

But she knows it is not for her, but for the king. For Arthur of Britain, his final gift.

For the briefest of moments she hesitates. This is wrong, she thinks. And for a moment she shivers with fear and indecision.

But there can be no turning back. The Darkness has been summoned. The Darkness will have its way.

So be it.

I fell asleep, exhausted from all I'd seen.

• • •

The amber dropped to the floor with a small click, and I awoke, stiff from my weird position on the chair. Slowly, painfully, I unpretzeled myself and sat blinking in the darkness.

Dark already! I must have slept all day. And my dream . . . how awful . . .

I shook myself like a dog to wake myself up fully. It had been a sickening dream, although I didn't remember much of it. All I knew was that I felt dirty in my own skin. Then I looked around, thinking about reading, about watching TV. Outside, the snow fell again like fat feathers, coating Gram's car in a thick white blanket under the strange blue of twilight.

Where will I go? The question hit me like a hammer, unexpected, startling. I needed more time to be awake before handling thoughts like that. I felt sick. My heart was beating like a drum in my chest. I wanted to run away. I would have, right then, if I'd had anywhere to run to.

But that was the problem. It was something I had to think about, whether I liked the subject or not. I needed to make some kind of plan about where I'd live after my father came back. But where would I go? Where does someone like me belong?

I answered myself: *In hell.*

"Oh, Gram," I whispered. "What am I going to do?" I buried my head in my hands. I hadn't asked to be poison. I hadn't made a deal with the devil.

Had Morgan?

I didn't know. Where was the line between innocence and guilt? If a bear in a zoo kills a child who squeezes between the bars, is the bear evil? Is it innocent? Is it the fault of the child's parents? The zookeeper? Does the bear deserve to die for its crime? Does the child, for its ignorance?

Why am I even thinking about this stuff?

Angrily I turned on the radio. It was tuned to an eighties station. A loud, funky man's voice was singing "You Can Leave Your Hat On," and for a moment I could almost pretend that life was normal. Or something.

But of course it wasn't. I was here like death, waiting to kill again.

With trembling fingers I picked up the amber pieces once more. *Take me away,* I thought. *Anywhere. Anywhere but here. And anyone but* me.

Even though I know where the ring came from and what it stands for, I cannot help but love it, in a way. There is such promise in that faintly glowing blue stone, such a feeling of good times to come. That is how evil works, I've learned. It is not some dark, spectral thing that sets your teeth on edge. Sometimes it's lovely, compelling, a mermaid on the rocks, something sweet and laughing, with a knife between its perfect teeth.

When I give King Arthur the ring, I make sure that the Merlin is absent at the time. I am one of many supplicants, sycophants, and court ladies seeking some special recognition from the king. Arthur is not a handsome man. He is slight and pale, attesting to a sickly childhood, and his ginger-colored hair is already thinning. But he is still the king, and everyone knows that his wife, Guinevere, is barren. All of his advisers have urged him to put her away in a convent and marry someone younger.

So there is never a shortage of women, young and old, the

reckless married ones and the innocent maidens prompted by their mothers, who try to catch Arthur's eye. Thinking I am one of these, he nods politely as he accepts my gift with a discreet questioning glance at his clerk, who murmurs that I am the Merlin's daughter. I notice the play of emotions that flit across his face: Oh, the Merlin! He has a daughter? But he's never mentioned her. Rather pretty. But of common blood, nothing special. Unless she's a witch, of course, like her father. Better to leave her alone. "Thank you," he says. And who is that behind her?

Then he places the ring on his finger, and the world lights up.

Oh, good heavens, my dear! He thinks the woman behind me has caused the sudden lift of his mood. I am forgotten.

My sigh of relief fills the room.

The stone takes time to do its work. Days pass, weeks. The Merlin is riding the countryside, conferring with the witch women of outlying provinces about the weather. There has been no rain since April, and that was scant. The first harvest, on Lammas, failed almost completely, and the second harvest at Mabon, soon approaching in mid-September, looks to be no better. Soon there will no longer be any deer or even songbirds in the forests; they will have all been eaten. Everyone on the entire island of Britain is in danger of starving over the winter.

The peasants blame the king, of course. In their minds they have invested him with powers even greater than the Merlin's. They believe that Arthur is the land, and the land is Arthur. If the land suffers, then it is because the king has broken some covenant with God.

And who knows? Perhaps they are right. The ring Arthur

wears is certainly nothing holy. God would not have approved of it.

To appease the people, the king sends Guinevere to a convent and strips her of her titles. The courtiers gossip that the queen is being punished for her infidelity with one of the Round Table knights, Lancelot, who has left Camelot under mysterious circumstances, but I have no interest in these court intrigues. As far as I can see, the king was only following the demands of his advisers to rid himself of a barren wife and find a new one in order to secure an heir for the kingdom.

But Arthur does not look for another queen. Instead he spends long hours alone in his chapel, praying to whatever gods will listen to save his people from famine. This, say the courtiers, is what is making Arthur sick. Worry, grief, guilt over discarding the woman he still loves, fear that his new nation—actually, still a loose bunch of tribes—will fall once more into anarchy and civil war. These are the things that are causing Arthur's hands to tremble and the flesh to fall from his body so that now he resembles an aging child. After a time he can no longer eat, and takes to his bed.

The advisers are in a panic now. If Arthur dies without an heir, Britain will revert to chaos, and an age of darkness will ensue for a thousand years.

And now I understand why the blue stone was given to me. This is what the Darkness wants.

The Knights of the Round Table decide, in the simpleminded way of soldiers, that what the king needs to cure his melancholy is some rare and expensive gewgaw. Personally I believe they just wanted a chance to go adventuring and looting again, but they swear that they are embarking on a quest to find, of all things, the Holy Grail. So there is a lot of handkerchief waving and brave smiles as the knights go off, leaving the sick Arthur in the hands of a bunch of freeloading, parasitical aristocrats who spend their days consulting with astrologers and drinking the last of the king's wine.

That is fine with me. I keep to myself and watch, telling myself that perhaps Arthur's decline is not due to the ring at all. The courtiers may be right. Worry can wear a person down. And the peasants may be right. Who's to say that the land is not somehow mystically tied to its ruler?

But I know it's the ring. Every day the thought passes through my mind that I should take it back. But then, what would I do with it? Give it back to the Darkness? Or does the Darkness even exist? I may have imagined it all, found a lost trinket in the woods after a dream encounter with a ghost from my childhood.

That's the thing about magic. You never know if it's real or not. It has to be believed to be seen.

But the king is sick, that much I know, and he may die. Is it my doing? Can I stop it? Am I evil? Do I belong to the Darkness? I don't feel any different from how I did when I was good. Is my evil in my own mind? Do my thoughts make me evil, or just guilty? And if I do belong to the Darkness now, what price will it exact from me?

I just don't know anything anymore. And I'm so scared.

I must have fallen asleep again, because the next thing I knew, the apartment was completely dark and there was an incessant pounding on the door.

I got up to answer it, smacking my sleepy lips and practicing what I would say if whoever was knocking was an irate student that my dad had flunked. "I'm sorry, but . . ." The words dried up in my mouth.

It was Morgan.

"Hiding out?" she asked, strolling past me. "Nice crib."

"Get out," I said.

"Hey." She spread her hands. "Who else is going to hang with you?" She switched on the overhead light. "Jeez, it's pitch-dark in here. You a vampire these days, or what?"

I leaned against the wall. What was I going to do, call the police? As if they could get here even if there were a real crime in progress.

Morgan rubbed her arms. "Think you could rustle up a cup

of tea or something? It's wicked cold out there." She was right. Outside, the cars parked on the street had become fat snow-covered shapes flanking a trackless river of white. "Please?"

I looked at her levelly. Okay, it was cold outside. I supposed I could spare a cup of tea, even if it was for her. "Why are you here?" I asked coldly as I tramped into the kitchen and put on the kettle.

"Just passing through," she said airily.

I held up my hand. "Forget it," I said. I wasn't in the mood for witty lies.

"Okay, okay. I looked for you. Feel better? I mean, it's not like you didn't want to be found."

"How do you know what I wanted?"

"Duh, you left a note."

"Oh." Right. That was for Gram, so she'd know where to find her car. "So you broke into my great-grandmother's house."

She shrugged. "No one saw me."

"I guess in your universe that makes it all right."

She made a face. "What's with you, prissy face?"

"What's with me?" I narrowed my eyes. "I'm poison, Morgan. I've killed people, including the person I loved most in the world. You want to know what's with me?" I shouted, almost screeching.

She stepped aside. "Relax, Wonder Girl," she said.

"Why don't you leave me alone?" I sobbed. My knees buckled, and I sank to the floor. "For God's sake, when will you stop?"

Her whole face changed then. It was as if she'd been wearing a mask that she'd suddenly dropped, revealing a face she'd never wanted anyone to see.

"Yeah, okay," she said quietly. "I'll go. I'm sorry about—"

"Don't," I said. I didn't want her to even try some phony declaration of remorse.

"Right." She put on her scarf and glanced out the window. It was the smallest moment, less than a second, but when she did that, looked out at the long expanse of snow that had put the whole city to sleep, I sensed how terribly lonely she was.

Or maybe I was just feeling my own loneliness. I didn't want to think that I had anything in common with Morgan le Fay, but in the eyes of anyone with a brain, we were both evil. Plus, there was no doubt that neither of us had anywhere to go or anyone to turn to. In that respect Morgan was my sister.

"Wait," I said.

She looked over at me and blinked once, slowly. "Why?"

"I want you to tell me the rest of your story. What happened after you gave the ring to King Arthur and he got sick?"

She smiled. "You've been spying on me?"

"Something like that."

"Okay." She laughed mirthlessly. "He recovered."

I didn't say anything as I fixed her tea. I just waited for her to go on.

"How do you know I won't lie?"

I shrugged. "Lie if you want to."

She looked at me oddly. I took the muffler from around her neck. She sat down and picked up her teacup, warming her hands on it. "I think the king would have died then if the Merlin hadn't come back."

"Could he sense the ring?"

"Oh, yes. And he knew how it had ended up on the king's finger too. The first thing he did was order me out of his sight." She smiled.

"That's not funny," I said.

"Of course it is. I'd sold my soul to get my father to love me, and he hated me for it. You of all people ought to find that extremely amusing."

"Why me 'of all people'?"

"Because it makes a fool out of me," Morgan said.

"It doesn't make me feel better that your dad didn't love you." I picked up the pieces of amber. "You've left memories in here."

She took them from my hand. "Ah, home," she said lightly, although I could hear a trembling in her voice. "Do you know how long I was imprisoned in here?"

"Yes," I said. "It must have been very hard for you."

Her eyes flickered toward me for an instant, but she didn't say anything. I put my hand over hers so that we could both feel the vibrations of the stone. She tried to pull away, but I held on to her. In the end I think she stayed only because of the novelty—and maybe the comfort—of being touched, even if it was by me. I sort of felt the same way.

"Do you know what you've done?" The Merlin's wrath was not often seen, which made it all the more terrifying. Instantly the hall cleared, and the courtiers fled to the corridors or the gardens, where they chattered like hungry birds.

"It was the girl, his daughter."

"Did she sleep with the king?"

"Much worse. She used witchcraft against him."

"She brought on his illness."

"With witchcraft!"

"Has she been arrested yet?"

A courtier laughed. "And who cares so little for his life that he will arrest the wizard's daughter under his nose?"

"Not that a cell could keep her, in any case."

The Merlin helped the ailing king to his feet, shouting over his shoulder at the girl, "You are no longer any child of mine!"

Inside the king's bedchamber the magician studied the strange and luminous ring on Arthur's finger. He could feel its power, its cold magic. When he touched it, it felt like a hot poker going down his throat.

"Can you take this off?" the Merlin asked, although he already knew the answer. The king was powerless against the ring with its glowing blue stone. For a moment the old man hesitated. He knew that what he was about to do would end his life.

The unification of the petty chiefdoms of Britain into one strong nation had become a reality, but it was still fragile. The king still needed Merlin's guidance. But the structure would break and fall without a king. That was the only thing that was certain. For Britain to survive, Arthur had to live.

He is the land, and the land is him. That was truer than even Arthur himself knew.

The Merlin scanned the room with weary eyes. Had he made a mistake by spending so much time in this temporal realm? He might have stayed in Avalon, increased his magic a thousandfold, lived the life of a king himself. Well, that was of no importance now, he thought as he assembled the tools he would need—a wand, a scrying mirror, a stone knife he kept in his robes.

He would have to work quickly if the king were to live. The Merlin had never performed this magic before, this last magic, but he knew what he was battling, and he knew what the cost would be.

"My child," *he said, taking Arthur's hand. The king's eyes fluttered open, confused. The lashes were crusted, the whites yellow, the rims red and swollen.* I could not have loved you more. *Thirty-four years before, the Merlin had saved the infant from certain death at the hands of Arthur's ignorant father, and had seen him safely reared in the home of a generous-hearted knight. From that moment the wizard had watched over the child as if Arthur were the son he'd never had. The magician had virtually abandoned Avalon, the land of his birth, and had brought its secrets with him into the chaotic, violent, changeable, uncertain world of cowen.*

With the spectacle of pulling the sword Excalibur from the stone—a clever piece of magic, and one that could not have occurred without some magic from Arthur himself—the boy had been assured of becoming high king over the petty chiefs, whose constant quarreling had kept Britain in the sorry state it had been in since the Romans had left a century before. And now it was so close, the prospect of a powerful Celtic nation ruled by a wise king who commanded the respect of all Britons . . . so close. Too close to let die.

No, my child, my destiny. You must live.

The Merlin touched the blue stone. With a gasp he felt its pulsating, glowing heart, its incalculable power. A fleeting thought: This may be worth my death, after all. *He wasn't referring to his sacrifice, to the fact that this last-ditch effort was mankind's last possibility to overcome the Darkness that had cast its shadow over the world. The Merlin was referring to the feeling itself. This was the Darkness in all its overwhelming power, coursing through the old man's body. And yes, it would kill him, would twist his mind to evil in the last moments before his death, would take all the magic he had and render it use-less. Yet still, it was worth it.*

A sound like the satisfied purr of a great cat poured out of his throat. Such a feeling of well-being. Really, I couldn't have asked for a better way to die.

And then, with a swift intake of air that signaled the first stopping of the old man's heart, he looked down to see the ring on his own finger.

"Yes," he whispered as the king's eyes fluttered open.

"Merlin?" Arthur asked in a small voice. "Merlin, have you come back?"

"Yes, Your Majesty," he answered, even as his knees buckled and he staggered over to the wall, where his hands slapped against the cool stone surface. The ring shot out a ray of white light. "But now I must rest. The journey has been . . . difficult."

The king breathed deeply. "Perhaps I will too," he said, closing his eyes once more. "I'm glad to see you again, old friend."

"As am I," the Merlin said, smiling for the last time at the man he had groomed to be Britain's greatest king. Then he wove his erratic way through the corridors and stairways of the castle to a subterranean place where the royal boats were kept. Beyond the docking channels, cut deeply into the rock, was a tunnel that led to a cave sparkling with crystal formations.

This was the Merlin's cave. When the wizard had first discovered it, he'd intended to suggest that it might be used as an emergency hiding place for the castle's inhabitants in case of attack. But as Arthur's power had solidified, it had seemed less and less likely that such a strategy would be necessary, and the Merlin had granted himself the small luxury of using the area as his personal retreat. This was where he had come in the past to reflect and plan in crystalline silence. This was where he had decided that Britain and its high king would be the central focus of his skill and his life. And now this unearthly chamber was where he had come to die.

"Father?"

The Merlin, who had collapsed against a column of sheer quartz, struggled to focus his eyes.

"It's me. Morgan."

He swallowed once. There was no longer any trace of anger in the haggard gray face.

"Would you have done it for me?" she asked.

"Wha . . . what?" His voice trembled with weakness.

"Would you have died in my place?"

He blinked, uncomprehending, then closed his eyes.

"Would you?" Her voice was high-pitched, urgent.

With a nearly imperceptible movement, the old man seemed to sink into the translucent rock as if it were something soft. "For you," he rasped, clutching Morgan's hand. "My son. My king."

CHAPTER

•

FORTY-EIGHT

With a strangled sound Morgan dropped the amber stones. Her eyes were flat and dull.

"I'm sorry," I whispered.

"Why?" she countered sharply. "Your father doesn't love you, either."

I didn't answer. My relationship with my father was too complicated for casual conversation. In the end, though, I believed he did love me. He wasn't very attentive or affectionate, true, but he'd allowed me to stay in Whitfield because he knew how important that was to me. That's love, in a way. His way. But it took me a long time to figure it out. Maybe if Morgan had taken the time, she'd have found that her father loved her too.

Or maybe he didn't. Sometimes you just had to live with things that hurt. It didn't justify destroying all of Avalon.

"Oh, hell. It was a long time ago," she added. Then she burst out laughing, a harsh, bitter, mirthless sound that let me know that even sixteen hundred years wasn't long enough to forget some things.

"When he died in my arms, he was delirious. He thought I was Arthur."

"I know."

"So I took the ring from him—it doesn't hurt me, and it had hurt him more than enough—and then I took his body back to Avalon."

"Why?"

"They didn't care for me there, but they revered my father. I wanted to bring him home. I thought they'd be happy that the great Merlin wasn't left in an English grave. I didn't think . . ." She took a deep breath. "I didn't think that witch would still be waiting to get even with me for knowing her secret."

"How many other children has she killed since then?" I asked.

"Shut *up*!" Morgan snapped. "Do you want to hear the rest of the story or not?"

I wasn't sure. Morgan's silence had guaranteed the death of countless babies like the one I had seen in my vision. After knowing that, her own suffering just didn't strike me as that terrible. But I knew she wanted to speak, so I nodded. "Go ahead," I said.

"As soon as I arrived, her cronies surrounded me. I made myself small so that I could get away, slip through their fingers. But she was fast. I hadn't even hit the ground before I was encased in this gloppy stuff, like liquid plastic. I remember struggling . . . and feeling like I was suffocating. . . ." Her eyes filled at the memory. Her hands shook. I took one of them in my own. It felt cold, and I realized how fragile she was, despite her evilness.

"Hey, no pity," she said, pulling her hand away. She just didn't know how to be close to anyone, in any way.

"Okay. Then what?" I asked quietly.

Morgan hesitated for a moment, then closed her eyes. "And then it was done. The resin hardened into amber, and I was trapped inside."

"Like the Muffy girls you put inside the antique dolls?"

Morgan gave me a disgusted look. "Yes, like that," she said.

"Did you at least feel bad that you did that to them?"

"No," she said. Then, miserably: "Yes, but what could I do about it?"

For a moment I could only blink at her. "What could you do?" I echoed hollowly. "How about letting them out?"

"Oh, that'd be smart. As if they wouldn't start blabbing all over the place."

"You could have erased their memories. That's easy magic."

She leaned in toward me. "They were *cowen*," she said, as if that explained everything.

I looked down at my hands. "A lot of people in Whitfield felt that way too," I said.

"And stupid. Every last one of them was really, really stupid."

"So they didn't count."

"Not much."

"And the girl in Avalon? The one I almost killed?"

"She brought that on herself."

"Then, what about how you're poisoning everyone else in Avalon?"

She laughed. "I'm not poisoning them, girlfriend. *You* are."

"How can you not take responsibility for that? For any of it?"

She shrugged. "I just don't want to. So I don't. If you do, then I guess it sucks to be you."

I clenched my teeth together, willing myself not to punch her.

"You'd understand if you'd been me," she added.

"Understand what?"

"That sometimes you have to forget about being a nice guy."

"You mean being fair."

"Fair." She spat out the word as if it were a bug that had flown into her mouth. "The last thing I saw before the resin hardened around me was my father's body. The Seer was moving her hands over it, trying to take his magic. Yeah, tell me about fair."

"What do you mean, take his magic?"

"Don't you people know anything?" She reached over and touched me lightly on my arm.

"Ouch!" It felt like a hard pinch.

"Ummm." She smacked her lips. "Your telekinesis tastes like chocolate."

"You took my magic?"

"Not much of it. Just a little. Here, take some of mine." She held out her arm.

I shook my head. If I didn't watch myself, I could pick up a person's entire history just by touching them. I'd learned how to keep that from happening, but I knew that if I touched Morgan for the purpose of taking something from her psyche or her memories, I'd probably get a lot more than I'd bargained for. Morgan was a liar and a cheat, and she'd called down the Darkness in order to hurt someone who had done her no harm. I didn't want those things to become a part of me, even for a second.

"Go ahead," She said.

"*No.*"

"All right, then. I'll give you some."

"Hey, I don't want—" With a touch of her index finger, she sent a shot of something that felt like an electric hum through my arm and down my spine.

"What was that?" I shouted, angry.

She grinned. "My magic. What does it taste like?"

"It doesn't taste like anything," I said testily. "Don't do that again."

Actually, it tasted like pears, and while I still had that taste in my mouth, Morgan said, "We could go to South America."

"What?"

"I've given you some of my magic. You can Travel, the way I do. Understand? You can go anywhere you want. The two of us could tear up Rio de Janeiro. Or São Paulo. Both are very nice this time of year." She held out her hand to me, wiggling her fingers in invitation. "Come on. Let's go."

I couldn't believe her gall. "What makes you think I'd go anywhere with you?" The pear taste in my mouth was turning as bitter as vinegar. "After what you've done to me—to everyone you've ever known—"

"But you're fine," she protested.

"The girl in Avalon isn't fine! Bryce isn't fine. And Peter—" My voice broke.

"All right, all right," she said, waving me away. "If you're going to be a drama queen about it, I'll go without you." She wrapped her muffler around her neck. "I just thought it'd be fun. We could be friends."

A wave of rage and hopelessness washed over me. "I can't

believe . . ." I let it drop. *She really doesn't care*, I thought. Not about me, or any of the people she'd destroyed through me. The only person in the world who mattered to her was herself.

But then, I knew that no one believed they were evil. People always had what they thought were good reasons for doing the horrible things they did. "We're not going to be friends," I said simply.

She shrugged. "Suit yourself."

Then she put on her coat and boots and opened the door. "You know, you won't have anyone else," she said, turning back to face me.

"I know."

I watched out the window as Morgan walked out of the building's front door into the snow. At one point she looked back and probably saw me at the window, but she didn't wave, and I didn't either.

Her feet sank deeply into the snow for a while, and then vanished as she slowly faded out of sight. Morgan was a Traveler, and she was traveling on. I was the only one who would have to live with what we had done. What we'd both become.

I lifted the window a crack and tossed the amber pieces into the street. Then I sat down and rested my head in my hands as the taste of pears danced in my mouth like a memory.

CHAPTER

•

FORTY-NINE

Yule.

Another sunny day, noisy with the sounds of water dripping everywhere. The neighborhood snowmen were shrinking, melting in the warm morning. Little rivers sloshed in the gutters. Cars made zipper sounds as water sprayed from under their moving tires. Police sirens wailed in the distance. People shouted to one another on the street below.

Life had gone back to normal, at least for most people. Here, though, in this apartment, the very air was heavy with memories. It didn't matter if those memories were mine or Morgan le Fay's. They were both crushing, suffocating, toxic. I had to get out.

Throwing on my jacket, I ran outside, my legs automatically making their way back to the park. There, at least, I could breathe. There were a lot of other people there too, more than I'd expected. Surely this wasn't another snow day.

I checked my phone. There were three messages, all from Becca. I ignored them.

The date was the twenty-second. I looked at the crowds again. Were all these people celebrating Yule? Then I almost laughed out loud. It was Sunday. That was why so many people were hanging out in the park at nine in the morning.

Some of them were there for Yule, though. On a nearby hill a group of women were gathered in a circle, chanting something that the wind brought to me in snatches of sound. Then one of them turned around to face the outside of the circle, raised her arms, and spoke. The wind must have been just right then, because I could understand every word:

"HAIL TO THEE, GREAT SPIRITS OF THE EAST, YE LORDS AND WATCHTOWERS OF THE EAST, LORDS OF AIR."

I knew those words. This was a ritual of High Magic, and these women were a coven of witches. Well, cowen witches, if there is such a thing. Cowen have invented all sorts of rituals to access the magic realms. Back when I'd lived in Palm Beach, I used to read about spells and rituals, feeling vaguely guilty for even wanting to learn about witchcraft. Now that I'd spent a year around real witches, all of the hocus-pocus seemed silly to me, but it probably wasn't to the women on the hill. They were trying to find their power in a place that taught them that such power didn't exist, especially for women.

I sent them a little love-bomb, a message some of them might be open enough to receive. They'd feel the power, and think it was the ritual that gave it to them. That was the thing about magic: Thinking was never the way to achieve it.

There are two basic kinds of magic. This was High Magic, as opposed to Practical Magic, which is magic designed to get things done. In High Magic no one expects anything to happen, but the experience can lead to a kind of enlightenment. It's like meditation, only performed by a group. Covens liked High Magic because it put everyone in the right state of mind for celebrating things, like the eight major witch holidays.

That made me stop breathing for a second. Last year I'd spent Yule with my aunt and great-grandmother, exchanging gifts and creating a cone of power. There had been a stocking with my name on it hanging over the fireplace, and the aromas of roast duck and apple cobbler wafting through the house.

Suddenly I felt as if all the air had gone out of my lungs. I would never see that beautiful old house again, or Gram, or Aunt Agnes, or Peter. A fat tear plopped onto my glove.

I had to get out of there, away from the ritual. It was just too painful. I started to run as fast as I could, my arms working like pistons as my feet raced along the pavement, splashing water onto the backs of my pant legs.

That was the best I'd felt in days. I never wanted to stop. Maybe I could just do this, I thought, run until I was out of the city, away from everything I knew. Run until nothing could ever catch me again.

Just do what you can, the homeless man had said.

"What . . . if you can't . . . do anything?" I huffed, still running at full tilt. "What . . . if . . ."

Just do

"No!"

what

"Stop!"

you can—

"Shut up!" I screamed, just as I ran full force into some-one's shoulder.

"Watch where you're going!" a girl screamed at me, so loudly that passersby stopped to stare.

I gasped, waiting for her to slump to the ground after com-ing into contact with me.

"What's wrong with you? Idiot!" She reeled around, rear-ranging a bunch of shopping bags hanging from her arms. But at least she didn't keel over dead. She didn't even throw up.

Relieved, I finally managed to close my mouth. My lungs filled with air for what seemed like the first time in an hour. "Excuse me," I said breathlessly. "I was just . . . " Then I looked up and saw her face. "Suzy?" I asked. "Suzy Dusset?"

"Who— Oh. You're from school," Suzy said, as if she were passing on information to me.

Great. It would be my luck to run into one of the meanest girls in school. But hey, at least I hadn't poisoned her. Might as well look on the bright side.

"Let's go," she said to her companion, whom I also saw for the first time. It was Summer Hayworth.

I stepped aside to let them pass, but Summer came up to me and, inexplicably, threw her arms around my neck.

"Stop!" I screamed, so loudly that she jumped backward. But it was too late. She'd touched me, cheek to cheek, skin on skin.

Summer blinked in surprise. "Okay," she said, holding her hands up in front of her. "I didn't mean to freak you out or anything."

I just stood there with my mouth hanging open for a while. "Er . . ." *Why wasn't she sick?* "Er . . ."

Because she's cowen, I remembered.

I couldn't hurt them.

Maybe living among cowen wouldn't be so bad, I thought. I could disappear here. I could pass.

The way I did back in Florida. Lying, hiding, pretending to be like everyone else. Trying to be someone besides myself.

"Are you all right?" Summer asked.

"Whatever," Suzy muttered, rustling her bags. "I'm the one she ran into."

"I'm . . . I'm fine," I managed to say.

"I dreamed about you," Summer said with a smile I'd never seen before. It looked genuine. Her face actually looked kind. "It was weird. I was trapped inside this giant doll, and I didn't think I'd ever get out, but then you recognized me through my eyes."

Suzy made snoring sounds.

"And then you came in and talked to me. You told me everything was going to be all right." She smiled again. "And it was."

"Positively riveting," Suzy said. "Can we go now? My arms are getting tired."

"And then Miss P came and gave me a message to give you."

"Me?" I asked, surprised.

"Miss N, you mean," Suzy said. "For 'Nerd.'"

"Shut up, Suzy," Summer said. "Yeah. She told me that I would never know what you'd done for me."

I looked around. "Er . . . Was that the message?"

"No. The message didn't really make sense."

"Too bad," Suzy said, yanking Summer's arm. "Maybe you can write her a letter."

Summer staggered a few steps toward Suzy. "She said 'Just do what you can.'"

I coughed. *"What?"*

"I know, dumb. But it was a dream. What can I say?" She laughed as Suzy dragged her away. "Hey, let's have lunch together once school starts again, okay?"

"Uh, sure," I said, although I knew I wouldn't be going back to school after break. Or ever again. Because even if half the population was immune to me, sooner or later someone was going to show up dead. And no one would know why except me.

No, my school days were done. Actually, my whole life was pretty much done, I guessed. What could I do?

Just do what you can.

Exactly the words the homeless man had used.

Were they supposed to be some kind of special message for me? What did they mean, anyway, "Do what you can"? Of course I would. Didn't everybody just *do what they could* all the time? And what about Summer's so-called dream, which actually really happened? Miss P was supposed to make them all forget everything, not pop into their subconscious minds to deliver homey messages of encouragement. *Do what you can.* Yeah, I'll keep that in mind while I'm living in the Alaskan tundra, Miss P. I kicked a can of Red Bull down the street, surprised to see that I'd walked back to the street where my father lived. I was less than a block away from his apartment building.

• • •

There was something about my great-grandmother's Cadillac that caused my heart to fall into my stomach. "Oh, no," I whispered as I crept closer.

There was someone inside.

I could see him only in silhouette at that distance, but it was pretty clear what he was doing. I ran toward him, not knowing what I was going to do with a car thief once I caught him. "Hey!" I shouted. "That's my car."

He heard me and turned toward me. It all seemed to happen very slowly, maybe because I was very scared, and maybe because I couldn't believe my eyes. But it was true.

It was Peter.

I gasped so hard that my lungs hurt with the inrush of cold air. A car behind me honked and swerved around me while I stood in the street, shaking and shocked.

"Katy," Peter said.

"Don't open the window!"

I could see the tension in his face. He wanted to touch me, but he knew I was right. "Gram sent me to get her car." He held up the extra set of keys.

I nodded.

"Eric . . . ," he said.

"Yes," I said. I knew Eric could bring him back. My heart was racing with joy. "Yes."

"And Hattie apologizes. I don't know exactly what for."

I couldn't talk, so I waved the words away, trying hard not to cry.

"And . . ." His eyes were pained. "I love you."

I covered my face with my hands.

"I'm going to fix this, Katy. "

A low moan escaped from my lips. I knew he would try. Peter would do everything he could for as long as he could, I knew, but he didn't have enough magic to overturn this. Avalon and everyone in it would die, and most of them would never even know why. I was poison, and would be poison forever. Some things, once started, just couldn't be stopped.

"I will. I promise." He pressed his hand against the window, his long fingers splayed. "Tell me you believe me."

I matched his handprint with my own. The glass between us grew warm.

"Tell me."

"I believe you," I croaked.

"And you're going to come home. To me."

I felt my heart breaking.

"Tell me!"

"I'll come home to you."

His jaw clenched, and I knew he was trying to hold things together for both of us.For a long time we just stood there, our hands touching opposite sides of the glass, looking into each other's eyes.

"Whatever happens, I'll always love you," I said quietly.

Peter swallowed. Then he started the car. "Remember your promise," he said before driving into the road.

I watched him until the car was out of sight. Then I looked at my hands. My fingers were still spread, remembering.

CHAPTER

•

FIFTY

He's alive!

Whatever else happened—and it would be very bad, I knew—at least Peter had been spared. Eric had brought him back from the death I had inflicted on him, and he would now have the life he was meant to live.

As long as I stayed away from him.

I could do that. I would. I just wished I'd been bright enough when he was there to ask him for something—anything, a handkerchief, a glove—just something of his I could hold.

I closed my eyes and remembered the smell of him, clean and healthy and full of love for me. I would never forget that, or the milky sweetness of the skin on his neck, or the electric velvet feel of his mouth touching mine. I knew just how his hand fit with my own, and how our bodies brushed together when we walked to class or worked side by side in the restaurant.

I never thought it would all end so soon.

Why had I walked away from him back at the Shaw mansion when he'd told me about his project? All I'd thought of at the time was that I wouldn't be able to see him as much as I wanted to. And I'd stomped away like a spoiled child. If I had that moment to live over again, I'd have told him to do whatever he needed to do, because knowing he was happy was more important than getting my own way. I wouldn't have ruined our time together. Our brief time.

I spent the rest of the day—all of it, I guess—looking out the window of my dad's apartment, watching the sun crest and then fall. The people on the street below were like insects in an ant farm, moving back and forth, performing what seemed to be meaningless tasks, going about the business of living while I looked on, disinterested, apart.

We are one. The homeless man's hands had looked cold when he'd held out the bottle of wine to me.

Bread and wine. In his way he had offered me Communion. But that hadn't happened, and not just because he'd been disgusting. It went deeper than that. We couldn't be one, whatever he'd meant by that, because I could never be a part of his world, or my own, either. That is, the world that used to be mine. I would never hold Peter in my arms again, or feel his lips against mine. We would never jump handfasted over the bonfire at Beltane, or lie together as lovers, or grow old with each other. He would be doing all those things with someone else.

And in the deepest part of my heart, I was glad. I wanted him to be happy, to have a life worth living, even if it was without me.

As the last of the sun sank in a wave of red that spread over the snow-topped buildings, my cell phone rang. It was Becca again. I guessed it wouldn't hurt to answer.

"Why didn't you tell me where you went?" she demanded immediately.

I sighed. I didn't even know where to start. "Who did tell you?" I asked.

"Bryce."

The phone felt frozen in my hand. "Bryce came back?"

"It wasn't easy. They put him in a *dungeon*, Katy. Like with *shackles* on his wrists. Do you believe that?"

"I do. They're horrible. But didn't they know he's a shape-shifter?"

"They didn't think he'd try to escape. And get this. He wasn't going to. Bryce said he was guilty and ought to be punished." She clucked. "Honestly, he needs looking after. But then they went too far. They brought him outside, and that so-called Seer told him to turn into a fly. He knew what they were going to do."

"Trap him in amber," I said.

"So Bryce stopped being the good boy, for once. He told them to take their guilt and shove it, and he turned into *smoke*." Becca laughed. "He appeared on top of the fireplace at my house. Unfortunately, that means my mom knows everything."

"Too bad," I said. Whenever Livia Fowler was involved, things had the potential to get complicated. "But thanks for telling me about Bryce. I'm glad he's okay."

"But he's not okay," Becca said. "He went back to Avalon."

"What? Why'd he do that?"

"It's for Peter's big stupid project."

I felt a shiver of alarm. "What project?"

"You don't know? He's been working on it for months."

"I don't know what you're talking about."

Becca sighed. "Well, from what Bryce told me, it's some kind of virtual video game system using touch-screen technology. You're supposed to be able to walk into the game itself—there are multiple screens involved—and you don't need special glasses. At least that's how it started out. After the dance he began to modify it so that instead of going into a game, the players or whoever go to Avalon."

I gasped. "To save the people there," I whispered. While I'd been hiding out feeling sorry for myself, Peter had actually been doing something to help those poor people whose world I'd poisoned.

"Whatever. Peter's calling them Travelers, like Bryce. Of course, they're nothing like him—if they were, they'd be able to come here on their own—"

"What?" I interrupted.

"He wants them to travel here, to Whitfield. He used some painting or something, and Hattie and a few other big-time witches are laying magic on top of Peter's electronics."

"Do you think it's going to work?"

"I think the guy I love is going to be killed!" Becca screeched. "All for some place that doesn't even exist on the same plane as us!"

"But it still exists," I tried to explain. "Those people—the Travelers—are real. And the trouble they're in is real." I knew that was the truth. I'd caused the trouble.

"Okay. Saving them's a noble thing. Everybody wants to help. The thing is, though, nobody seems to remember Eric's prediction about how Peter was going to destroy Whitfield, along with a great witch who was going to help him."

A shiver ran through me. I did remember. I was the witch in that prophecy.

But Becca barreled on. "Well, who's a greater witch than Hattie Scott? Don't you see, it's all going to be a terrible disaster. And Bryce is going to be right in the middle of it."

What did she say? *Hattie? Hattie* was the witch who was going to help Peter?

"You've got to stop him," Becca said. "It's the only way."

My head was still spinning. "Stop who?" I asked numbly.

"*Peter*, Katy," she said irritably. "Pay attention. You've got to stop Peter."

"Be-because of the prophecy?" Suddenly I could see what Hattie's point had been when she'd said it was all ridiculous. Eric might have been the greatest healer that Whitfield had ever produced, but he was still a brain-damaged kid who barely knew his own name. No one in his right mind was going to take anything Eric said seriously.

Becca made a conciliatory noise. "Okay. Actually, it's my mother who's saying we shouldn't be bringing all those people into Whitfield. But a lot of people are agreeing with her. Personally, I don't care. I just want to get Bryce out of danger. He's all alone over there, trying to get most of the population of Avalon to come to Whitfield while a bunch of demonic witches in Avalon are using all their magic to stop him. The only way he'll come back is if Peter shuts the whole thing down. You can make him do that, Katy. Just tell him to stop."

It was hard to take in everything she was saying. All I was getting was that Peter and Bryce were trying to rescue the people of Avalon, and people on both sides of the border were trying to stop them.

"Becca, what—" There was a commotion at the front door to my dad's apartment.

"Hello?" Becca said, but I was concentrating on the door, which was swinging open. I looked around to see if there was anything I could use for a weapon. I didn't think it was likely that burglars would be witches, so my poison, deadly as it was, wouldn't affect them.

"Hey, are you there?" Becca's voice floated tinnily through the phone.

Then my dad and Mim walked in, carrying about a dozen suitcases and packages apiece.

"Katy?" Becca said.

I'd forgotten about Becca. "I've got to go," I said, and hung up.

"Don't tell me we forgot to turn off the lights when we— Oh, hello, Katherine," my dad said. "What are you doing here?"

I froze. *Oh, God*, I thought. *What if I kill my father?* I mean, the encounter with Summer and Suzy might have been a fluke. They'd been involved with magic, whether they knew it or not, but . . . I backed up slowly. "I . . . That is, I've got . . . I mean . . ."

"Kathy!" Ignoring anything I said, as usual—although I have to admit, I wasn't saying much—Mim swept past Dad in a cloud of exotic perfume. "Give us a kiss, darling."

I flattened against the wall. "No!" I exclaimed, my voice cracking. "Er, that is, you can't . . . er . . ."

"How many times have I told you not to say 'er,'" Mim said, grabbing my shoulders and planting two lipstick-reddened kisses on my cheeks.

I choked noisily.

"What? Oh, for Christ's sake, say what you mean. And why are you staring at me like that?"

"Are . . . Are you all right?" I asked in a squeak.

"Of course I'm all right. What's wrong with you?" Her eyes narrowed. "You're not pregnant, are you?"

"Madison," my father chided.

"Well, it wouldn't surprise me."

I heard myself breathing again. Mim was as good as ever. Well, she was alive, anyway. She'd touched me, and she was still standing. Apparently the no-cowen rule was still in effect.

"I'm not pregnant," I whispered.

"Excellent," Dad said, setting down his parcels.

"Oh, Dad," I said, feeling my facial muscles smiling for the first time in what seemed like years. I ran into his arms.

He seemed surprised. And glad. "That's my angel," he cooed. "Are *you* all right, hormonal changes notwithstanding?"

"I'm fine," I said. "I'm glad to see you."

"Didn't I tell you I was going to India?" he asked, dumping a box filled with Mim's cosmetics onto the dining room table.

"*We,*" Mim corrected. "*We* went to India." She batted her eyelashes at him. "And we lived in an ashram where a lot of movie stars go."

"I didn't see any movie stars," Dad said.

"It's the off-season. And we chanted. And became vegetarians."

"God, I need a steak," Dad said. "Tonight." He turned toward me. "Will you join us?"

I almost said yes. I was hungry. The two bites of bagel I'd eaten in the park yesterday morning had been used up long ago. But then I remembered the message. The homeless guy's message. Miss P's.

Just do what you can. That meant doing something, even if I wasn't sure what that was. It meant being where I belonged, even if no one wanted me. It meant finding a way, no matter what.

"I can't," I began, "because—"

"What a pity," Mim said, too quickly. "I suppose it'll just have to be a little romantic tête-à-tête with just the two of us." She blew Dad a kiss. "Communal living can be such a bore," she added as an aside to me. "No privacy *at all.*"

I took a deep breath. *Might as well get this part over with,* I thought. "I have to get back to Whitfield," I said in a rush. "Can you take me?"

Dad looked at Mim, who was shaking her head resolutely while stabbing at her iPhone.

"Er . . . we can discuss it later," Dad said, waffling. That was a normal reaction for him. Whenever there was any sort of disagreement, he waited for whoever won, and then did what that person wanted. Naturally, the winner was almost always Mim, but I had to at least give it a try.

"Please, Dad," I begged. "It's important."

"Aha." Mim looked up from her phone, beaming. "There's a flight out of Teterboro in forty minutes. I'll call you a cab."

"Problem solved, I guess," Dad said. "It'll be faster than driving."

And you'll get your steak.

For a moment—just the quickest, flickering moment—I wondered if my father would love me if Mim weren't around. But that wasn't worth thinking about right now. Getting back to Whitfield was the only thing that mattered.

Getting back, and finding a way to help.

CHAPTER

·

FIFTY-ONE

The six-seater prop plane I was on landed at Lynne-Graham airport, about ten miles outside of Whitfield. At first I was worried about finding a cabdriver who would be immune to me, but then I remembered that it was the winter solstice, one of the eight Wiccan holidays. Our people didn't work on holidays unless we absolutely had to, but just to make sure, I asked the driver of the only taxi at the airport if he'd been in the Meadow that day. If he said yes, I'd know he was a witch, and that I'd be SOL as far as transportation was concerned.

Fortunately, he answered, "Huh?" So he was safe from me. "Never mind," I said.

The cab took me straight to the Shaw mansion, where a number of witches I knew were gathered outside. I could tell from the looks on their faces that they weren't happy. As I'd expected, Becca's mother, Livia Fowler, was in the thick of them. She appeared to be their ringleader, standing on top of a low stone wall bordering the front entrance so that she stood above the crowd.

"There have been twenty-seven families in Whitfield for the past three hundred and fifty years!" she boomed. She was talking about the twenty-seven magical families who had come over from England on the same boat in the 1600s. Some Whitfield residents believed that the number should always be kept at twenty-seven because twenty-seven is a magical number, a multiple of nine, which is the number of completion. It all seemed a little silly to me, but apparently it meant a lot to Mrs. Fowler.

"Twenty-seven! No more!"

"No more!" shouted someone in the crowd. One man shook his fist.

"And now some brainless teenagers"—she pronounced the word "teenagers" as if she were talking about ax murderers—"have taken it upon themselves to bring the *entire population* of a distant community into our midst. Now, these may be fine people, but we don't know that. We don't know what they are, or what they want to do to us."

"Where's Jeremiah Shaw?" someone called out.

"Where indeed?" Mrs. Fowler pointed to the mansion. "The ringleader of the gang of hooligans at the center of this is himself a Shaw, and one of precious little magic. This is no doubt just another scheme to add more gold to the Shaw family's already overflowing coffers."

"At our expense!" a woman near me called out.

So far I'd gone unnoticed in my hooded jacket and muffler. Fortunately, my layers of clothing insulated the poison I carried. But the closer I got to the big stone staircase leading to the mansion's front door, the more conspicuous I became. It couldn't be helped. I had to get inside.

"Well, look who's here," Mrs. Fowler said, crossing her arms as I neared her podium. "The criminal's little girlfriend." She raised her chin to snarl at me. "Come to cheer the traitor on? Or just go to jail with him?"

This last was just rhetoric, I knew, because no witch from Whitfield would ever call the police for something that involved magic. It was our first rule—*keep silent*. But Mrs. Fowler and her small crowd of followers could make life difficult. They already had. At least she didn't know about the poison inside me. If she had, those people might have panicked.

Still, Livia Fowler didn't look as if she was going to let me pass. She grabbed the sleeve of my coat—she didn't know how dangerous that was—and then let go with a shriek, clutching her heart. "What . . ." She narrowed her eyes at me. "You did this," she rasped.

I shrank back, but people were already approaching me. *Please leave me alone*, I thought. I didn't want to hurt them. No matter what they thought of me or my friends, they didn't deserve to die.

"Stop her!" Mrs. Fowler said, fanning herself.

"Better not," I said, holding up my hands. A blue-white light emanated from them.

Mrs. Fowler reached out for me, then thought better of it. The others backed away too, parting to form a path for me. But as I got to the massive front door, someone threw a stick at me from behind. Fortunately, I was wearing so many heavy garments that it didn't really hurt. Still, I was very eager to get inside.

I pounded on the door, but no one came. Well, I reasoned, if I'd been inside, I wouldn't have let me in either. Then something hit me hard on the shoulder, and I saw a rock glance off me and land at my feet. At first I couldn't believe it. Would they actually *stone* me out there in the open?

Another rock struck me in the middle of my back. That one hurt. Then someone hurled a handful of small stones that broke the glass of the door, and I knew I had to get out of there.

It was just like being back in Avalon, with witches pelting me with rocks. In fact, I thought as I looked for an avenue of escape, there was a lot about Whitfield that was like Avalon: a lot of judgment and punishment and fighting for power, and rules made so long ago that they no longer had any meaning. And this crazy prejudice against outsiders, as if "we" were somehow always better than "them," no matter what.

Were my own people so weak? But I already knew the answer. They were. We all were. It was too easy for human beings to turn into monsters. Look at me. I hadn't done anything except pick the wrong friend, and I'd become a walking bomb. And Morgan, who'd only wanted her dad to love her. And Mrs. Fowler, who was just scared. And even the Seer of Avalon, who had sold out her people for a stab at immortality.

So easy.

I tried to shake off those feelings. Even if they were true, they weren't going to help me do what I'd come to do. For that I had to get inside the house, and that meant I had to get away from Livia Fowler and her rock-throwing cronies.

First I leaped out of the way of the next projectile, onto the low wall that was on either side of the stairway. This, I discovered to my dismay, made me more of a target than ever. As a tree branch whizzed over my head, I looked down. The wall may have been low from the front, but behind it was a drop of nearly ten feet. For a moment I hesitated, trying to decide which would be easier to run with, a broken leg or a broken head. Then another rock hit me hard in my back, and I jumped.

As it turned out I didn't break either my leg or my head, but the crowd wasn't about to give up. I took off in a sprint, taking care to keep between the house and the boxwood hedge that surrounded it. My plan, such as it was, was to get to the rear of the mansion, out of sight of the protesters, and then run for the woods on the far side of the lawn, where maybe I'd be able to call someone inside on my cell phone. It wasn't much of a plan, I admit, but it was *something*, at least some kind of effort.

Just do what you can. Right then I didn't know what the best thing to do was. Would it be best to talk Peter out of the whole project? Or help Bryce lead those doomed people out of Avalon? Or would I be of more help casting spells with Gram and the other witches? I only hoped I'd be able to figure out what I was meant to do before it was too late to do anything. As I ran through the knee-high snow with the ugly sounds of the crowd receding behind me, I was becoming aware of a feeling I hadn't experienced in a very long time. It was the feeling—the *knowledge*—that, however I might have screwed up in the past, I had something to offer now. And I had to get into the house.

"Katy!" someone whispered. I looked up. Becca was peering out from behind a narrow door at the back of the house. "I saw what happened out front," she said, waving me inside. "I can hide you. Hurry."

"Just get me a blanket," I said, running up the back steps.

They led to the laundry room, where Becca held out a comforter thick enough to protect her—and whoever else was in the house—from me.

"It was in the dryer," she said. "So I guess it's clean."

"I don't care." I snatched it out of her hands and covered myself with it.

"Notice I didn't ask you what you wanted the blanket for."

"Good," I said.

"Because I know," she said quietly. "Everyone knows."

I looked at the floor. "Are you saying I'm not welcome?"

"You are to me," she said. That meant a lot. "And to Peter."

I swallowed. I wished she hadn't said that. This was no time to get emotional. "I just want to help," I said, trying to act casual as I nodded toward the interior of the house. "So what's going on?"

She sighed. "You're too late," she said. "It's already started."

Well, that's one option I don't have to think about anymore, I reasoned. "Okay. There are still some things—"

"You were supposed to stop Peter!" she screeched, planting her hands on her hips. "I mean, I asked you, *begged* you, but you hung up on me."

"I'm sorry," I said, remembering that I'd been on the phone with Becca when my dad and Mim had come home. "I got here as fast as I could."

She blew air out between her lips. "Well, Bryce is already in Avalon."

"And Peter?"

"Peter's at the controls in the lab here while Bryce is on the other side, trying to get the Travelers through. Only there are a lot of witches over there trying to stop them."

"Are the Travelers fighting back?"

"What with? Those guys don't even have pitchforks, let alone weapons. All they've been able to do so far is put up a kind of wall made out of whatever they could get their hands on. But they won't be able to hold out long. Those shape-shifters are going to kill Bryce the second they get the chance. They'll kill them all. And then they'll come here and kill us, too."

And then I knew. I understood the message. There was something I could do, after all. Something I could do that no one else could.

"Maybe not," I said.

"Look, even if you get Peter to shut it down, I don't think Bryce is going to leave without the Travelers at this point."

I didn't have time to talk, but she needn't have worried about that. I knew that Peter wouldn't shut it down for me or anyone else. "Which way is the lab?" I asked.

Becca pointed. "Through the kitchen and down the long hall. Hey, what are you going to do?"

"Whatever I can," I said.

The lab was full of people, including Hattie, Miss P, and Gram, who were pressed together in a circle, deep in concentration. I think Peter was the first to notice me, although I don't know how he did, since I was behind him. But at the moment I walked in, before the room quieted and people started to flee in panic, Peter turned away from the console where he was sitting and looked right into my eyes.

Then the fear in the room took root.

"Who is that?"

"What's she doing here?"

"Get her away!"

"Clear out! It's the poison girl!"

The crowded room suddenly split into two groups with a wide space in the center with only me in it. Me, and the console where Peter sat before a huge screen at the front of the room. On the screen three vultures were flying from a familiar outcropping of rock toward a ragged group of people huddled behind a makeshift barrier.

"Katy!" I heard Gram call out, but I was already running.

"Let me through," I said. Peter closed his eyes in anguish. He knew. He knew me, and he knew what had to happen if the Travelers were going to be saved. "Now!" I shouted.

Peter nodded once. *Good-bye, my love*, I thought as I leaped through the screen into Avalon.

CHAPTER

•

FIFTY-TWO

"Katy?" Bryce was so surprised that he almost touched me.

"Keep the Travelers away from me," I said as I moved past the barrier Bryce had built to protect the Avalonians from the Seer's witches. The blanket was still wrapped tightly around me. "I'll try to cover you."

Once I was in the open, I took off the blanket and my winter coat. The vultures recognized me immediately. For a moment they seemed to hesitate in midflight, shimmering between the glamour that made them appear as birds and their true human forms. I knew they were afraid of me. One of them even tried to turn back, but was attacked by the others until it wheeled around and hurtled forward toward me, shrieking, its talons out, the shadow of its black wings spreading over me.

I knew I had to kill it, but when the actual moment came to strike, I think I would have preferred almost anything else. As the vulture speeded toward me, I had a very strong impulse to run back behind the barrier and hide with my hands over my head. But then, I knew, I'd really be of no use to anyone.

I gathered all the strength of the terrible power in my hands and shot it out at the vulture. It fell to earth, not a bird at all but an old woman who seemed to grow older with every second until, by the time she might have struck the ground, there was nothing left of her but dust.

Behind me the Travelers cheered. "Go, Katy!" Bryce shouted, pumping his fist in the air. But I didn't feel like it had been any kind of victory. I kept seeing the old woman's face as she fell, her rags flapping around her like broken wings.

"Look out!" Bryce shouted, pointing at the sky behind me. I whirled around before I could think anymore about the vulture—the person—I'd just killed. Because that was what I was there for. To kill. I'd known it when I'd come. It was what I was good for, maybe the only thing I was good for anymore.

So I choked down the bile in my throat and shot the poison out of my hands. It lit up the sky like a forest fire. Four of the witches fell, disintegrating before they hit the ground. But two others managed to escape by changing themselves into snakes that shot through the crowd of Travelers like lightning bolts, attacking the line of people waiting to come through the narrow portal that Peter had created.

The Travelers screamed and scattered while Bryce tried vainly to round them up as the snakes slithered from one person to another, biting indiscriminately.

"Help us," someone wailed. I couldn't use my poison this close to the crowd. I knew I'd kill them all. All I could do was find the snakes.

I lumbered behind the barrier. A few people fled from me in terror. Some had already tried to run away, back to the caves and huts where they had lived all their lives. They now lay dead in the field. The others were too panicked by the snakes in their midst to notice them, or me. Trying not to get too close to anyone, I walked toward where the two snakes were slithering among the Travelers. One of them hissed malevolently as I approached.

"What are you going to do, poison me?" I asked softly as I grabbed the snakes in my two hands. They squirmed wildly before the inevitable happened, and they disintegrated.

I shuddered, wishing I could have removed my hands from my body, from my memory.

But I had come to kill. I tried to remember that as the snakes became rats and swarmed toward the barrier. One of them bit me hard on my leg before it fell down dead. I gasped at the pain, but I couldn't stop to look at the wound. More were coming, and behind them, birds.

A wall of birds.

"Hurry, Bryce," I called, my voice shaking.

The sky was black with them. I'd had no idea there were so many of the Seer's followers. They'd come out in force, though, to stop the exodus of the Travelers. And me.

I shot out my hands at them, but there were too many of them, and I couldn't take them all from a distance. As poisonous as I was, I just didn't have that much power anymore. Even when they got closer, it was taking a lot longer for them to die. I was getting tired, and my poison was being spent. *Oh, man*, I thought. What a time to run out of juice.

Meanwhile, the people behind me screamed in panic as they tumbled through the narrow portal, looking over their shoulders at the snakes, rats, and vultures that were bearing down on them. But they weren't the target now. I was the one the Seer's followers were after. In a suicidal frenzy they swarmed around me, biting and scratching my legs until my knees buckled and I found myself on the ground in the middle of a moving sea of repulsive creatures bent on destroying me.

I struggled against them, but I was exhausted. There was nothing more I could do. A rat tangled in my hair, chattering. I gagged in revulsion but was too weak even to stand. I had no power left in my hands. The stone in my ring was the flat gray of limestone.

With the last of my strength I pulled myself upright and picked up two of the rats. They bit my fingers until my blood washed over them and dripped onto the ground. When they fell out of my hands, they changed back into human witches, still clawing at me with their gray fingernails. Their mouths opened into weird, perverted smiles, their rank breath spewing through brown stubs of rotten teeth, their eyes glinting with malice and victory.

They pulled me up by my hair until I dangled with my feet off the ground. "Bryce," I panted. I don't know if he heard me. "Hurry. Please." But I knew in my heart that nothing he could do would help me now. I only wished I could have won this battle. I might have felt that my life had been worth something after all.

But even this, I thought, *even this pain, this failure, was worthwhile.* Because I'd tried. I'd done my best, and I would keep trying until the very end, and that meant I was something more than poison. I was a human being—flawed, maybe, wrong, but still a person whose life had been worth living.

"Forgive me," I whispered, knowing that I was worthy of

forgiveness. That we all were, no matter what we'd done, and why.

I blinked away my tears. I wasn't the only one who needed forgiveness. We all had something of the Darkness in us. We all just did what we could.

"I forgive you, Dad," I said. Immediately I felt as if a weight of a thousand pounds had lifted off my chest. "And Mim," I went on. "And Mrs. Fowler." I took a deep breath. "And Morgan, too," I managed. "I forgive you all." My words flew into the wind like the fragrance of flowers. They left my heart clean and full of peace, and I knew at last that I was free.

Suddenly there was a brilliant light that bleached out everything in sight. A gasp of wonder went up from the crowd of Travelers, and I felt the witches' fingernails scrape against my skin as they released me. Wobbling, I stood on my own feet again, shielding my eyes from the light.

Eventually I could see a shape in the center of the blinding light. At first the shape was amorphous and nearly blue, like the cobalt heart of a flame, but as the light began to ebb, it grew more distinct, revealing a human figure.

My heart was pounding. What new horror had the Seer sent? It was a woman. I could see that much. An alien, then? Or a hologram? Or had one of the Avalon witches shape-shifted into something like a burning sun come to kill us all with its heat?

"I should have known you'd screw up without me," the figure inside the light said conversationally.

"What?" I squinted at the bright halo.

"You're supposed to be the hero here," she went on, stepping out of the nimbus of light.

"Morgan," I whispered.

"Who else? You summoned me, didn't you?"

"Summoned?"

"Okay, you *thought* of me. That counts." She pulled a wand out of her sleeve and shot it at a pile of sniffing rats. They dissolved into jelly. "Good thing too. Somebody had to bail out your sorry butt."

Clumsily I lumbered toward her. "Morgan," I began, looking warily at the Travelers, who recognized her and were tripping over one another in a frantic attempt to reach the portal. "Please don't hurt them. They haven't—"

"Oh, shut up," she snapped. "I won't touch your precious people."

"They're *your* people," I said.

"Stop talking and touch my wand."

I wasn't sure what she was planning, but a new wave of vultures was heading toward us, so I did as she said. The moment my hand came in contact with the tip of Morgan's wand, I felt a powerful surge like nothing I'd ever felt before. The shock of it was so strong that it nearly knocked me backward. Instantly the ring on my finger glowed a brilliant blue that shot out across the sky in Klieg-like rays, and the vultures fell.

"Go now!" I shouted to Bryce.

"Almost done," he called back. "But you have to come, too. Once the portal's closed—"

"Just *go*!" I screamed.

Then I couldn't hear him any longer.

The sky, so bright now that involuntary tears streamed out of my eyes, reeked of burning flesh. "I think they're gone," I said, mostly to myself, but Morgan answered me.

"Good," she said, breaking the contact with me. For a second I could see the space between us. "Because the next wave is coming, and it's going to be rough."

She nodded toward the grove of trees from where the Seer and her followers had come. Something that looked like a thick snake was winding out of it now, twisting like a long rope toward us.

"Listen," Morgan said. The snake was talking.

"I call thee to my aid, O mighty one, thou who is greater than all things. . . ."

The sound dissipated as the wind changed. I looked at Morgan, frowning in bewilderment. "What is that?"

"The Seer," she said. "She's calling the Darkness."

That was when the snake began to hiss, and then to grow, squirming upright like a giant cobra.

"The . . . the Seer?" I asked numbly.

"Old friendships die hard," she said with a mocking smile.

The snake rose up over us, looming so large that it blotted out the sun.

"But you're not still her . . . friend," I said uncertainly.

"I made a deal with her, remember?"

I looked down at the ring whose poison was destroying this whole magical universe. "You aren't that person anymore," I said softly.

Morgan shrugged. "Does it matter?" She looked over at me. "I think she's come to tell me that a deal's a deal."

The snake crept closer, and I saw that it had transformed into a twister, a hundred feet high, picking up everything in its path as it grew darker and denser. And it was coming at us with the speed of a locomotive.

"Oh, Gram," I squeaked. I could feel myself shaking.

"Stop thinking about yourself," Morgan said. I thought it was an odd thing to say, especially since I was only thinking of myself in terms of my imminent death, but it brought me to my senses. She was right—it wasn't about me, and it hadn't been ever since I'd had to leave Whitfield. As far as the future went, I had none. I'd known that when I'd gotten to Avalon. Either I would leave every last bit of myself out on this field or everything I'd been through would have been for nothing.

"Okay," I said. "I'm ready." Morgan turned to look straight at me. "What?" I asked, hoping she wasn't going to show me another monster on the horizon.

"I just want to tell you . . ." She hesitated.

Can this wait? I thought. I looked at the snake slithering at incredible speed across the field. "What *is* it, Morgan?" I nearly shouted.

". . . that I'm sorry," she finished. "About everything. I wish I hadn't brought you into this."

I swallowed. Could she have waited? And I answered myself. *No, she couldn't.* Because she wasn't expecting us to live through what was ahead either. Whatever had to be said, whatever had to be mended, it had to be done now.

"Forget that," I said, reaching over to squeeze her hand.

Suddenly it was as if the sky exploded around me. Debris flew everywhere as the wind increased to hurricane proportions and the perennial sunny spring of Avalon was engulfed in pitch blackness. In the distance I heard Bryce's voice call my name, but it was too late to talk. Too late for everything, really. The Travelers were all safely away. There was nothing to do anymore but take whatever the Darkness had to give.

Just do what you can, I told myself as Morgan and I stepped hand in hand into the heart of the Darkness. I screamed, not out of fear but to let the Darkness know that the two of us were there, in its belly, and that these two women would not go meekly to their deaths.

I felt my hair standing on end as I reached out my free hand. Through even this primeval blackness my ring glowed, a dot of light in the dark depths of space that had descended on us.

Morgan's grip on me loosened. I looked over to see her vanishing into the blackness. "No!" I shouted as I realized that she was leaving. "No!"

But in an instant she was gone.

Well, that's just fricking great, I thought, furious. But then, what had I expected? Morgan and the Seer had made a pact with the Darkness a long time ago. She'd told me herself: A deal's a deal. Had I really thought she'd help me do anything except die?

A strangled sound shrilled out of my throat. Forgiveness, my tuchus. I wished I had her throat between my hands.

"Oh, hell," I said out loud, allowing myself to breathe again. What did it even matter, really? Dying alone or holding hands, it was still dying. The Travelers were safe. I'd done my job. It was time for the poison girl to move on.

I thought of Peter. He would miss me. I'd been faced with death before, but Peter had been with me then. It was better this way, because I knew he'd at least have a chance to be safe.

But he would miss me. My thoughts raced back to when I'd last seen him in New York. When we'd held our hands to opposite sides of Gram's car window, all I'd been able to feel was the glass, but through it I could imagine his skin, his soft lips, his beating heart. I would never know these things again, even if I lived. And so it didn't matter to me that I wouldn't live. Only that I would never touch him again.

As the Native Americans used to say, it was a good day to die.

But Peter would miss me.

Then the speed of the black whirlwind around me picked up with a wild sound like bagpipes from hell. In the center of it the face of the Seer seemed to emerge, ancient and mad, its rotting teeth sharpened to daggerlike points, its mouth open wide.

Just do what you can, I reminded myself, willing my hands to stop shaking. Dying wouldn't be so hard if it weren't for the fear that came with it. "I love you, Peter," I whispered. I knew he couldn't hear me, but I hoped that maybe he would feel it anyway.

That centered me a little, although the Darkness was pressing upon me like a huge weight. The wind was so forceful that I could barely breathe. In another moment, I knew, the whirlwind would pick me up and tear me to pieces.

Just then I saw my ring glowing brighter, brighter than I'd ever seen it, until, in what had to be a trick of the light, it seemed to lift off my finger.

It formed a still ball of light in the whirling Darkness. I gasped with what I thought must be my last breath as the floating ball of light elongated into the form of a woman, shimmering like a goddess in the dark vacuum where I stood.

I watched, astonished, as Morgan's face appeared in the glow, as if she had become the ring itself. Before my eyes she had transformed into something eternal and beautiful, and powerful beyond imagining.

"Thank you for being my friend," the ethereal being breathed into my ear before she leaped into the Darkness like a diver slicing through water.

She whirled inside the cone of the Darkness, a blur of gold. It was her life force I was watching, everything about Morgan that the Darkness had not taken from her. She thought she had traded her soul for power, but a soul can never really be lost. Now she had found it again, and she had used it to save me.

The light that was Morgan exploded into a million fragments. I heard the Seer scream as the Darkness slowly vanished into fog, consumed by the power of Morgan le Fay's beautiful, blessed soul.

CHAPTER

•

FIFTY-THREE

The sky cleared. The ring, now a flat, spent stone, still sat on my finger. Some things really were forever, and evil was one of them. Somewhere, I knew, the Darkness still existed. It always would. Goodness—or love, or whatever was the Darkness's opposite—was different. It came from tiny dots of light inside each of us. Morgan's light had saved my life. Mine had saved the Travelers' lives. And theirs would pass through the Darkness too, in their own ways, in their own time. In the end we would always have a fighting chance.

"Good job, Morgan," I said, allowing myself to sit on the soft grass of Avalon.

The birds began to sing once again. In the forest I could see the eyes of wild creatures blinking with wonder that the light had returned. It would be a good day, after all, even though I was alone in this place, on this plane, where I would remain alone for the rest of my life.

I shivered. The portal to Whitfield had been closed, and a

good thing too. The last thing those poor people needed after being uprooted from their homes was a dose of walking poison infecting their new home.

Could they see me from the other side? I wondered. Would I be like an animal in a zoo, a pastime for any observers who cared to see how I managed to live from day to day? Maybe taking bets on how long it would take me to go crazy and hang myself from a tree?

"Are you out there?" I asked out loud, leaning toward the portal. "Because if you are, I'm going to ask you to stop." I paused for a moment, gathering my thoughts. "But first I've got something to say. It's about Morgan. Whatever you've heard about her, forget it. She saved you all, even though it cost her her life. No matter what else she did, that should count for something."

I tried to compose myself. "Gram, I want to tell you how much it's meant to me to be part of your family," I said. "I don't remember my mother, and my dad—well, you know how he is. Busy. Tell him I'm okay. And don't let him blame you for what happened. This whole thing was my fault, and it has turned out as well as it could, so I'm not complaining.

"All of you—Aunt Agnes, Miss P, Hattie, Bryce, Becca— I'll never forget you. I love you all."

I was feeling myself choke up at this point, but I had to finish what I needed to say. "And, Peter . . ." I cleared my throat and tried to keep my voice from trembling. "I'm so proud of you. You've always been my hero."

I could hear my voice starting to wobble then, so I stopped talking. There was more I could have said, I supposed, about why I didn't want any further communication with Whitfield or my family, but I didn't think they would have understood. They couldn't. They were *good*.

People like Gram and Hattie and Miss P thought of the Darkness as something outside of themselves, something dirty to be brushed away before it touched them. But it had already touched me, and more. The Darkness had crawled inside me like a worm, and I knew that for the rest of my life that worm, that dark thing, would always be a part of me, as much as it had been a part of Morgan.

She had died honorably, and I believed that when she gave up her life, that fragment of the Darkness that had made a monster of her flew away like dust in the wind. She'd gone out clean.

But I was still alive, and as long as I was, I would never be clean again. My innocence was gone. That small, pure space in my soul—that place that still existed intact for the others—was, for me, now filled by the Darkness, and always would be.

No, they wouldn't understand. And I wouldn't want them to.

"Katy." A whisper. I looked up with a gasp. Peter was standing beside me. A soft breeze ruffled through his hair. He held out his arms to me.

"No," I said, lunging backward. "Please go. You shouldn't even have come through the portal."

He shook his head slowly. "I'm not going anywhere," he said.

My eyes flooded. I wanted so much to run to him, to touch him, but I knew I couldn't. Not without killing him. "Don't do this to me," I begged.

"You said I was your hero, but that was wrong. You've

always been the heroic one." His face was filled with sorrow. "I hated watching you fight alone."

"I wasn't alone," I said. "You were making everything possible."

He put his hands into his pockets and grinned a small, lopsided smile. "Do you think this was what Eric's prophecy meant? That we'd destroy this place together?"

I blinked. "I thought it was Whitfield we were going to destroy."

He shrugged. "I don't remember."

"I don't believe in prophecies, anyway," I said. "People can change everything." I looked down at my ring. "Well, almost everything." I tried to smile. "Go back, Peter," I said as gently as I could. "We both know it's the only smart thing to do."

"Who says I'm smart?"

"Peter—"

"I'm not leaving you, Katy. Not now, not ever."

"Yes, you are!" I shouted. "You have to. Staying with me will *kill* you! Don't you understand?"

"No," he said softly. "I don't understand. Whatever happens, I don't care. I don't want to live without you."

"Stop it!" I screamed. "I'm not even worth it! I'm not worth . . . anything . . ." I sobbed into my hands.

"You're wrong there," he said, wrapping his arms around me. Panicking for his safety, I tried desperately to push him away, but he held me fast. "You're worth everything to me," he whispered in my ear. "Everything I am, everything I ever will be, is because of you. And I will never, *never* let you go."

I pounded my fists against him. "Go away!" I pleaded. "Please, Peter . . ."

But he crushed me against his body until I had to stop struggling. Then he kissed me full on my mouth. Even then I tried to pull away, but he caught my face in his big hands and turned it back toward his.

"I love you," he whispered, pressing so closely against me that I could feel his heart beating in his chest, could feel his thighs move hard against me as he kissed me more deeply. "I love you," he said. The words were as soft as the breeze that touched us, and as sweet.

I gave in then, kissing him back, feeling the hardness of his tongue against mine. I felt as if I were melting beneath his heat. "Oh, Peter," I said, filled with regret and confusion. "Do you even know what you've done by coming here? By being with me?"

"I've told you that I'm going to be with you for the rest of my life." He looked deep into my eyes. "However long that may be."

I hung my head. I knew I would not be able to live with another death. Not his death.

"Hey," he said gently, lifting my chin. "The rest of my life may be longer than you think." He took my hand and touched the flat, cold stone of the ring. Then, with no effort at all, he pulled it off my finger.

I choked. "How did you . . ."

"It's got no more power," Peter said, tossing it away. "Morgan used it all when she threw herself into the Darkness."

"But . . ." I stared at my naked finger. "How did you know that? How did you know I was safe to be around?"

Peter kissed my forehead. "I didn't," he said, moving his

lips down to kiss my eyes, my cheeks, my lips. The place where the ring had been had left a white mark on my finger. He kissed that, too.

"I can't believe it," I said. "It's over."

"For now," Peter said.

"Right," I said hollowly. "For now."

He tousled my hair. "Now's enough." I pressed my face against his chest. "Come home, Katy," he whispered, holding me tight. "You promised."

"Home," I repeated. "But I—" I couldn't stop smiling.

"With me."

I thought about it for a moment. "With you," I said, and I knew that would make all the difference. Whatever I might be, whatever I might face, I'd be with him.

"Come on," he said.

Then he led me by the hand through the portal back to Whitfield.

Back to life.

31901055504072